THE
LONG SUN

THE
LONG SUN

A Novel

Janice Lucas

Published by

Soho Press Inc.
853 Broadway
New York, NY 10003

Library of Congress Cataloging-in-Publication Data

Lucas, Janice, 1937–
The long sun/Janice Lucas.
p.   cm.
ISBN 1–56947–013–8
1. Frontier and pioneer life—Appalachian Region—History—17th
century—Fiction.   2. Appalachian Region—Ethnic relations—Fiction.
3. Tuscarora Indians—Fiction.   I. Title.
PS3562.U2365L66   1994
813′.54—dc20   93-48028
                                                                      CIP

Manufactured in the United States

In memory
of my Grandmothers
Lydia Elizabeth Billips,
    née Beavers, whose family was British,
and Lockie Alice Spriggs,
    née Taylor, whose people were Cherokee.
To them and their descendants
    this story is dedicated.

ONE

1

The white man had moved into the hunting range of the Tuscarora three springs ago. He brought with him a woman and two children. They all slept in an open mountain meadow until the man put up a shelter.

The clan did not understand his ways, but he seemed harmless and they accepted him. They began to drop food at his cabin door during that first summer and continued to help feed him through the next three winters. Several clan members approached the whiteskins during these years, exchanging signs and attempting conversation. The first to speak with the man was Lame Crow. After observing the small group for several hours, Lame Crow stepped out of the woods just before sundown one evening. He tried to impress upon the white man that he should move his family into the protection of the forest. The man's reaction was to place his family behind him and assume a firm stance, holding a long-handled ax in front of him.

Lame Crow made the sweeping sign with both of his arms for them to move toward the woods. The white man retained his position. Lame Crow then pantomimed a person being attacked in the clearing and dragged toward the treeline. Finally, the white man understood the Indian was trying to help.

The white man laid his ax down but did not move far away from it. He pointed to himself and said, "Billips."

Lame Crow pointed to Billips, and on his first attempt firmly and correctly pronounced, "Bill-ips."

John Billips tried to explain by word and gesture that his family was more afraid of sleeping in the woods than of being attacked in the clearing. Lame Crow, understanding Billips's declaration, stopped belaboring the point.

Fearing for the safety of the little group, Lame Crow decided to stay on with the family. In the days that followed, both Lame Crow and the Billips family lost their fear of one another.

The young boy followed Lame Crow everywhere he went. His name was Jackson and he was nine years old. As soon as Jackson's morning chores were done he would tug on Lame Crow's arm. "Take me hunting in the woods," he'd say, or "Take me to the creek, take me to a hickory tree for wood to make a bow."

Take me, take me. Lame Crow thought the boy's name was "Tak-i-me" and when he had free time he would call out in his language, "Come, Tak-i-me. We go."

Jackson's mother, Lydia, smiled whenever she heard this. She felt that it was good to see a new face and hear a different voice. The spring and summer that Lame Crow spent with them was the best they had had in several years. Since they moved to the mountains, life had been extremely hard for them all. The clothes they had brought with them were almost threadbare and the fabric in Lydia's trunk was nearly gone. There was not enough of summer and far too much winter.

Lame Crow taught them new trapping and hunting tricks and how to work the different animal skins. He showed them a great many wild plants that they could make teas from or eat.

Lame Crow made himself so useful that one day Lydia spoke to her husband about him. "John, could we build a permanent place beside the cabin for Lame Crow to live in? He teaches Jackson so many things that he needs to know and he is such a help to me. Though I worry about the way Sassy is also following him around. I am sure that it is just that we have never had neighbors. It does not seem right for a little girl to follow an Indian around through the woods. But I guess she will get over that." Lydia sighed. "I really would like to have him here through the winter."

"No," her husband answered. "He is leaving soon. He told me so. He has some kind of celebration to go to. I think it is in late summer. He has made all new weapons. I saw him working on some sort of kilt for the celebration. I do not think that he is coming back. His clan lives about sixty some miles northwest of here and he wants to see them. He probably has a family, too. We cannot ask a man to stay away from his own family in order to help us."

Just as Billips suspected, Lame Crow left the family in the year of 1703 in the moon of the green corn ceremony. Before leaving, he stood straight and tall with folded arms and endured the hugs of the woman and the backslaps and handshakes of Billips and the sad eyes of Jackson—Takime now to everyone. As a token of friendship, Lame Crow gave each family member a precious gift to help get them through the coming winter.

"Sassy, keep when snows come," he said as he handed her a cape of fine fur. "Lydia, too." They took the capes and held the soft fur up to their cheeks. Priscilla Billips, who was called "Sassy," covered her eyes with the cape so nobody would see the tears that were spilling over.

"Keep long time," Lame Crow said as he handed his gift to Jackson. "Tak-i-me, grow big. You need hunt. Here fine, strong hickory bow and arrows with feathers. Hunt for family."

The bow was beautiful, curved downward in the middle with a hole placed at one end where the sinew was passed through and knotted. The arrows were light and straight with heads of flaked chert. Jackson Billips accepted the gift with the same dignity with

5

which it was given. Lame Crow ceremoniously presented John Billips with a larger version of Takime's gift.

When he was finished giving his gifts, Lame Crow raised his arms toward the heavens and asked Grandfather Sky to stay with the family during the coming winter. He turned to go.

"Lame Crow, wait! We have something for you, too." Billips reached just inside the door of the cabin and returned with his arms full. He passed out the things to his family to present to Lame Crow. First Sassy. She gave him her precious copy of *A Child's First Reader.* It was filled with pictures Lame Crow had always been charmed by. Sassy had read it to him so many times that he could repeat the text by rote.

"I know you would like to have this for yourself," Sassy said. "Please take this as my going-away gift."

Lame Crow held the book to his heart and smiled down at Priscilla, then quickly put it in the bag attached to his trump line.

Lydia handed him an iron pot with a swinging handle. The pot was one of her smaller ones, weighing about five pounds. She knew that anything heavier would be a burden for him to carry. He accepted the pot with great seriousness. He did not know where to put it so he set it down on the ground between his feet just as Takime presented him with a slingshot.

"I noticed that you did not have a slingshot, so I made you one. And I carved a crow with a broke foot on the handle, so you would know whose it was," Jackson said.

Lame Crow solemnly accepted the gift and nodded at the boy. He examined the carving closely. It looked exactly like a crow with a broken foot. His respect for the boy shot upwards. Never in his lifetime had he seen anything so accurate as this carving.

It was Billips's turn. He hated to see his friend go, but he knew that he could not keep him. He handed Lame Crow a strong and well-made knife of iron.

Lame Crow accepted the gift and examined it carefully. Without a word, he put it back in its sheath, picked up the iron pot, turned on his heel, and walked into the forest. Once out of sight, he sat down, leaned back against a tree, and closely examined his new possessions. He grinned with satisfaction. Good friends give good gifts.

Excitement marked his arrival back at the village. Lame Crow came home with many stories to tell and he even taught a few English words to anyone who asked. But the tribe's greatest interest was in the gifts the white people had bestowed. Lame Crow gave the iron pot to his wife, kept the knife and the slingshot for himself, and placed the book in the meeting lodge for all to see. Sometimes, in the evenings, he would "read" the book aloud to anyone who would listen. The most interested was Bear Paw's son, Runs With The Wind. Lame Crow watched the boy as he recited the primer to him. Runs With The Wind took in the strange sounds like someone thirsting.

It was midafternoon. It would take Runs With The Wind another day and a half before he would reach the Billips's cabin. He paced himself carefully for the long journey, taking the old winter path. Usually there was little chance of meeting anyone on the trail this time of year so he felt free and happy. If all went well, he would find his evening meal and sleep beside the Big Tree River.

The sun was falling behind Peelnut Mountain when he stopped suddenly and in one swift motion unsheathed an arrow and sent it flying. Thirty feet away, a young red fox dropped. Without ceremony, Runs With The Wind dragged the fox off the path and split open its belly, removing the entrails. That finished, he fastened its feet to his side by the thong encircling his breechclout and continued on his way.

Just before sundown he arrived at Big Tree River. He squatted under a virgin oak and prepared his meal. He skinned the fox, quickly removing most of the hair from the hide, then started a small fire and carried the hide to the river to fill it with water. He sharpened the ends of several small tree branches and stuck them in the ground, attaching the hide to the branches so that it was positioned over the flames. Placing all but one strip of meat into the water-filled hide, he slowly lifted the lone piece toward the sun in the four directions of the universe. He thanked the fox spirit for sending this one across his path for his evening meal and returned the piece of raw meat to the timberland as his gift to the animal spirits. Leaving his meal cooking in the skin pot, he walked along the riverbank in search of edibles to add to his supper.

After his meal, Runs With The Wind poured the juice from the soup over the fire to put it out. He buried all evidence of it and the remains of the fox skin, and wrapped the leftover meat in leaves for protection until his next meal. Having taken these precautions, he carefully checked his weapons for damage, replacing the arrows in their worked quiver and the stone knife in the back of his breechclout. This done, he looked for a secluded place to spend the night.

Slipping back into the trees, he trekked a mile downriver through the woods before finding a perfect spot beneath low-hanging boughs of a fir tree. Pine needles supplied a soft bed and the fir boughs protected him from the elements and from discovery. He placed his weapons alongside and lay down, settling into the needles and thanking the fir for its protection during the night.

With the first light he gathered his possessions, took a long drink from the river, and resumed his journey, crossing the river and traveling without interruption for several hours. Along the way, a small herd of white-tailed deer crossed his path. Runs With The Wind spoke softly to them. "Eat well," he whispered, "and grow strong before the winter. I will need your coats and flesh when the heavy snows fall."

His voice frightened the doe and they bounded away. He laughed at the sight of their retreating rumps and said, "We will meet again."

At midmorning, he stopped by a swift, racing creek and ate. He stripped and bathed in the cold water, wasting no time in replacing his breechclout and getting under way along the creek.

By mid day sweat trickled across his forehead and chest. He began to silently recite the clan history to take his mind away from his exertions. He conjured up the faces of all his relatives and whispered their names to the forest. He named those from his own village and those who had migrated to others. He recited close to fifteen Xs of names—one hundred and fifty clan members—tallying every ten with an X until he had notched all of them into a stick.

There were moments when Runs With The Wind forgot that his mission was a serious one, for he was happiest when alone and on a journey. It had been so for as far back as he could remember. When he was very young and small, a gentle warm breeze had passed through the summer camp and he had tried to keep ahead of it. In his wanderings, he had crossed a stream and scampered down the valley floor. He was lost for over half a day. He could still feel the wonder of his feet touching the new ground and his happiness from being all by himself. He had explored the banks and the creeks and the edge of the forest, feeling no fear of the unknown. He was startled when his father found him. He had been so busy exploring that he did not hear him coming.

When his father picked him up in his arms, he squirmed and tried to get down. He was not ready to go home. His father laughed and called him "Child That Runs With The Wind." And such would be his name until the time of his vision.

Rounding the next bend, Runs With The Wind halted abruptly. There in front of him lay a small grouping of stones. The sight sent fear rippling along his skin. He swiftly slipped into the woods without a sound. He waited motionless, even after the birds took up their singing again and the squirrels resumed their chatter. He felt no one else near. Cautiously, he went back to the stones and examined them without touching anything. Their formation was a puzzlement. He could not read the message or discern for whom it was intended. Someone from a distant and unfamiliar tribe had placed them there, presumably for others to decipher and follow. Many others.

Runs With The Wind was uncertain as to what to do. The village council had sent him to check on the white man and he had to report Billips's situation back to them. If he tried to find the messenger who left the stones, it would delay his passage. If he ignored the stones without investigating, the tribe could be in danger. If he did not continue to the Billips homestead, he would be disobeying his elders, and Billips and his family might be in danger.

Runs With The Wind made up his mind. He would look for more evidence of intruders by continuing to the white family's cabin along a different trail. He would pass north of their cabin and come upon it from the east. It was a much longer and more difficult route to travel, but he could look for signs. In less than two nights he would be on Billips's ground. He pressed on.

The next hours were easy. Then he came to the base of the first mountain he had to cross. There was no time to hunt food but he was able to drink from the water running down the side of the mountain along huge gray rocks. He had never been on this ground before, but had listened intently to his uncles describe the mountains in their talk around the evening fire. They had made many winter forays into this same wilderness.

So Runs With The Wind knew to proceed in a straight direction until he saw the flat rock crest of a place called Hard Top. Through the years, some young men from his clan had chosen Hard Top for their isolation before they entered into the spirit world of visions. Maybe, when his time came, he would go there too. Runs With The Wind went on.

He did not come across a human trail over the mountain and he did not particularly look for one. Sometimes he used deer trails, but they often ended in large patches of greenbrier and underbrush that the deer could slip through but he could not. Several times he snatched up a plant, roots and all. Later he would make them into a drink that would help keep up his energy. He had no time to find solid food. He shook the earth from the roots as he climbed, and stuck the plant in his waist thong to dry. The sun was edging toward the west when he topped the mountain. The only notice he took was to pick up his pace.

The Tuscarora did not travel in darkness unless it was a great emergency. Spirits moved about in the dark and he did not want to get in their way. Provoking spirits could bring trouble down on the clan. He crawled into the center of a low-lying bearberry stand and fell asleep, confident that he had left no trace of his passing.

2

Runs With The Wind headed up the incline of the last peak before Billips's mountain. The going was much easier now. When he reached the top, he came upon the remains of a temporary camp. The party had stayed in place for several days and had been gone for at least two.

They had built a small bark-and-limb shelter.

It had rained heavily four days ago. The marks were still in the earth from the rain dripping from the shelter's roof. He poked about the campsite, picking up several white feathers from a bird unknown to him and estimated the band at twenty to forty braves. A war party from the south. Their trail led off to the southeast, which could only mean that they were circling the area.

Not far from the camp clearing was a stick marker balanced on a small group of stones. Seeing it, Runs With The Wind departed, his pace quickened. He would warn Billips and then his own clan. The People from the South seldom entered the mountain country, but when they did, there was trouble. Chances were that they had sighted Billips and his family on the next mountain.

. . .

He arrived at the Billips's cabin just before dark. He saw a woman at the door. She called out to the man working in the small clearing. The man stopped his work and motioned to two children who were with him. They all went inside the cabin together.

The girl came back outside. She bent over, looking for something among the long grass cuttings. Runs With The Wind rose up on his knees to get a better view, making sure to keep the high grass between himself and the girl. He estimated she was perhaps eight winters old.

She had found what she was searching for and picked it up. It was a lump of cloth with long appendages attached. She bowed her head and brushed her cheek across the thing. The Tuscarora boy's curiosity overrode his caution. He lifted his body higher, just enough to peer over the grass. At the same instant, the girl raised her eyes in his direction.

She stood perfectly still. The great sunset inflamed her hair. She narrowed her eyes in order to keep the glare from distorting her vision and met his steady gaze. Neither moved. Then, slowly, Runs With The Wind stood up. He had not expected discovery and his heart was racing, but his face did not betray him.

Her arms went slack. The doll slid to the ground. Silently she bolted for the cabin.

Runs With The Wind walked up to the door and pushed it open. He stood on the threshold with his arms folded across his chest. The startled occupants of the cabin did not move at first, and then everyone moved at once.

Billips reached for his rifle, but realizing the intruder was a boy and brandished no weapon, Billips dropped his arm and remained still. Lydia had gasped and backed into a corner by the bed. Her hand was over her mouth, stifling a scream. Young Jackson stood transfixed. Sassy surprised them all with a scream, her eyes flying from her father to the boy and back again.

Runs With The Wind stood motionless. He knew the white people needed time to look him over and get used to him. He had the advantage, having observed them all, except for the baby asleep in the cradle.

Finally, Runs With The Wind spoke a word Lame Crow had taught him. "Welcome," he said.

At this, Billips glanced around at his family and smiled. As soon as the boy spoke, he knew he was of Lame Crow's tribe. Lame Crow had never really understood exactly what *welcome* meant, only that it was a greeting. It never mattered to him who spoke the greeting, the guest or the host.

"Welcome," they all said, almost in unison.

Runs With The Wind pointed at Billips and said, "Billips."

Billips nodded.

Then the boy pointed at each in turn and spoke their names. "Sassy, Tak-i-me, Lydi-a. Lame Crow teach." Then he pointed to himself and said in his own language, "Tahitnekah."

Using sign language, he explained to Billips as best he could that there were enemy warriors wandering around in the woods and that they were no longer safe on the mountaintop. He made the "X" sign three times, shrugged, and made another X, indicating the thirty, perhaps forty, braves in the party. He signed that he must take them to his village at sunrise. A three-sleep journey. He wanted them to discuss the situation and decide if they would come. When he finished, he walked outside and stood leaning against the cabin. He had done all that he could. It was up to the family to make their choice. Either way, he would head for home in the morning.

Billips closed the door and spoke to his wife: "I know he is very young, but we will have to trust him. We will pack up tonight. We can only take what we can carry. A little food, some clothes, a couple of pots, our weapons. Lydia, you'll have to carry the baby." He turned to the children. "Each one of you pick one thing of your own that you want to keep. If and when we come back, there might not be anything left here."

Lydia nodded. "Priscilla, get the sacks from the loft. You can carry the clothes. Make sure our winter things go. John, call the boy in. He looks hungry."

Billips spoke to Jackson: "Son, first thing in the morning, catch a couple of roosters and a few hens. You know how your mother treasures those hens. We must try to take some with us." Then he opened the door and motioned for Runs With The Wind to come in and sit at the table.

Runs With The Wind came in but then hesitated. In winter he sat inside the lodge on the ground before the fire to eat, and in summer he ate outside on the ground. Awkwardly he eased onto the bench. It was the first time he had ever sat at a table. It felt uncomfortable. He knew they were going to offer him food. It was in containers on the table. At home, he sat on his bed oftentimes, but not to eat.

Billips hand-signed that they would leave the cabin and go with him in the morning. Runs With The Wind nodded, glad of their decision. Meanwhile, Lydia placed a plate filled with chicken stew and a huge slice of corn bread before him. He ignored the metal spoon beside his plate. Instead, he broke the bread in half and used it to dip up the stew, first with one hand and then the other. He was famished and did not stop until it was all gone. Then he turned to the cup of dark, hot liquid. Lydia had made coffee from her store of dried dandelion roots. Runs With The Wind seldom drank anything except water or weak, lukewarm teas, but it was not polite to refuse food or drink offered by a friend. He picked up the cup and gulped down the liquid in two swallows. He kept a straight face as the hot coffee seared his tongue and mouth.

Sassy was totally fascinated by their guest. Although he was not unusually large for his age, his presence seemed to fill the cabin. She knew the coffee burned him, but he gave no sign of it. They all knew that the coffee burned him, but no one was going to mention it unless he did.

Jackson Billips was beaming. He had been without a friend since Lame Crow left, and never in his life had he enjoyed a friend near his own age. This Indian boy could only be a couple of years older than he was—thirteen maybe—but he acted like a grown man.

Lydia removed the plate from in front of Runs With The Wind while Billips tried to explain that he could sleep on the floor. Runs With The Wind shook his head and headed for the door.

Billips stopped him and handed him an old blanket of rough cloth. Runs With The Wind headed for the door. A second time Jackson stopped him, grabbed up another blanket, and went out the door with him.

"Poppy, I will stay the night in the woods with Runs With The Wind." He pronounced the name as best he could. "If you need me, ring the bell."

Once outside, Runs With The Wind seemed nervous. It was completely dark now, and he quickly crossed the field and entered the woods. Jackson was beginning to get nervous too. Maybe the warriors were close by. Runs With The Wind found the place where he wanted to sleep and spread his blanket on the ground. Jackson spread his there too, but the Indian boy shook his head and pointed to the woods on the other side of the field.

"Tak-i-me," he said.

Jackson Billips had not counted on this. He knew what was meant: they must keep the cabin in between them in case of trouble. He had never spent the night alone in the woods before, but he could not show cowardice now, so he rolled up his blanket and carefully crossed the field and went into the woods alone.

The morning songbirds woke Jackson just before daylight. He folded his blanket and slipped across the field to where Runs With The Wind had been. No one was there. He crossed the field again, this time heading for the cabin. As he was about to enter, he saw Runs With The Wind inside the lean-to, standing there staring at the chickens.

Runs With The Wind said nothing but it was obvious that he had never seen so many tame birds. He was perplexed. Where was the honor in wearing the feathers from a yard bird? Why would anyone feed an animal and then eat it? This was not a good thing for the spirit of the animal or the spirit of the man. One day he would ask Takime or Billips about this. Today, they had to hurry. He motioned for young Takime to enter the cabin.

The table was already set and Lydia was dishing up food. They hurried through breakfast. Afterwards, Billips placed his pack and weapons by the door while Sassy tried to decide which of her two most loved possessions to take, her book or her doll. She sat on the corner of her mother's bed and held them both. It was a difficult decision to make.

Runs With The Wind saw the puzzlement on her face. He knew that she was deciding what to place in her pack. He was familiar with Lame Crow's book and knew that it had provided hours of entertainment in the council house. He walked over and took the book and stuck it in Sassy's pack. He could see no need for carrying the doll on a journey such as theirs.

"Quit it," Sassy snapped, grabbing the book out of the pack and flinging it on the bed. Runs With The Wind was taken aback. She stared at him, blue eyes flashing anger. When she met his steady, dark gaze, the angry look turned into a troubled look. She seemed so worried about the decision she must make that he forgave her the outburst and left with Takime to help put chickens in a carrying sack.

After he was gone, Sassy changed her mind and laid the doll down on the bed and put the book back in the sack. She picked the doll up one more time and kissed it on the forehead before replacing it on the bed. She took one last look around the room that had been her home for three years and walked slowly outside to stand beside her mother and baby brother.

Billips made another round inside and outside the cabin to see if he had missed any necessity.

Runs With The Wind had followed him into the cabin. Spying the doll on the bed, the boy glanced around to make sure Billips was not watching, and stuffed it into the pack Billips had given him to carry.

Satisfied that all the right things had been packed, they started out across the field with Runs With The Wind in the lead. Jackson was next, followed by Lydia carrying the baby. Then Sassy, close behind her mother, and Billips at the rear. Runs With The Wind could easily make the trip in two sleeps, but he kept to a slow, steady pace instead of his usual lengthy stride. Their speed would be that of the weakest. He was not yet sure if that was going to be the daughter, Sassy, or Lydia carrying the baby. Billips did not have a cradleboard for the infant and there was no time to make one now.

They stopped at high sun beside the magnificence of the Big Tree River. Jackson released the chickens for a little pecking and exercise and packed them up again. Lydia breast-fed the baby. Afterwards, Sassy pulled dried cedar shavings from one of her sacks and placed them in the baby's cloth to keep him dry.

The beauty of the place was not lost on the Billips family. This undisturbed land was a balm to their spirits. Runs With The Wind had known nothing else but these mountains and valleys, rivers and streams, and wilderness trails. He was as much a part of it as the running water or the oak trees, and to his way of thinking, they were all equals. All were alive and imbued with spirit. Each blade of grass, each twittering bird, and each fish in the river carried the stamp of a greater design. He was watching Sassy as she made a circlet of wildflowers and placed it on her mother's head, then made one for herself.

"Poppy, we look just like the pictures in my book," she laughed, and danced around John Billips on her tiptoes.

Billips smiled. It was good to see his daughter so happy. She had nothing but her imagination for a playmate and sometimes he felt guilty for having brought her so far into the wilderness. She never complained. Sometimes she behaved just like Jackson and spent whole days in the woods with him, following animal trails, building little rush houses, making traps. She would try to tame any animal or bird she could get her hands on, then set it free.

He put his hand on her head. "Hold still, Sunshine. We have a few more minutes to spare. How about making us all a hat of flowers while I take a little walk in the woods?"

"Oh, Poppy. Would you really wear it?" Without waiting for an answer, she ran along the bank to gather more blooms. Her adroit fingers flew. Whenever she thought she had gathered enough, she flopped on the ground and made another band.

Jackson and Runs With The Wind glanced uneasily at each other with the certain knowledge that they were going to have to put on one of the awful things. If Poppy was going to wear one, he was surely going to make them wear one.

Lydia leaned back against a tree, resting, watching the children. She understood the thoughts running through the boys' heads and the fever and excitement running through Sassy's hands. The baby lay contentedly on the ground beside her. She smiled. The baby never gave any trouble at all and seldom cried. He was five months old now, and sometimes she worried about him. He seemed alert enough, but different from the way his siblings had been at the same age. He was watching a butterfly and he carefully followed its progress with his eyes. She knew that if she called to him, he would ignore her, continuing to watch the butterfly. Once his attention was taken by something, it was difficult to distract him.

Her father had not returned by the time Sassy finished. She placed a small flower band on the baby's head, then skipped over to Jackson. Resignedly, he bent his head to receive the gift. Before he even straightened, Sassy was already on her way to Runs With The Wind. With all the dignity he could muster, Runs With The Wind bent his head, too. Sassy took his head between the palms of her hands and gave him a hasty kiss on the forehead, just below the crown of flowers, then quickly danced away.

Runs With The Wind stood stunned. He refused to look at anyone, hoping that no one had seen the invasion of his person.

Lydia was the only one to take notice but quickly turned away, whether out of shame over her daughter's behavior or embarrassment, she could not be sure. Either way, she intended to speak privately to Sassy about this.

John Billips came out of the woods and Sassy wordlessly placed a garland on his head and skipped over to help her mother gather up their belongings.

"Priscilla, you should not have done that to Runs With The Wind. Young girls do not kiss young men. Even in fun. Besides, it is not his custom and he might not understand what you meant."

"Oh, Mommy, I was just playing. He looks so mean all the time, I wanted to bring him down." She changed her expression into a sweet smile and added, "Everybody looks so happy with their flowers." As an afterthought, she whispered, "Please, you must not tell Poppy."

Everyone picked up their sacks and Runs With The Wind took the lead again. The vivid colors of the flowers they wore gave new life to the group. They made good time. After several miles, Runs With The Wind lost his seriousness and his face took on a grin. He was thinking of the silly flowers Sassy made them wear and the little lip peck. He wondered what the elders back at the lodge were going to think of this white clan that he was bringing to them.

In the late afternoon, they came across the first stone grouping that had startled Runs With The Wind several days earlier. He lifted his hand for them to halt and bent down to examine the stones again. Nothing was changed. As best he could tell, no one had used or crossed the trail since he had. Billips came to stand beside him. He too studied the design. Suddenly, he kicked it apart, sending the stones flying in all directions.

Frightened by his action, Runs With The Wind almost ran but made himself stand and face Billips. "No. No touch," he scolded. He did not know the words in Billips's language so he spoke in his native language. He explained that the grouping could be sacred. "No touch!" he said again, in English.

Billips did not understand the boy's speech or why he was so concerned. "I destroyed it because it might be a message to an enemy.

Now they cannot read it." Billips shrugged. "It seemed the best thing to do."

Runs With The Wind stood looking at the stones scattered about. He tried to remember how they were placed. Maybe he could remember well enough to rebuild it for the elders and one of them might recognize the tribe who made it or the significance of it. There was nothing else he could do for now. In exasperation, he ripped the flowers from his hair and threw them deep into the undergrowth. He turned on his heel and motioned for them to follow.

The fun was gone out of the day. As they walked on, they removed the flowers from their hair.

When they stopped for supper, Sassy broke the silence, saying, "Mommy, I will look after the baby for you. I will carry him while I find plants for supper."

Supper was over and all traces cleaned up before first dark. Billips, carrying the baby, went for one of his walks. Runs With The Wind was searching the surrounding area for signs of the intruders. Takime guarded the camp and Lydia and Sassy gathered leaves and soft pine boughs for bedding. They had not done that since before the cabin was built when they had slept in the open meadow. It was fun to be sleeping outside again. By full dark, they were all comfortably nestled for the night.

Runs With The Wind roused the others at dawn. He grunted and pushed Billips and then Takime in the side with his foot. He left it to Billips to wake up the women. He wanted to get an early start and reach the Winding Waters before noon so that he could fish and gather greens for their meal. Billips and his family seemed to need to eat three times a day and he did not want to change their habits if it was not necessary. He was no longer angry with Billips. The white man had different ways. He would watch him more closely and try to stop him before he did anything foolish again.

3

Such stories he would have to tell around the warriors' fire. Yesterday, they had left the white boy alone with the women. Although he had had every opportunity to do so, he had not attacked. He waited and watched. Tonight would be different.

Lone Runner's war paint glistened in the noonday sun as he considered his approach. He had been following them since midday. There were too many of them to fight, but surely he could steal the woman or the girl. All he had to do was wait until evening.

His raven hair was gathered tightly to the right side of his head and entwined with a leather strip to which a single white feather was attached. His calf-high moccasins protected him from brambles and snakes. He wore only a breechclout, with no shirt or jewelry for an enemy to grasp, and carried his knife, club, bow and arrows. His medicine bag, attached to his breechclout, was strong. He could feel it in every bone and muscle of his body.

The little band below him began to gather up their belongings and repack for their journey. Lone Runner threw his head back and laughed out loud at the white boy chasing down birds and stuffing them into a sack. These were foolish people. Perhaps some of them would not live to see their journey's end. Only the Indian boy was cautious. The big white man made more noise as he traveled than a bear on the warpath. The women sang and chattered most of the time. The melody of their songs floated back to Lone Runner. It was a strange but pleasant sound, like the wind gently whipping through the willows. He would not mind having those songs in his camp.

They were setting off. Lone Runner eased down the hillside toward the little group, always staying far enough behind not to be heard or seen.

Runs With The Wind was becoming more nervous as the afternoon wore on. He figured on two sleeps and one more sun before reaching his lodge. He did not hear anything out of the ordinary, but he could sense eyes upon him. He cautioned Billips and the women to keep quiet. He was pleased with Takime's progress on the trail. Despite his cumbersome burdens, the boy was learning to travel sensibly. Takime's eyes darted here and there as he moved forward. He imitated the way Runs With The Wind lowered his feet across fallen leaves and dried twigs and imitated his steps, heels down first, and had discovered that this gave him a surer footing and a quieter tread.

When they stopped for the last meal of the day, Runs With The Wind decided to backtrack the trail they had taken to search for anything out of the ordinary. Before leaving their temporary camp, he instructed Takime to explore the forest's edge and Billips to remain at the camp's center. The women were to stay by the supplies and prepare a cold supper. No one was to make a fire until Runs With The Wind returned.

Runs With The Wind had backtracked a mile when he bent to examine some disturbing footprints. In one of the scattered, sandy spots in the trail, someone had walked several paces, placing his footsteps inside Billips's tracks. It would have gone unnoticed except for the buildup of sand at the heel edge. The stranger's track was a tiny bit smaller than Billips's, but the depth was identical. Other than the fact that he probably weighed about the same as Billips, there was no clue as to his identity.

The double tracks lasted for several yards and then disappeared. Runs With The Wind explored first one side of the trail and then the other, looking for further clues. He found nothing. In his search, he stepped deeper into the shadow of the forest.

At camp, Jackson was taking his orders seriously. He cautiously surveyed the perimeter of the campsite. Lydia prepared a cold supper while Billips watched the chickens peck and scratch in the soft earth around the supply sacks.

Sassy walked around with the baby on her hip and looked for sweet grass to chew on until supper time. She wandered by the edge of the woods, keeping her eyes focused on the ground so she had no chance to scream or struggle when Lone Runner came from behind her. He clamped his hand over her mouth, jerking the baby from her with his other hand. He held both children tightly against his chest, swerving back into the woods without breaking his stride.

Billips caught the movement from the corner of his eye and yelled, "Son, quick! That way." He pointed toward the place where the children had disappeared. "A savage grabbed Sassy and the baby. Follow them. I'll get the carbine."

Jackson crashed into the woods. Billips followed close behind. They thrashed about for several minutes, first in one direction, then another. There was no sign of the Indian or the children.

"We will have to split up, Poppy," Jackson stammered. "He is getting farther away all the time and we are not doing any good this way."

"Stop a minute, son. Go back to your mother. I will do what I can to find them. You wait for Runs With The Wind. See what he thinks we should do. Look after your mother while I am gone. Comfort her the best you can."

Billips left. Jackson obediently made his way to the edge of the clearing. He could see his mother silently running back and forth, wringing her hands and shaking her head. When she saw her son, she ran to him and hysterically shook him by the shoulders.

"Did you find them?"

"No! There was no sign of which a way they went. Poppy made me come back to wait for Runs With The Wind. He went on to look for them."

Tears spilled down his mother's cheeks. "Mommy, now stop crying," he said in a much softer tone. "Get me something to eat, and you eat, too. Pack some food for Poppy and Runs With The Wind. I think Poppy wants me to stay with you."

The boy was almost as tall as his mother. For the first time in his life, he realized how vulnerable she was. He put his arm around her waist and walked her back to the supplies. She dried her eyes and got busy packing food and repacking the supplies. She was afraid that if she stopped moving, she would give in to the fear clutching at her heart and become totally useless.

Jackson ate whatever food she handed him. He knew her anguish because it was his as well. Somehow, they would get Sassy and the baby back.

His eyes scanned the woods as he ate.

"Mommy, we will have to stay here tonight and maybe for a day or two longer. We will have to find a safer place to make camp."

Just then, Runs With The Wind appeared in the clearing. He sensed that something was terribly wrong. He did not see Billips or Sassy. As he came closer to camp, he could tell that Lydia was crying and Takime seemed to be trying hard to keep from it. He knew without being told that Sassy was gone. The man whose tracks he had seen had taken her. Billips was either dead or tracking him. He looked around for the baby, but did not see him either.

The Indian boy listened intently as Takime tried to explain everything that had happened. When Takime finished, Runs With The Wind moved some distance away and squatted on the ground. He sat there thinking about what to do next. He knew that he would go after the children, but he must decide what to do about Lydia. He had found only one set of tracks, but there could be others that he missed. It was too dangerous for her to stay here and too cumbersome to take her with him. He needed Takime to go with him, but Lydia needed Takime to stay with her. He made his decision and called Takime to him.

"Takime, go lodge. Lydia too. Leave sacks."

Jackson nodded and leaned down to watch Runs With The Wind take a stick and draw the trail in the earth. It seemed fairly simple. The trail they had been following was well worn and Takime assumed the rest of the trail would be the same. Runs With The Wind drew several lines indicating intersecting trails, but the one to the lodge was consistently northwest.

Runs With The Wind stood up and walked over to Lydia. He said, "Me get Sassy." He pointed to Takime and then the trail and said, "Go lodge."

Lydia nodded. She placed her hands on Runs With The Wind's forearms and gently squeezed them. He turned and, stepping into the woods, vanished. She stumbled over to the supplies and sat down, placing her elbows on a sack. She bowed her head and prayed aloud for her family's safe return. The prayer had a calming effect on her. She rose and handed food to Jackson, then finished packing the sacks.

She spoke to her son: "We will take all the sacks and hide them beneath the brush in the woods. Turn the chickens loose and leave them here."

Jackson gathered the sacks from the clearing and moved them to the edge of the woods. There was very little time before dark. They would have to quickly hide the sacks and find a place to sleep. Lydia pulled her thoughts together. She must work alongside her son.

They removed extra clothes and a little food from the sacks, then dragged them quickly into a thicket. They scavenged for light tree limbs with leaves still attached and brushed away the traces of the dragging. When finished, they went back to the trail and continued northwest. It was a bright night and they decided to walk as far as they could before settling down. They went on until they were very tired and walking so slowly that they decided they might as well stop. Leaving the trail, they took shelter under a pine tree, put on their extra clothing for warmth, and lay down for the night.

Runs With The Wind had tried to find the intruder's trail. The only tracks visible were Billips's. He followed them until second dark when he could not see well enough to go any further for he was deep in the woods, not on any trail. The moonlight was not sufficient for tracking.

He needed to intercept the stranger before he reached the rest of his party. Even if he found Billips, the two of them would be no match for thirty braves.

He tried to sleep, but his mind kept him awake. He knew how badly he needed rest and silently talked himself into slumber. His breathing became heavy and he slid into the world of dreams.

As day was breaking he awoke with a start. Instantly he was on his feet. He went back to the place where he had last seen signs of Billips. Billips was heading directly south and walking in the clear spaces of the woods, although he was not taking any of the animal trails. He was not trying to hide his passing at all and his path was easy to follow.

For about an hour, Runs With The Wind continued in the direction that he thought Billips would go. He came across a small tree limb broken and dangling from a tree. He bent down close to examine it. The shape of an arrow was dug into the ground beneath it, pointing directly east. For some reason, Billips had made a turn. If any of The People From The South were around, they too could follow the arrow and know which way to go.

Even so, Runs With The Wind left everything just the way it was. After moving on several paces, he turned and went back to the arrow drawn on the ground. He knelt beside it and with his finger traced an inverted "V," the sign of The People of the Mountains. If any of his

27

people passed the spot, they would know that he had gone in that direction.

A little farther along, he saw the broad back of Billips. Billips was standing still, looking at something in his hand. He turned as the boy approached and did not seem surprised to find him there.

"Look," he said, as he held his hand out to Runs With The Wind. It was a small crushed leaf. "I found one of these back there and another one right here."

Runs With The Wind took the leaf and smelled it. The odor of its juice was still strong.

Runs With The Wind took the lead and Billips followed. They traveled quickly but carefully. The stranger, with two children in tow, could not travel as fast. Also, Runs With The Wind reasoned, those children would be making enough noise to cover any small sounds their pursuers might make. With any luck, Runs With The Wind and Billips should come across them well before the sun was high.

They saw a small stream. Runs With The Wind held up his hand for Billips to stop. He went down the slight incline and followed the stream for several hundred feet while Billips waited up above. He found what he thought he would—footprints in the slightly damp bank, those of the stranger and smaller impressions belonging to Sassy. He was not carrying her anymore. They had knelt down to drink. The man's knee had left an imprint. A little way up the hillside was another crushed leaf.

Run With The Wind could not see Billips from his position so he bird-called to him. Billips came quickly. Runs With The Wind pointed out the footprints and the mashed leaf. They both drank deeply of the cold, running water and headed back up the hillside. It was not long before they came across another path going east. This was several inches deep and well used, but not much lately. A thick growth of grass and weeds covered it. They were almost certain that the stranger had taken it. He was becoming careless and not even trying to hide his direction.

"Many braves near. Man not care if followed," Runs With The Wind noted. "No noise. Kill quick."

He put his hand on Billips's carbine and pushed it away. Except for his knife, it was Billips's only weapon. He thought about leaving it, but decided against it in case they ran into the rest of the war party. Better to slay one of them than none of them, he thought. They moved on down the path.

Neither Lydia nor Jackson had rested well and both were awake as dawn filtered down through the boughs. The nightmare of the previous day's events struck at Lydia like physical blows. Her children. The savages had them. It was real, it was not a horror to be shaken off with the coming of day. A wave of dizziness swept over her. Her hands shook. She lay still until it passed, then tried to think calmly. There was nothing she could do. The best thing was to go on to the Indian village as she had been told. But she promised herself that she would never be caught so helpless again. She sat up and saw Jackson staring at her from his pallet of pine needles.

"Son, when this is over, I want you to show me how to use that bow and arrow. And maybe that knife . . . and a carbine too."

She knelt and silently prayed for God to save the lives of her children, her husband, and the Indian boy. She asked God to protect her and Jackson on their journey. Jackson gathered up their few items and urged her onto the trail.

It took them through a valley, winding its way south for a while, then north again. With so little to carry, they made good time. In midafternoon, just as they were approaching the base of a mountain, a man appeared in front of them. He carried a bow but made no attempt to draw it. No one moved. Jackson raised his arm in greeting. The Indian returned the gesture and stepped aside. No one spoke. Jackson and Lydia cautiously walked past. They continued along the trail, looking behind them from time to time. The Indian was following. He seemed always the same distance from them. If they rounded a bend, he did not hurry to catch up, but on the straight path, they would see him again. It was impossible to tell what he might be thinking. His expression never changed. They hoped that he was from Runs With The Wind's tribe, but they could not be sure.

The trail led them up the mountain. Greenbrier was so thick on both sides of the path that no man could enter the forest. Someone had recently hacked it on each side of the trail, clearing stray tendrils away, leaving just enough room to walk single file. The greenbrier patch went on for yards and yards.

Jackson said, "Mommy, that Indian back there better be friendly, because there is nowhere for us to go but straight up."

Lydia nodded agreement and glanced back again at the man following them.

They rounded another bend and saw a platform built above and across the path. It was suspended by a network of woven vines, each attached high up in oak trees on both sides of the path. A man sitting cross-legged on the platform was watching them. From his position, he could see anyone coming up the path for quite some distance. He remained motionless as they passed under the platform. From somewhere far away, they could hear a dog barking.

The path began to level off. They reached a plateau heavily planted with corn and continued along the worn path that skirted the field until they came to a small group of trees. Lydia and Jackson stopped to rest in their shade. All of the lower limbs were removed from the trees as high as a tall man could reach. Here and there, lying up against the tree trunks, were tightly woven baskets with lids attached. A crude shelter, open on one end, stood in the center of the grove of trees. It had a small second story about a foot and a half high with handles of farming implements protruding from its opening.

Lydia and Jackson took up their march along the path. They came to another clearing and stopped. Before them lay a village. From their vantage point, they could see several dozen lodges circling a huge rectangular building. There were no trees, bushes, or even grass growing around the lodges. The ground was packed hard from the weight of many feet over a span of years. There was a tiny cooking fire burning outside each lodge that the women were attending. Children and dogs were everywhere.

The Indian who had trailed them to the village now took the lead and motioned for them to follow. As they entered the precincts of the village, dogs yapped at their heels and young children began to shyly follow.

Young men and boys about Jackson's age stared openly at him, but when he looked back, they turned their eyes away. The women, Lydia noticed, were simply dressed in lightweight doeskins seamed together on the sides and shoulders with one or two necklaces for decoration. Lydia smiled and nodded at them but they too would not allow their eyes to meet hers.

The Indian they were following stopped before one of the lodges and indicated for Jackson and Lydia to wait. He entered and soon reappeared with another.

"Tak-i-me," the man exclaimed to Jackson's and Lydia's delight.

"Lame Crow!" Jackson shouted. He jumped on his old friend and hugged him. Lame Crow laughed and held Takime at arm's length, inspecting him for growth. The boy had grown taller but he was not yet very muscular.

"Where Billips? Where Runs With The Wind? Where Sassy?"

"Somebody took Sassy and my brother. Poppy and Runs With The Wind went after him."

Hearing this, Lame Crow turned to face Lydia. He saw the sorrow of a grieving mother and his spirit went out to her. Her long chestnut hair, usually pinned up, had fallen loose. Her blue eyes, a shade darker than Sassy's, had a bewildered look. With her arms folded across her waist, she held her back straight. She was very shaken, but otherwise all right.

With a wave of his arms, he scattered the children surrounding the visitors. Obediently, but not quietly, they dispersed among the many lodges. They ran excitedly to their mothers, chattering and asking questions and describing the white people to them.

Lame Crow led his guests inside the lodge and stepped back out to tell the woman at the fire to bring food. He returned and sat quietly beside his guest.

"Tak-i-me, speak," he said.

In the best way he could, Jackson explained everything that had happened since Runs With The Wind first appeared at their cabin door. When he was finished, he waited for Lame Crow's comment.

Lame Crow said, "Eat, rest. I will speak to the People on your behalf. They might help and they might not. I will try my best for you, old friends."

Runs With The Wind and Billips heard them before they saw them. The baby was crying. They stayed far enough behind so that they could not themselves be detected. Over the sound of crying, the warrior said something. The pair realized the little group had stopped just around the next turn in the path.

Billips and Runs With The Wind swerved into the woods and dropped to the ground just as Lone Runner came back around the bend in the trail and looked. Seeing nothing there, he retreated.

Billips and Runs With The Wind crept forward until they saw Sassy and the baby. There was a vine tied around Sassy's neck. It was long and dragged on the ground behind her. A piece of rawhide was tied across her mouth. Why had he not tied a rawhide around the baby's mouth as well? For lack of anything else, Sassy was gathering large, soft leaves from a sassafras tree to put in the baby's cloth.

The stranger stood guard. His bow was in his hand but the arrows were still in their quiver. The baby was propped against a tree trunk beside Sassy. He had stopped crying and was watching her.

Runs With The Wind set and aimed his bow. At the same instant he loosed his arrow, Billips broke out of the woods with his knife raised.

The arrow struck Lone Runner in the side, just below his ribs. It was in deep; the pain, agonizing. He dropped his bow and clutched the shaft, his eyes dazed. Billips was on top of him, knocking him to the ground. Lone Runner fought back with a surge of strength, but the battle was already lost, he knew. He opened his mouth to sing his death song but nothing came out. The only sound was the baby laughing as Billips drove his knife into the brave's throat and pulled it all the way across. He stood above the Indian and watched as the man's life poured onto the ground. The head was almost severed. Billips was smeared with blood.

Sassy stood by the tree, her eyes terror stricken. The baby's squealing laughter brought her to her senses. She thought to grab him and run, and bent to pick him up.

"Priscilla."

Runs With The Wind came alongside her. Tears filled her eyes and ran down her cheeks as soon as she recognized him. He untied the rawhide from her mouth and the vine from her neck. Her mouth was stuffed with pine needles. Her stomach heaved as he tried to clean out her mouth. She retched but her stomach was empty. There was nothing he could do until she was finished, then he motioned for her to be as quiet as possible. Her neck was raw from the vine and there were welts across her face from the rawhide. She was dirty and tired and hungry, but she was alive and his heart was glad.

Billips picked up his son and walked over to them. The baby was hungry but there were no marks on him. Billips put his free arm around his daughter and hugged her to him. His face turned a shade darker when he saw the marks on her neck and face.

"Poppy, I tried to run away," she said, "but . . ."

"Shh, Sunshine," he warned. "This place is full of enemies. We have to be quiet and get far away from here as quickly as we can. You can tell me all of it later."

He handed her the baby and went to pick up his knife. He passed Runs With The Wind kneeling over Lone Runner's body. It looked like he was carving a deep, inverted "V" in the motionless chest. When the boy was finished with that, he systematically destroyed Lone Runner's weapons.

He broke the bow and each of the arrows in half. He took the carved wooden club and beat the stone knife until it snapped in two, then smashed the club against a boulder until it cracked. When he was done, a smile of satisfaction crossed his face. The dead Indian had no weapons. He would be one less threat to Runs With The Wind's ancestors in the spirit world.

Lame Crow retrieved the ceremonial drum from just inside the entrance of the huge meeting lodge in the center of the village and beat a simple cadence. The village fell silent. The women ceased their chores and looked first toward the main lodge and then toward Lame Crow's woman, Wananada.

Wananada, standing alone by her fire, continued to prepare the evening meal as though nothing out of the ordinary was happening. She kept her head down and would not look at the other women. She knew it was her husband beating the drum. He had not taken the time to explain to her why he was doing this. There was nothing she could do but trust in him and stand by him if he needed her.

The men of the village left their lodges and approached Lame Crow. They entered the council house in single file, gathering around the small fire in the center of the large room. Lame Crow continued drumming until the last man settled himself in the circle of life. Then he took his place beside the fire.

All was silent. His friend Great Hawk stood up and said, "My brother, why do you beat the drum of war? Many fields of corn lived and were harvested since I last heard the drum of war. The drum of war is beat against an enemy. Where is our enemy?" Great Hawk spread his arms out to encompass the group. "I see no enemy here."

"Our enemy comes from the south," Lame Crow answered. "Your grandson tracks our enemy as we speak. They have taken the white woman's children. Your grandson is brave, but he is only thirteen winters. He has not seen his vision. He travels with the white man, Billips, and they track one of many."

"The white woman's enemy is not our enemy," Little Badger reasoned. "Let the ones from the south have her children."

"Be sensible, Little Badger. The ones from the south did not come here for white children. They did not know white children were here. We are The People of the Mountains. They came to the mountains for us. If we do not track them down before they find our village, they will burn our cornfields and steal our women and children."

Lame Crow waited for his message to reach everyone. Then he continued, "Our fathers spoke of such times. Remember?"

Great Hawk said, "When I was a young man, the people of my village were attacked by the Apalachees from the south. We could not live in safety or peace so we left our village and searched for a safe place. It was then that our old *sachem*, Squint Eye, had a dream. In his dream, the mountaintops touched Grandfather Sky and asked our people to live between them. The mountains promised our people peace if we would live upon them. We found these mountains and built our lodges upon them. We planted our crops upon them. And, true to their promise, we have lived in peace. Now the Apalachees come again. We must not let them chase us from our homes once again. We must fight!"

"Lame Crow and Great Hawk speak well. I will make war against the ones from the south. My son is brave and wise. How can a father behave less bravely and less wisely than his son?" So saying, Bear Paw, father of Runs With The Wind, lifted his tomahawk above his head and sang, "*Hiieeee, hiieeee.*"

His singing pierced the silence of the camp. Yellow Bird, wife of Bear Paw, heard her husband's war cry and moved toward the door of her lodge. She would prepare: food for his journey, clothes for war. She would set out his paint pots, but she would not open them lest she accidentally touch the paint. It was too sacred for a woman to touch.

Yellow Bird had never before made such preparations but she knew how to do it all. Stories handed down by her mother and her mother's mother had anticipated this inevitable day. She would put on her best clothes for the ceremony that would surely be held before the men departed.

One by one, the women of the camp heard the war cry of each husband and son and entered their lodges to make ready for the ceremony of war. Only Oak Leaf, the medicine woman of the tribe, remained outside. She waited to be called by the council and formally told of their plans. She, in turn, would pass them on to the women. In this way, the warriors would not have to speak to their wives or mothers before leaving. Once a man called the spirit of war to him, he spent no more of his energy or time on women until battle was over.

Oak Leaf had many medicines in her dwelling. Those for healing wounds she would give to old Leather Face. She would say the sacred words over each one and he would carry them for the warriors.

Lydia and Takime sat in Lame Crow's lodge, listening to the strange cries. The sound frightened them.

Lydia said, "What do you think they are doing?"

"Making themselves angry."

They sat on the edge of a bed curtained with animal skins, the remains of a cold fire before them. Directly across was another sleeping place; two more were at the other end of the room.

They did not know what all the commotion was and there was no one to ask. Wananada entered and handed them food without even looking at them. Then she busied herself around the room, totally ignoring them.

It was first dark before Lame Crow returned to the lodge. He came in quickly, acknowledging no one. He gathered up his belongings and left. Wananada put some clothing over her arm and followed him. Jackson started for the door but Lydia pulled him back.

"Say nothing. Do nothing," she said. "We are guests. Please do not do anything that would stop them from going after Sassy and the baby. That must be what they are doing."

Jackson sat back down beside his mother. There was no light inside the lodge, and the glow from the small fire outside the door was not enough to see by. A great deal of noise and activity was going on around them. When they heard the sound of drums beating again, his curiosity won out.

"Mommy, I must go outside and see what is happening."

"Do not leave me here by myself," Lydia begged. But she sensed his disappointment. "Never mind. I will go with you," she added. Nervously she went to the door and stepped outside.

The entire village had gathered at the ceremonial grounds in front of the meeting lodge. The children were dressed in finely sewn and exquisitely decorated clothing. There were small bones strung around their arms and legs that jangled as they walked. The women wore many necklaces and dresses embellished with dyed porcupine quills.

No one seemed to notice Lydia or Jackson, so they followed the people toward the huge bonfire burning in the middle of the grounds. Off to the side of the earthen arena, three men sat at a large drum. They were fearful to look upon, their bodies covered with bear grease. They glistened in the firelight, and their faces and bodies were harshly painted in patterns of white and red and black and yellow. Weapons lay at their feet. Their hair and the weapons were decorated with feathers and strips of fur.

As the men hammered the drums, the women formed a large circle, leaving an opening in front of the meeting-lodge door. They lifted first one foot and then the other in time to the drums, standing in the same positions for a long time. The drummers sang out in high-pitched, feminine voices.

Suddenly, with a great cry, the warriors burst from the lodge, swinging their tomahawks and posturing threateningly. They grouped themselves in a circle inside that made by the women and began a masquerade of war.

No two warriors were dressed alike or had painted their bodies the same way. Some wore animal heads above their own, others wore capes or loincloths made of fur. They grunted and groaned and waved their weapons in the air before bringing them down on the heads of their imagined victims. All the while, they kept step to the cadence of the drums, never breaking the circle of life.

Lydia searched for Lame Crow among the dancers. She could not find him, then realized she would not be able to recognize him. The scene before her was so savage that she was tempted to run back down the greenbrier path toward home. She turned to the other women for solace, but their faces were set as though in stone. They swayed to the drums. Cries and moans escaped their lips.

Lydia turned to Jackson, standing next to her. She saw a look of rapture on her young son's face such as she had never seen there before. The light from the fire glittered in his eyes and strangely shadowed his face. He was totally unaware of her beside him, so lost was he in the ceremony. For an instant she was afraid for him. Then she saw his face relax and he turned toward her and smiled.

"Have you ever seen anything like it?" he said.

"No, son," she murmured. "No. Never."

The ceremony continued. After several hours, the menacing warriors no longer frightened her as much as they had at the beginning. She even recognized a few of them.

The constant sound of the drum lulled her into a stupor. She was so fatigued from the strain of the day that she decided to make her way back to the lodge alone in the dark. Jackson was somewhere about, but she did not see him when she left the circling dancers.

Inside the lodge where she would sleep, a small glow of light from the fire outside illuminated the interior. She threw a few sticks on it from the stack beside the entryway and lay down across the closest bed. There were no windows, only the doorway. She fell asleep to incessant drums.

Some time later the silence woke her. She did not know when the drumming had stopped but all was quiet now. There was just enough light to see that she was alone in the lodge. Her body was aching. She must have lain in one position since she fell asleep. She stood up and stretched just as Jackson entered.

"I tried to go with them, but they would not let me. 'Not enough winters,' they said. 'Not enough winters.'" He looked crestfallen, ashen in the moonlight. "They're gone."

4

The Tuscarora were exhausted after traveling at a lope since morning. The warriors ate a cold supper and spread out in the woods at first dark to sleep.

Many Arrows, the war man, chose the first watch. It was his hope to find the Apalachees before sundown the next day. He needed time alone to consider a plan of action.

He had been chosen war man because of his strength and intelligence, his gift for strategy, and his hunting prowess. He was a handsome man, brawny and agile with deep-set eyes, a strong chin, and prominent nose. He feared nothing. Defeat did not enter his mind.

Like most of his clan, he had never been to war. He had been two winters old when the clan moved to the mountains from the place by the rivers where three trails meet. Thirty winters had passed since then. He had heard of skirmishes among neighboring tribes—The People of the Skaruren visited often and brought rumors of wars to the east of them—but no tribe considered the Tuscaroras' mountain range valuable enough to fight over. Many Arrows knew that the white eyes were moving further west and pushing the friendly Delaware and other tribes in front of them. The red man was fighting for his homeland hunting grounds. When he lost, he moved west. In times past, he had gone north or south, but now more and more of those southern and northern tracts were in the hands of the whites. West lay the only hope.

He sat thoughtfully, mulling every detail of past battles that had been recounted endlessly around evening campfires, handed down from generation to generation.

He considered the carbines of the white man. Many Indians used them now. They got them through trading or took them in battle. Several of his friends had carried theirs to the last green corn festival. But there was not even one carbine among his clan. Blackbird discouraged trading with the white man or using the white man's tools.

Only one trader had ever come into their mountains; he did not come with guns. He came with blankets and beads and other precious things. They had eagerly traded with him. When he left, he stole their furs and took back some of the blankets. When they found out, Great Hawk and Bear Paw were chosen to follow him. Great Hawk and Bear Paw hacked him to pieces and left his body for the animals to feast on.

Five winters had passed since then, and no other white trader had ever come into the mountains as far as their village.

If possible, he thought, this battle with the hostage takers must be fought in the forest until he could determine if the Apalachees had carbines. He knew the rifles were not as effective in the dense woods. There were too many hiding places, and a warrior could shoot several arrows while a carbine was reloaded.

At dawn the warriors continued south and southeast. Runners were sent ahead. The rest traveled more slowly and cautiously.

About midday, High Step, a young runner, came back to meet them. He had spotted the Apalachees' camp. It lay nearly two hours away. Many Arrows sent two men to find the other runners, Winter Sun and Red Dog, to tell them where the Apalachees were located. High Step stayed behind to lead the main body of warriors to the encampment.

At the outskirts of the camp, they spread out through the forest and approached cautiously. Several men went ahead, their main responsibility being to quietly wipe out any sentinels.

The first to encounter an Apalachee was Red Dog. He was sprinting down an old and well-worn path when he came face to face with an enemy warrior. Neither man had the time or the distance to draw his bow. Each gave his victory cry and attacked. Red Dog took a glancing tomahawk blow on his shoulder even as he delivered a crushing swipe to the side of the Apalachee's head. Again and again, he struck the man. Ignoring the hot blood from his own body running down his back, he savaged his opponent long after the life was gone from the warrior. When Red Dog finally stopped, the corpse at his feet was beyond recognition. Red Dog dropped his club and bent over, gasping for breath. He lifted his hand to the wound on his shoulder, testing it, and to see if he could halt the bleeding. It felt as though part of him was shorn away. The bleeding would not stop. He tried to think of a way to stanch the flow. He staggered into the woods as far as he could manage. He was afraid that he might faint.

Red Dog thought of his new baby and his wife and wondered if the dead man had a son to avenge him. He went down on his knees and rolled onto his back, pressing his wound against the ground. It did not hurt as much in that position. He needed to rest before seeking the main party again. He gazed up at the sun through the pattern of leaves from the great trees. He was very tired. He closed his eyes and rested, and slowly bled to death. Red Dog was the first from his clan to die in battle in more than thirty years.

When the main body of warriors reached the Apalachee camp they found it empty. Many Arrows instructed several men to search for signs of the white children and to determine if Billips or Runs With The Wind had been taken prisoner. They discovered a small stack of books like the one the white child had given Lame Crow. They looked through the pages and passed the books around, laughing and mimicking the pictures and posing and prancing across the ground. They ran their fingers across the words and repeated some of the dialogue from Lame Crow's book. Mostly, their English words sounded like gibberish. Lame Crow looked at them and laughed, but secretly he watched closely to see that no one harmed the precious books.

Many Arrows interrupted their revelry. "These talking leaves are Billips's. Put them the way you found them. The Apalachees must not know we were here. They stole them from Billips and they have probably burned his cabin. They will come back here. We will hide in the woods, waiting. We will attack when they reach the open. If they have carbines, they cannot hit us among the trees." He glanced around the deserted campsite. "I see no sign of captives or the children."

That was all the instruction they would get from Many Arrows. It was up to each man to choose his own hiding spot in the surrounding forest. Each man was raised from early childhood to think and act for himself and there would be no practice or drills for this battle. They left the camp as they had found it and quietly faded into the woods.

Some chose to hide in the surrounding thickets, others behind or up in the branches of trees. Once concealed, they did not move again. They waited several hours. The first Apalachee to appear was a runner. He sprinted ahead to make sure no one was on the path or at the camp. Lame Crow was furthermost from the camp and closest to the approaching runner.

Lame Crow sat high in an old oak tree, camouflaged by its many branches and leaves. He had selected a spot giving a clear view of nearly a hundred yards of a well-worn and hard-packed path. He raised his bow as soon as the Apalachee came into view. When the distance was right, he let the arrow fly, hitting the Apalachee in the stomach with great force.

Lame Crow was out of the tree and on the ground almost as soon as the Apalachee fell. He dragged the still living man into the woods and killed him with his knife.

Lame Crow intended to rush back onto the path and clear up any evidence of the runner's fate before the main party came into view. When he reached the edge of the woods, he saw that old Leather Face was already there, carefully brushing away all signs of the struggle. When Leather Face was finished, he stepped back into the woods and disappeared.

Lame Crow decided to stay near the path in case a second runner preceded the main party. A good while passed. He heard the Apalachee approaching. He counted off two tens—two Xs of them. They were in good spirits and talking among themselves. Near the back of the group, two were carrying deer on their shoulders. Lame Crow itched to let another arrow fly, but he let the Apalachees pass without harm. They did not notice anything out of the ordinary as they crossed the place where he had shot the runner.

Lame Crow stayed in position until he heard war cries in the distance and knew his tribe was attacking. He started for the camp, then stopped abruptly. Another Apalachee was running up the path toward his camp. He had heard the commotion and his bow was ready. Just as he passed, Lame Crow shot him in the back. The warrior pitched forward on his face. Leather Face ran from the woods and attacked, beating the man to death with his club.

Lame Crow watched for a moment and then ran toward the main battle. As he ran he was thinking that the old man had been brought along mainly for his knowledge of healing and medicines, but he was proving himself a valuable fighter.

There was no time for strategy when Lame Crow reached the bloody scene at the camp. An Apalachee warrior, just rising up from hacking a Tuscarora brave to pieces, spotted Lame Crow entering the clearing. Lame Crow recognized him as one of the deer carriers. The Apalachee struck with a knife, gashing Lame Crow's upper arm. Lame Crow fell to his knees, expecting a continued attack, but the Apalachee ran past into the woods.

Lame Crow struggled to a standing position and surveyed the killing ground. Dead and dying men were strewn about. Another Apalachee dashed away toward the woods in a different direction.

The outnumbered Apalachees were not staying and fighting. They were scurrying away at first opportunity. This was strange behavior for warriors. Once engaged in direct combat, a warrior fought to the death, but not these.

Lame Crow tried to follow the last Apalachee he saw fleeing. He ran a few steps and halted. He was losing blood and with it his strength. He walked back to the edge of the clearing and leaned against a tree. Although his vision was blurring, he could see that the battle was already almost over. Many Arrows had a prisoner in tow. Other than being bound and gagged, the man looked in good condition. He had no visible wounds and was able to walk.

Three Tuscarora were dead and two wounded, unable to rise. Lame Crow saw one of his clan chase into the woods after an Apalachee. There were eleven dead Apalachees and three more engaged in a death battle, the odds against them. About half of his own clan were missing. They were probably running down Apalachees who were trying to escape.

"Come." Leather Face was suddenly beside him, tugging at his good arm. "Let me mend your shoulder."

Lame Crow turned away from what remained of the battle and followed Leather Face into the woods.

Tired and aching, John Billips and the youngsters arrived at the village in the afternoon. A young boy of nine or ten winters was on the platform that straddled the greenbrier barrier. He hailed Runs With The Wind.

"The warriors have all gone. They left two moons ago. Only the very young boys and the very old men remain to guard the women and the crops." He waved his small bow proudly. "I am the one chosen to protect the greenbrier pathway."

"They have chosen well, my little friend. None but a winged mosquito will get by you," said Runs With The Wind. "Did a white woman and her son come here?"

"Yes," the boy said. "They are with Wananada."

The little group eased past the sentry and down the corn path toward the village.

Billips spied his wife sitting on the ground outside one of the lodges, making moccasins. She looked up and saw them coming.

"Jackson, they are here! They have them! *They have them!*" she screamed as she threw the leather work down and ran to her husband and children.

She grabbed the baby in one arm and hugged Priscilla with the other. At the same time she stretched up to kiss Billips.

"I knew you would bring them back to me," she said with deep emotion. Clutching her children, she turned to Runs With The Wind and said, "I count you among my sons, now and forever."

The Indian boy understood and gave her a broad smile. He had many aunts and now he had two mothers. Life was very good.

Jackson had come out of the lodge and was watching. Sassy broke loose from her mother's grip and ran and hugged him.

"Oh, Jackson. It is so good. Sometimes I thought I would never see any of you again."

Although he did not say so, there had been moments when Jackson had been afraid of that, too. With great relief, he returned Sassy's embrace and then he noticed the mark on her neck. The same dark look that had spread across Billips's face now swept over his. He ran his finger across the wound. Part of it was an open sore, inflamed where the vine had rubbed it raw and dirt had lain in it. Sassy flinched in pain.

"Please, don't do that," she said.

"All right, little sister, but it makes me mad to see it."

Sassy looked around. "Lame Crow? Is this where Lame Crow lives?"

Lydia answered. "He does, but he is gone now. I will tell you all about it soon."

Wananada appeared in the door of the lodge and walked over to the girl to inspect her neck. As the rest went inside the lodge to talk, Wananada left to get the medicine woman, Oak Leaf. A small smile played across her lips. She was smiling for the first time since the white people had come. The big man, Billips, had arrived. He had not been killed. Now Wananada would not have to share her lodge with the white woman. Her husband would not be considering taking another wife.

Although the lodge belonged to her, if Lame Crow chose to hunt for a woman who had no husband, it would be unseemly to object. If the woman were one of the People, Wananada would not object. But this strange creature, with her skin turned inside out and her eyes a shocking color, was not wanted in her lodge. Wananada had examined her several times and saw that she was perfectly formed. That did not help. The woman smelled peculiar, and her body looked too soft, like the shining mud beside the riverbank.

There was a bounce in Wananada's step that had not been there that morning. Yes, she thought, I have much to be happy about. Everything will be the same in my lodge since the big man has come.

"The man grabbed me and took the baby away," Sassy explained. "He hurt my face . . . my neck. He held me by the hair, with his hand across my mouth, and my feet could not touch the ground. He ran for a long time like that. He ran until he was breathing so hard I thought he would die." Sassy took a deep breath. "I hoped he would."

She glanced at her mother to see how she had taken that last declaration. Lydia was listening intently but there was no change in her when she heard her daughter announce that she had wished the death of another.

"But then he started to walk," Sassy said. "After a while, he put me down. I fell and he dragged me off further into the woods. He never did put his hand over the baby's mouth, and the baby never cried all that time. He liked the running. I could hear him laughing sometimes.

"Anyhow," she continued, "we rested, and then he gave me the baby to carry. He took us to a little creek and we drank some water. He made a funnel from leaves and gave the baby water. The baby choked some but drank it. I fixed the baby's cloth with moss, but that did not work too good. It was too damp."

Oak Leaf came in and silently inspected Priscilla's face and neck as she talked. The marks on the little girl's face would be gone soon but there were several bad places on her neck. Oak Leaf decided which medicines she would need to help heal the wounds and quietly left to get them.

Sassy went on with her story: "He seemed to be fascinated with the baby. He came over and watched when I fixed the cloth. He touched the baby all over and the baby laughed and that savage kept grunting at him.

"He gave us some food to eat and I chewed it first and then gave it to the baby. Then that *Indian* did the same thing. I pushed his hand away from the baby's mouth, but he knocked me down and fed the baby anyway.

"We did not walk too much farther after that. He found the place he wanted to sleep for the night. I made a bed for me and the baby. After he fell asleep, I picked up the baby and we left." Sassy's eyes darkened a little at the memory. She had been very frightened of traveling alone with the baby in the night.

She shrugged her thin little shoulders and went on. "We were gone just a little ways when he came from out of nowhere and found us and carried us back. That is when he put the vine on me. He never took it off again. He tied me to a tree and the next day, he pulled on me all day long. I could not go as fast as him. He carried the baby and pulled on me all the time. At least he didn't hurt the baby."

Her eyes brightened as they rested on her father for an instant. "And then Poppy and Runs With The Wind found us and they killed that dirty, mean Indian." Finished with her story, she sat back, exhausted.

"You were very brave," her father said. "And you took care of your baby brother just fine." He noticed a woman coming back in, carrying several baskets of herbs. "After she treats your neck, I want you to eat something and then lie down and sleep a good while. Do not worry about anything. We will be right outside."

Billips, Lydia, Jackson, and Runs With The Wind went walking through the village. Lydia told Billips of the experiences she and Jackson had had since he had left them in the woods, including one involving a young woman of the village who had brought an infant to Lydia to suckle. The woman's name was Day Star.

Day Star had quietly walked into the lodge early in the morning and handed the infant to Lydia, motioning for her to feed it. Lydia recoiled at the idea. The baby had not been fed and was restlessly moving around and whimpering. But just from the sight of the infant, Lydia's breast began leaking milk, staining the top of her dress. She knew she needed to empty her breast even though she balked at the idea of feeding this Indian baby.

At the time, she did not know when, or even if, her own baby would be rescued so she finally accepted the infant. All pangs of doubt left her as she held the infant in her arms and hoped that somewhere somebody was feeding hers.

"After I fed the infant, Wananada took me to the fields to work," Lydia said, looking at her husband. "I told Jackson to help but Wananada would not permit it. The men do not work in the fields."

Runs With the Wind interrupted: "Billips, come," he said and led the way to the lodge of the shaman Blackbird, which stood at the far end of the village.

. . .

The old man had lived at least eighty winters and he looked it. His bright brown eyes were almost hidden in the cracks and folds of his skin. His body had shrunk with the passing years so that he was not much taller than Sassy. He sat by the ever-burning fire in the center of his lodge warming his old bones and lit a clay pipe. Runs With The Wind sat down beside him. Billips folded his long legs beneath him and joined them.

"I am Blackbird," the old one said in his own tongue. Runs With The Wind interpreted as best he could: "Welcome to the village of The People of the Mountains. It is with sorrow that I greet you in times of trouble. We have lived in peace for many years, but now we must speak of war."

Runs With The Wind took the pipe from Blackbird, puffed on it, and passed it to Billips.

"Changes are taking place in our village," Blackbird continued. "Runs With The Wind smokes the pipe even before he has had his vision. But he has counted coup. Trouble has taken the child from this boy and left a man sitting beside me." He gave Runs With The Wind a long, hard look. "You will be a great warrior someday. You will see many changes take place during your lifetime. They will not all be good."

He turned his attention to Billips. "Your people offer rewards for the scalps of Indians, they capture and sell them into slavery whenever possible and drive the tribes of the south from their lands and, in turn, The People of the South want our lands. The Iroquois will not let us join the Five Nations so that we might better protect ourselves in concert. Soon, there will be nowhere for us to go. Meanwhile, we must shield our women and children. We beat the drum tonight for all to gather. Then, after the council, you and Runs With The Wind must enter the sweat lodge. You have killed a man. Killing a man is a serious undertaking. Even in time of war. You must be purified in order to become acceptable again."

Blackbird sat, staring into the fire. Then he said, "There is among us now a special one. He has strong medicine. I speak of the white baby. Bring him to me an hour before sundown. I wish to be with him for a while."

John Billips blinked rapidly, totally surprised and not knowing what to reply. The old man returned to staring into the fire. Billips and Runs With The Wind waited patiently until the old man said, "You may leave now."

Lydia, on the way to the meeting, was surprised to see how many people remained in and around the village. She could see that some lodges were scattered along the mountainsides. Others were further away and out of sight of the majority.

Arriving at the meeting, she easily found her family and took her place near John. When several minutes passed and no one else entered the meeting room, the leather curtain was dropped over the doorway. At such an important event, she learned, the curtain was closed so the night birds and wild animals could not overhear and carry tales to the enemy.

Blackbird, considered the wisest among them, began the proceedings. "People, we are at war," he said. "We are here to decide the best way to protect our women and children and crops while our warriors are gone. We must prepare for the return of our warriors. We must prepare for the coming snows . . . for invasion by our enemies. And we must prepare to move, if we have to. We must consider and be ready for many alternatives since we have chosen the path of war."

He paused.

"The heart of each of you is touched by war." Blackbird swept the gathering with his strong eyes. "Blackbird has spoken. Now we will hear the voice of every man, woman, or child who wishes to speak." The old man nodded at the crowd and sat down.

There was a great deal of discussion but little disagreement on decisions. Although few understood her words, the most moving speech was given by Lydia. Runs With The Wind interpreted for her how ever much he understood and made up the rest. The people listened attentively, as though she had been among them forever.

"Few of you have known the horror of having your children stolen, but most of you can imagine how a mother feels sitting helpless and wringing her hands, unable to do anything about it. You can imagine how it feels to be a burden instead of a help."

Lydia kept her eyes on the women in the group. "I watched while my husband and Runs With The Wind left to go after that man. I saw my son's great sadness when he found out that he must stay and protect me instead of going with them. And all I could do was cry and beat my breast.

Lydia braced herself before the people and calmly folded her hands. "I have worked hard all my life. But when the day came that I was needed the most, I could do nothing. That is why I am going to ask something that will seem strange to you. What I am going to suggest to you is not your custom. It is not my custom either."

Lydia paused a moment to catch her breath, then she said in a strong voice, "I want to learn to shoot the arrow. I want you to teach me to use the knife. I do not propose to go to war, but if war comes to me, I want to fight for my children and for my life."

There was a great deal of squirming and mumbling as Lydia and Runs With The Wind sat down. Many of the young girls already knew how to use a bow but not proficiently. They had often played with their brothers and cousins. But as they grew older, and custom separated them, they seldom continued the practice.

The older women could also remember pretending they were warriors when they were small children. A few of them hunted small game from time to time. But none considered competing with the boys or young men. The thought was totally foreign to them. But then, so was war. Uneasily, they glanced at the wounds on Priscilla's neck and thought of their own children.

Those women who had had direct contact with Lydia were the first to speak. Oak Leaf stood and declared, "I have no children, but I am willing to learn the use of weapons. It is time." She nodded toward Lydia. "My white sister speaks bravely and logically. We, The People of the Mountains, will be cunning like the fox and slay our unsuspecting enemies. For what nation has taught its women war? None that I have heard of."

Wananada and Runs With The Wind's mother, Yellow Bird, agreed. Day Star stood with her infant in her arms and gave the sign of approval. One by one, the women conceded.

It was a very good thing that mostly young boys and old men attended the gathering, for the warriors certainly would have objected. Old Blackbird would not object. In his many years he had seen enough to know that the enemy would destroy defenseless women and children as quickly as they would destroy an armed foe.

Having watched the settlement of most of the issues brought forward, Blackbird spoke once again before calling the meeting to a close.

"There is a baby among us," he began, "who has special powers. The Apalachee enemy was aware of this and would not hurt the baby. I have laid hands on this baby and a vision came from him and reached out to me."

Blackbird opened his arms wide. "Brilliant white clouds came from him, moving so quickly that an eagle could not catch them. They ran into my forehead. They entered my head and stayed there."

Blackbird tapped his forehead. "This is a good sign. This means that our warriors will win this battle and we may stay here among these mountains for a time longer. But later, other clouds came and passed by me and ran quickly toward the west. One right after another. There were many, many clouds." Blackbird shook his head. "This is not a good sign. The day will come when we must journey to the west. Many, many tribes will travel toward the sleeping sun."

Blackbird waited for the People to understand what he said before proceeding. "It is too soon to name this baby, but I will call him White Cloud, because of the vision that came to me. With his appearance come many changes in our village. Already our young boys must be men. And never in my time, my father's time, or his father's time, have the women thought to be warriors. You have decided that the women will be warriors. It is your decision and so it will be.

"I call upon Bright Eyes, son of Little Badger, to be the mentor of White Cloud as long as he is with us. He is to teach White Cloud the ways of our people and to always be with him in his waking hours, for this child of the spirits cannot hear the human voice. This child hears only the inner voices."

Blackbird bent low to make the People listen closely. "This child, as he grows, may learn all the things that we have failed to learn. We know the song of the bird but he may learn the flight of the bird. We hear the words of a man but he may hear the thoughts of a man. We sometimes make bad decisions by listening to the words of a man, but he will be able to make decisions based on what is in the heart of a man.

"Can we let all of this knowledge remain locked up inside of this boy because he cannot hear or speak?" Blackbird asked. "No, and that is why Bright Eyes must learn to talk with the speechless one. Bright Eyes will be his silent teacher and interpreter. In time, they will speak, the one to the other. That is the way of children. Then they will teach us that way of speaking. In so doing, we, the Tuscarora, will raise up an uncommon one who will strengthen our people in the very difficult times to come."

Blackbird had said all he had to and abruptly sat down. Billips and his family were completely caught off guard when made to understand what Blackbird had said. They had not realized their infant son was deaf.

5

It was amusing how the Tuscarora paid little attention to the time of day, yet the women would begin sauntering toward the fields at about the same hour. They worked hard, they worked together, talking and laughing all the while.

Lydia and Sassy walked to the two small sheds and placed their tools in the storage bin along with all the other tools.

"Mommy, later on today we are going to practice with the bow and arrows. Since you were the one who thought it up, are you coming with us?"

Lydia studied her daughter's face and wondered if it had been a mistake to suggest that she learn to shoot. She behaved so much like a boy now. Teaching her to shoot a bow and arrow would not help make her any more of a lady.

"Yes, I will be there," Lydia said. "But for now, how would you like to take a nice long walk with me? We will stay within sight of the sentinels."

The threat of Apalachee was ever present. Sassy nodded. It would be pleasant to spend time alone with her mother.

"First, I have to stop and feed . . . White Cloud," Lydia said, getting used to the name. How appropriate the silence of passing clouds now seemed. Lydia tamped down the sadness creeping into her mind about his deafness.

The mother of Bright Eyes was taking care of the baby. Lydia fed White Cloud and put him down for a nap. Then she and Sassy climbed the hill behind Lame Crow's lodge. Most of the lodges were in the main clearing, but lodges were sprinkled around the surrounding hillsides, too. Some were very large, holding several families, while others looked like one-family dwellings.

The village was very high up in the mountains to begin with, but this particular peak rose several hundred feet more on two sides behind the clearing. They chose one of the many paths and began to climb. Sometimes the going was easy, but part of the way they had to cling to rocks and overhanging branches. When they reached the very top, they found a shady spot on the ridge and sat down to rest.

The view was overpowering. Directly below them lay the village. On the other side of the mountain behind them was a sheer rock decline that even a mountain goat could not manage and certainly not marauders. In every direction were rolling mountains. Lydia could see water coming from the rocks. There were meadows and valleys at different levels.

The scene made Lydia feel both elated and sad. She appreciated the beauty but the visible isolation was disheartening. But then, she had lived in isolation for several years now. Thoughts of warm fireplaces and curtained bedposts came into her mind. She shrugged and tried to rid her mind of such musings.

Since John had fought with and killed a drunken English soldier outside Philadelphia, there was little chance of ever enjoying the amenities of home again. They had known that there was no justice for them so they had run away. Now there was no turning back. They had spent almost a year traveling from one community to another before deciding to move into the wilderness, alone. They had trekked deeper and deeper into the unbroken forest.

The sweet sound of Priscilla's childish voice rose in song—"Elliott's Consent"—and broke in upon Lydia's reverie. She could not help but to join in:

"'Twas a bloody battle Sir Elliott fought,
A top o' yonder hill,
While brown-eyed Mary, all distraught
Sang from her window sill.

"Oh, Sir, wa' you come,
Come to London Town,
Oh, Sir, wa' you come wi' me.
For I be bound for London Town,
I will arrive in time for tea.

"Sir Elliott never heard a single word,
Of sweet Mary's lonely lament,
So against her will she climbed the hill
To gain Elliott's consent."

Lydia suddenly felt dizzy.

"Mommy, what is wrong?" Sassy said.

"I'm fine. I just got dizzy. The dizziness is already gone." Lydia took several deep breaths. "Oh, dear," Lydia said. "I think I am going to have another baby." Smilingly, she turned to her daughter. "Sassy, you may be having a little brother or sister."

Although smiling, Lydia was deeply troubled. Here they were, stranded in an Indian village. Her newly named White Cloud was only a little over five months old and deaf. It was much too soon to be having another, and perhaps she was no longer strong enough to produce healthy children.

Sassy happily waved her arms in the air, repeating over and over, "A baby, a baby. We are having a baby."

Lydia shook her head as though to make all the bad thoughts go away along with the recurring dizziness.

"Do not get your hopes up too high, Priscilla. I cannot be sure yet about the new baby."

Sassy ignored her mother's doubts.

"I want a sister. I want a baby sister. I have two brothers and I want a sister." She grinned at Lydia impishly.

"Well, a sister would be just fine now that we are turning into savages. She can plow the fields and plant the corn alongside of us just like Jackson used to do alongside your father," Lydia said sarcastically. She slowly stood up, testing her legs.

Sassy said, "Mommy, I like taking care of the corn. I like working with the Tuscarora. I like it here!"

Lydia was taken aback by Sassy's declaration. But then, like Jackson, Sassy knew little else besides the wilderness. And there were children here her own age to play with—bright-eyed, energetic children who were always doing something. The People were a closely knit group. They did everything together.

It was time to get back for the afternoon lesson. Sassy and Lydia reluctantly surrendered their private perch and struggled back down from the peak.

The women and children gathered at the end of the ceremonial grounds to begin their instruction in shooting. Billips was overseeing the procedure since the villagers had never had a formal plan for teaching the use of weapons. The children learned by watching older children and their uncles and fathers, and by joining in the many games using weapons. By the age of five, they were proficient with their small bows and arrows without feathers.

Billips had borrowed the children's bows and old ones left behind by the warriors. He decided that the women could help make their own weapons.

Before such a sacred undertaking as teaching the women and children the games of war, Blackbird spoke to the Great Spirit on behalf of his people: "We have chosen to shelter a white family," he said. "They may stay with us as long as they need to.

"It is true that they have brought strange customs with them. Can we take a new brother in and ask him to leave his customs outside our village?" Blackbird paused. "No. We cannot. It has not been the practice of The People of the Mountains to teach their women in the ways of war. Yet White Sister has asked to be trained in these ways. With our enemy crossing our hunting grounds, how can we refuse?

"We thank the Great Spirit for the day and for the gathering of the people. May their eyes be keen and their arms be strong." He raised his arms to the sky with a flourish. "Let the training commence."

"Anyone wanting to learn to shoot the bow can do so," John Billips announced. He had planned for each pair of women to have a teacher. He had not planned on such a large group. Children barely past the toddling stage came forward as well as several very old women. Given their respect for wisdom and age, the first to step forward was an elderly woman well into her seventieth year. The old woman nodded at the doubtful Billips and grinned a jagged-toothed grin. Nodding and smiling, she accepted the small bow and featherless arrow and, without instruction, shot the arrow accurately into its mark. The clan burst into laughter at the astonished look on Billips's face. They had played a grand joke on him. Old Hekanawaw was an expert markswoman in her youth and had not yet lost her touch. Even now, she would sometimes disappear into the woods and return with small game.

"I see you are learned in the spirit of the bow," Billips acknowledged. "Will you help us teach the others?"

With a little interpretation from Runs With The Wind, she understood his words and nodded yes. Billips paired her up with two young females and sent them off to the side of the arena to practice. He took the very young males and, watching them shoot once or twice, paired them with even younger children. He gave Sassy and another girl about her age to Runs With The Wind. Meanwhile, Blackbird took over the training of Lydia and Oak Leaf.

It took almost an hour to pair everyone up and find a place for each group to practice. By the time he finished, Billips noted that few of them were actually practicing with their assigned partners. He did not understand much of what was being said, yet he knew their soft voices were constantly giving advice to one another and disagreeing with each other's teaching techniques. There was absolutely no order to their methods, yet he could see improvement.

Unsolicited advice was prolific. Partners were changed and switched back again. Some stopped practicing altogether and engaged in private conversation. There was no discipline. Yet, mostly they practiced. They learned. They were great mimics, watching a demonstration once or twice and then executing it precisely. Given a little time, they could be shooting against some of the best men.

Later that day, in the lodge of Wananada, Billips discussed the first training session.

"I was surprised at the progress we made," he said. "They are a strong and healthy group. Everyone could shoot."

"Poppy, did you watch me?" Sassy exclaimed. "I love it here, Poppy. Do we have to go back to the cabin? I want to live here, Poppy. Can we stay?"

Before he could answer, Jackson interrupted. "I want to stay here, too," Jackson nearly shouted, "and I want to be called Takime. Did you see me teaching the little daughters of Many Arrows? They call me Takime. They laugh and giggle all the time, but both of them learned to shoot today."

Billips was at a loss for words. This wilderness did not have much in the way of a life to offer his children or his wife. Isolation and loneliness and hard work were all they had known for a long time. There had been no community.

He enjoyed the company of these villagers, too. What a relief it was to share the responsibility of providing for his family. What a difference it made, living with the Tuscarora instead of alone on a mountaintop? No one in the world outside knew where they were—

59

that was unchanged. By this time, probably no one cared. He turned to Lydia.

"Well, what do you think?"

"There is something I must tell you before I answer," she said. She had been thinking things over all day. "I could be with child. Rather than face another hard winter without another woman around for help and companionship, I would prefer to stay here a while, too."

Billips's face broke into a big grin. He picked her up and swung her around. "A baby! How wonderful. I thought these three little savages were all the family we would ever have. Well, that settles it. Of course, we will have to bring the question before the council when the warriors return." Then he frowned and added, "If they return."

"Blackbird says they will return," Sassy interjected. "Remember? He says they will return and there will be peace in the mountains again."

"Yes, Sunshine. I remember what Blackbird said." John Billips gazed down at his sleeping infant son. "White Cloud," he murmured. He turned to Jackson and said, "Son, if the council says we can stay, then you and I will have a lodge to build. We cannot live in Lame Crow and Wananada's lodge forever."

Lydia said, "Why *do* they have their own lodge? A lot of the families live together. Is it because they're childless? Oak Leaf is childless, too. She also lives alone in a lodge all by herself."

John Billips shrugged. "They can live any way they want. There are no rules. Listen," he continued, "there is a great deal of work to be done. Before you know it, winter will be upon us. With most of the men gone, we will have to bring in as much meat and fish and firewood as we can. The women will not have a lot of help harvesting the crops or smoking fish this year since the men are away."

Lydia placed her hand on her husband's shoulder. "John, they have been living here for many years and they have done well. Stop worrying so much."

"Yes, but they were at peace. Now there is war. It could just be a skirmish with these raiders or it could be more serious. I do not have to tell you how hard it is to get through a bad winter in this mountain wilderness. We have had our share of winter shortages. Without this tribe's help, we might not have made it."

"No, you don't have to tell me," Lydia said, and promptly changed the subject. "I have so many things to learn here, right down to the cooking. They do it differently and they set such store by it. I will have to learn their ways in everything. Such as how they will not look you in the eye when they first see you. They just look past you and do not speak. Don't even pretend to recognize you. Then, the next thing you know, they are talking and laughing like you were together all day." Lydia sighed and picked up a moccasin to finish.

"That is their way of showing respect," Billips said. "They consider it an insult to stare into another person's eyes before greeting them. You do not have to be like them. You can be yourself. Most will accept us the way we are. But some of them will not like us and will not want us here . . . for whatever reason. So be careful if you encounter those who do not want us to remain. They could cause . . . a lot of trouble. Maybe turn others against us."

He touched Priscilla. "Come outside with me. You might as well learn to bank these fires the right way. It's going to be one of your jobs when your mother is too busy."

The others began to settle down for their second night together as a family in their new dwelling. There was as much room in the lodge as in the old cabin, but it was laid out differently. The children slept at the far end, having removed all the items from the beds that were stored there—mostly corn and beans from an earlier harvest. John and Priscilla returned.

Priscilla was pleased that she had accomplished so much in one day. She ran her finger along her neck where a large scab had formed over her encircling wound. This would not happen again. She would work very hard at becoming proficient with the bow and arrow. She would not fail.

6

When the women and children reached the creek, the youngsters dropped their clothing on the bank and waded into the cool running water. Standing knee deep, they drank their fill.

As Lydia watched aghast, Day Star placed her baby's cradleboard on an overhanging branch and lifted her soft deerskin dress over her head. She hung it on the branch beside the baby and waded into the water along with the children. The other women followed suit. The creek was dammed a little further upstream, leaving a small area for dipping. Before Lydia could stop her, Sassy was stripped and running toward the dammed pool. Lydia gasped, horrified, as Sassy plunged naked into the water. The other women poked one another and giggled at Lydia's reaction.

"Sassy!" Lydia shouted above the noise of the water and the children playing. "Sassy, put your clothes on!"

Sassy either did not hear her mother or chose to ignore her. She was romping with the rest and did not even turn around. She did not see the ghostly white of Lydia's face.

Never in her entire life had Lydia felt such embarrassment as at that moment. Stripping naked with the heathens and bouncing around in the water! Someone touched her shoulder and she spun to face Oak Leaf. There was amusement in her eyes as she motioned for Lydia to shed her dress and join them. Lydia jerked away and walked over to lean against a black willow tree. She felt as though she would faint. Oak Leaf calmly discarded her own covering and stepped into the water. Lydia slid down the tree trunk and plopped on the ground.

There was nothing for Lydia to do but watch or avert her eyes from the entire scene before her. She turned her head away to compose herself only to find Blackbird propped against another tree, watching the women and children at play. Unlike the men she had known in the past, young or old, there was not even a hint of lust on his face. He seemed to be simply smiling at a group having fun. The few men spared to guard the group were not even paying attention to the women in the water. The only conclusion Lydia could come to was that this was typical in their lives, although certainly not in hers. How could they act this way? They were behaving as though they were at a church supper.

Except for John, Lydia had never been entirely naked before another human being. And here was Sassy, at such a young age, totally bare, dancing around in broad daylight as though she had been doing it all her life. Her white skin stood out among the darker ones, her bright hair plastered to her head by the water. She was holding hands with two other children. They jumped up into the air and fell down into the water without letting go of one another. Then they scrambled to their feet and began again.

Lydia sat under the tree, big eyed and tight lipped. The simple laughter of the children and the soft voices of the tribeswomen finally penetrated her anger. She began to calm down. In truth, she had never seen her child so happy, so active. She studied the firm bodies and supple movements of the young women as they played with their children. They were truly beautiful, out there in the full sun with rivulets of water running down their backs and arms. Neither shame nor self-consciousness marred their day. She wondered why she was letting apprehension ruin hers.

Oh well, she thought. I can never be one of them or behave the way they do, but I can stop this sulking and cool off a little at the same time.

She stood up and walked over to the creek's edge. Lifting her skirt calf high, she stepped in. The cool water swirled around her ankles and she took another step forward. The current was whipping about the hem of her skirt. She would go no further but just stood there, letting the water do its soothing work.

In a little while Lydia noticed that things were quieting down. She looked around. People were leaving the water and gathering up their clothes. Sassy came to stand beside her, water trickling down the bridge of her upturned nose.

"Mommy, you look so pretty. You should have come in with the rest of us."

Her mother's face changed from its soft reverie to a stern look of disapproval.

"Sassy. Why did you do that?"

"Do what, Mommy?"

"Take your clothes off. I told you to put them back on."

"I did not hear you," the child replied, hanging her head, the lie apparent.

"Sassy, this time do not ask me not to tell Poppy. You know that you did wrong and you must be punished for that. Now put your clothes on!"

With that, Lydia strode out of the water, dropping her skirt into place. Sassy quickly slipped her dress on and followed closely behind.

Upon reaching the base of the mountain, the women collected their heavily loaded baskets of picked berries and began the walk back to the village. It was much more difficult and tiring, carrying full baskets and walking uphill all the way.

Lydia's thoughts were uneasy. She was genuinely worried about Sassy's behavior. Along with that, she could feel a small pain in her pelvis. Sometimes it went away, but other times it came back to daunt her. And the child. It was bad enough that Sassy had been raised alone in the mountains and even worse now that she was living among savages. What chance was there of her becoming a good Christian?

She and John tried to provide spiritual training. One or the other read aloud to the children from the Bible several times a week and always on Sunday. The girl was beautiful and would grow even more so, given time. But what would she do for a husband? If she were in England she would have her choice of good men. But here?

Lydia was so deep in thought that she failed to notice a tree root in her path. She stumbled over it and caught her balance by grabbing Sassy's shoulder. The girl helped set her mother right and flashed one of her elfish smiles.

"Mommy, no harm was done," she said. "Why do you have to tell Poppy?" The thought of her favorite person in the whole wide world being disappointed in her was more than Sassy could abide.

Lydia looked into the dear face, which was gazing at her with such innocence that she almost had a change of heart.

"We will see."

It was enough for Sassy. The heavy mood lifted, and she went into her tippy-toe dance, spinning up the trail for all her newfound companions to see. A few of the toddlers tried the little dance, much to the amusement of their mothers. The older children watched out of the corners of their eyes, noting the movements for practicing when no one else was around.

In spite of all her recent misgivings, Lydia smiled and shook her head. How could anyone stay angry with Sassy? It was impossible. The girl was so full of spirit and life and happiness. Sassy came twirling back to her mother and fell into step alongside her for the rest of the trek.

Lydia was exhausted by the time they arrived back at the village.

She brought her berries into the lodge to get them out of the sun until she could dry them properly. She told Sassy to do the same.

Lydia sat on the edge of the bed, unwinding her hair. "Run along outside and play with the others," she said. "If the archery lessons begin before I get there, go ahead without me. I will be along soon."

Sassy nodded and left. Lydia found a comb and combed out her long auburn hair. She poured cool water from the huge storage basket into a smaller one, pinned her hair back into its usual knot at the nape of her neck, and used a piece of soft leather to sponge herself. She ran the water all over her body. She would replenish it later. Right now, she wanted to feel clean and to rest a while. She lay back on her bed.

The pain deep within her had risen to full crescendo. Beads of sweat broke out across her forehead. She turned on her side and doubled up her knees almost to her chin to gain some relief.

She knew the child within her was forsaking her body. There was nothing she could do but wait and bear the pains as they came. Sassy's happy, smiling face flashed before her. No little sister for you now, she thought. It was her last coherent thought.

Hekanawaw held her hand several inches above Lydia's face. She could feel the bad medicine. White Sister was in grave danger. Old Hekanawaw left the lodge and went to find Oak Leaf.

When Oak Leaf arrived she found Billips placing wet cloths on Lydia's face. He had ripped the bottom from his shirt and torn the strip into several squares. He had removed Lydia's dress and loosened her undergarments. In her delirium, she tossed her head madly. At odd moments, Billips would grasp her head in both his hands and firmly hold it in place. For all his strength, he could not stop her from thrashing.

Oak Leaf turned to Hekanawaw. "Prepare the women's sweat lodge. Tell Blackbird to ready his strongest medicine. Tell him to make something that will expel this baby quickly or White Sister may die."

Oak Leaf stripped the rest of Lydia's undergarments from her and Billips carried his wife's naked body through the village to the women's sweat lodge.

Jackson and Sassy and Runs With The Wind followed the hurried procession. Only Sassy knew how sick her mother really was. Only Sassy knew how shamed her mother would be to know that she was carried naked across the village grounds. Tears spilled from her eyes. If God would grant her the morning back, she would not go into the water undressed again. She would not cause her mother concern.

The women took Lydia from Billips at the small entrance to the sweat lodge. Men were not allowed inside. Blackbird came and lay his medicines on the stone at the lodge door and sat down close by. He began a chant. As he sang, he removed two small turtle rattles from inside his shirt and shook them in time to the chant. After a while it soothed and calmed Billips.

The chanting was also a message to the villagers that someone was gravely ill. From time to time, those passing would pause beside Blackbird. They joined him in chanting the song for Lydia.

Inside the lodge, Oak Leaf steamed the air by pouring water over heated stones. Half Moon and Day Star were heating more. Yellow Bird summoned a small group of youngsters to carry water from the spring to the sweat lodge door. Everyone asked to help.

Lydia lay on a pallet beside the heated stones. Soon her whole body was drenched with sweat. The women took turns taking care of her. The room was much too hot for anyone other than Lydia to stay inside for very long. Periodically, Oak Leaf returned and lifted Lydia up by the shoulders. She poured small amounts of liquid down her throat. Lydia gagged, but eventually swallowed the foul-tasting medication.

When her fever broke, the women stopped pouring the water over the heated stones. Still, it was many hours before any real progress was made. Then Lydia's pains returned. She tossed and turned in agony. Several more hours passed before she expelled the fetus. Then she lay back, limp and exhausted, but alive.

.   .   .

Oak Leaf cleaned Lydia's naked skin with warm water and covered her with a skin. She gave the white woman herbs to make her sleep, then opened the sweat lodge door just enough to sluice the boiling air slowly out and the cooler air in. Oak Leaf did not want the chill night to envelop Lydia before her body cooled itself. Oak Leaf motioned for Yellow Bird to watch Lydia while she went to speak to Billips.

She found him sitting outside his lodge with his children and Runs With The Wind. Oak Leaf appeared before the anxious cluster like a welcome vision. Runs With The Wind interpreted.

"The medicine is working," she said. "The baby is gone. Lydia sleeps. Fever may come again. The medicine is very strong. Strong enough to kill baby, maybe enough to kill White Sister."

John Billips paled. "Poison! You *poisoned* my wife?"

Oak Leaf stepped back from his accusatory tone. She spoke to Runs With The Wind, who again translated:

"She say, 'Lydia is good. Come to lodge, see her soon.'"

Oak Leaf turned to go but paused. "I did not have two choices," she said to Runs With The Wind, pointing at Billips. "There was no other. Tell him. I gave it to her slowly, just a sufficient amount to suit my purpose."

Runs With The Wind translated and Billips quickly strode to the sweat lodge. Custom or no custom, he had to see his wife.

Yellow Bird blocked his way at the entrance. Hot vapors billowed out around her. Billips was about to brush her aside when Runs With The Wind took his arm firmly. Sassy held the other.

"No," said Runs With The Wind.

"Poppy," said his daughter, holding tightly. "Give her a chance."

Billips had been delayed long enough for Oak Leaf and Yellow Bird to lift Lydia from her pallet and help her to the entry. They passed her to Billips.

"You carry," Oak Leaf said, pointing to her own lodge. She rushed ahead to ready a sleeping place.

Billips lifted Lydia tenderly and carried her into Oak Leaf's dwelling, gently laying her down on the soft wadding of animal hides.

"Sassy," he said. "Jackson. Come here. Kiss your mother and then go to bed."

When the children had reluctantly gone, Billips eased himself onto the earthen floor beside his wife and took her hand. During the long night she tossed and moaned but never once opened her eyes or realized he was there. From time to time Oak Leaf left her own bed and compelled Lydia to take a dark liquid. Just at sunrise Lydia opened her eyes and looked directly into her husband's. She showed no recognition at first, then smiled faintly and fell into a deep, calm sleep.

"Thank you," Billips whispered into her ear. "You are still here. You are still here. You will get better."

He released her hand and stood, stretching his aches, then lay down beside her and instantly fell into sleep.

When John Billips awoke the sun was high. Someone was calling his name. Runs With The Wind stood in the entry opening. Glancing about, Billips saw that Oak Leaf was gone. Lydia was sleeping soundly. Her brow was cool to his touch, her breathing normal.

Billips staggered to his feet and followed Runs With The Wind outside. The harsh sun made him blink.

The boy said excitedly, "Lame Crow has returned. He is wounded. Other wounded men have come too. One prisoner." He held up a lone finger. "Meeting." He pointed to the council house. He and Billips hurried to the meeting called for the men of the village.

Inside, a prisoner was tied in a sitting position to the centermost pole, his arms high above his head, his legs straight in front of him and secured with rawhide. His long hair was wild and unkempt, falling across his face. The trussed position he was in barely allowed him to move his head. His feet were unshod and cut, bleeding. Billips doubted the prisoner had eaten for days.

The Tuscarora braves sat in their circle, waiting silently for the other men to arrive. No business could be conducted until everyone was there. Billips could not help staring. So these were the warriors. They were hard muscled and strong, their war paint smeared. Several were injured, including Lame Crow. Billips was excited to see him, but it was clear that they wouldn't be permitted to converse until after the council had deliberated.

John Billips counted thirty warriors. Could that be all of them? Had the others been killed? Perhaps they were still skirmishing. He would have to be patient. They waited. Several more men arrived. Blackbird and Oak Leaf entered, followed by two men and a group of women, young and old.

A tall young Tuscarora rose and spoke in a soft voice. "Our warriors killed many. Our war man, Many Arrows, and our brothers are still chasing from our hunting grounds what few of the enemy are left. The People of the Mountains stand strong and brave before the Spirit. No enemy can destroy us."

He smiled and looked about. The men grunted and nodded affirmation. Very solemnly, he said, "The Great Spirit saw the breath taken from some of our brothers on the battleground and they no longer walk among us. They died bravely but not before they helped kill sixteen enemy. We have brought their still bodies home to rest with their ancestors in our sacred burial grounds." He paused a moment before continuing. "Blackbird has two brothers in his lodge who will rise no more. We will sing the healing words and dance the dance for healing them tonight."

He stopped and pointed at the prisoner. "Take him outside and tie him to the ceremonial tree. There is nothing for him to hear."

Two braves rose, untied the prisoner, and dragged him out. When they returned, the tall young warrior continued: "Our prisoner spoke of terrible times. Warring tribes killed many braves and women and children of his tribe. White men burned their homes, their crops. White men stole their brothers and sisters and sold them as slaves. To escape these horrors some of the tribe ran away and have never been seen again. Their tribe has fallen in numbers. Their clans are almost gone. Few are left alive."

The youthful warrior gazed at Billips. "And brothers, we have a white man who has come to live with us. We must decide today whether to adopt the white man and his family for all time. We cannot wait for Many Arrows to return before we make this decision. He will be gone too long." He motioned toward the curtained doorway. "We must decide, too, whether to adopt the prisoner. The prisoner has asked us to stop warring against his brothers and to make peace with them. He asks that we let them gather what is left of their clan and bring them among us to live.

"Our warriors saw that when we fought the Apalachee, they did not fight and die as warriors should. Instead, they ran . . . into the forest. This is not customary behavior for warriors. This is cowardice. When we spoke to the prisoner about this conduct, he denied their cowardice. His people had held a council concerning the consequences of battle. It was decided among them that it was more important to save the remnant of the Apalachee men than to die honorably."

The speaker shook his head in disbelief. "If their warriors saw that they were losing, they were to desert the battleground and return to their women and children. Although not everyone agreed, this decision is what was concluded. They would try to protect the future of their depleted circle. Each man was sworn to protect the clan above all else. So they hid their children and their women far from the fighting places. When they knew they would lose to us, they ran, back to their clan, rather than risk death and fewer still in the tribe."

The speaker looked aggrieved. "Such thoughts were unheard of in my father's time, or in my grandfather's. But in those days, the white man had not profaned the land and destroyed everything along his trail. Never was there such affliction as now. We know the Apalachee is a brave warrior. Now we know why he ran. It is for us to decide if he will live among us. If we decide yes, then we must find Many Arrows and tell him, so that he will not kill any more Apalachee." He turned to the man beside him and said, "Bring Blackbird and any remaining men of the village. Bring Oak Leaf and all the women who wish to vote."

The warrior went out to summon the stragglers and those gathered waited. The men spoke among themselves. Billips quietly asked Runs With The Wind, "Who is the warrior who spoke?"

"He is village peace man. He is fair man, thinking man. He uses many words but even small children understand him."

"What do they call him?"

"Racing Fox."

"Why is he deciding whether to take us into the tribe forever?"

"Apalachee burned your cabin. Nothing stands. No crops. No shelter. Winter is too close. You need much food. Clothes. We have plenty . . . from before the last snows. Enough for Apalachees, enough for Billips and his family."

Billips had not known nor had he been told that his cabin was gone, along with all of his crops and possessions. He had feared that the intruders might burn his cabin but had clung to the hope that they might not find it.

When the time was right, he would have to go back and see if anything was left to salvage, especially the sacks hidden by Takime and Lydia. So much had happened. A wave of sadness washed over him. Lydia was sick; there would be no new baby. Jackson had succumbed completely to the way of life of the Tuscarora and had become Takime. And now their baby was named White Cloud. Would Priscilla follow suit and change? Would they even know their own children in a year's time if the tribe took them in? His little family had endured so much in so short a while.

Racing Fox, the peace man, raised his arm and all fell silent.

"We will decide now if Billips and his kin are to live with The People of the Mountains." He motioned to the gathering. "Speak now or not at all."

Runs With The Wind stepped forward. "Billips is my uncle.

He has fought beside me. Together we killed an enemy. He has taught me much."

He told them of sighting the strange array of stones and sticks along the trail, about Sassy's flowery headbands, and of carrying the chickens. The surrounding faces laughed aloud at the chickens being put in and taken out of their sacks, and frowned at the thought of men wearing flowers in their hair and Billips kicking the message stones. They tensed when told of the theft of the children. Their eyes glittered on hearing Runs With The Wind recount his trailing the Apalachee. And they grunted aloud and made all manner of noises when he reached the part where he and Billips spotted Lone Runner with the children. There was almost a frenzy when they were told of the killing of the enemy, and then quiet satisfaction when the Apalachee lay dead on the lonely back trail.

Although Billips only understood some of the elaborate description, he could follow the story from the gestures Runs With The Wind was making. If only he could join in the telling, Billips thought. There was never a more appreciative audience. Each would carry the story, the listeners would pass it on to the children of their children.

It was time for the ballot. Billips and his family were unanimously accepted. The children beamed. From that moment on they were an acknowledged clan and would participate in every decision made by the council. The first—the fate of the captive.

Racing Fox put forth the question of the prisoner's adoption. This was a separate matter from the adoption of the survivors of his clan. The council again voted unanimously. Adoption. The vote finished, the same two who had secured the prisoner to the ceremonial tree outside left to bring him back.

This time the prisoner entered unbound. The old wounds on his feet shed new blood as he walked toward the fire and stood before the gathered tribe. Racing Fox motioned for him to take his place in the circle and the brave's whole being changed. He straightened and tossed his head back several times to throw his hair out of his face. Suddenly the man showed no sign of hunger or pain as he proudly sat in the circle of life with his new brothers and sisters. A strength of will radiated from him.

By sign and speech Racing Fox put the next question before the council: the fate of the Apalachee's clan.

"We have accepted new brothers today, three white children, and a white woman. Are we willing to accept our new brother's clan as well? Or will we be like the warring tribes and the white tribes, and hunt them down and kill them until the land knows them no more?" He looked to the left of the circle and then to the right. "If you have words to say, say them now."

A man of forty or so spoke: "My father lies wounded in Blackbird's lodge. If he dies, my mother and sister will need someone to hunt for them and to make their tools and repair their lodge for winter. I have no time for this because I must hunt for my own family. A strong Apalachee man could do this for them."

Another spoke up, a young man barely twenty: "Few women come to these mountains so our men must leave to find women. A good Apalachee woman could tend our fires and bear children for us."

John Billips listened intently, straining to understand. The people were willing to ignore the murders and hardships to follow in order to adopt the Apalachees. They were all saying only what would make the Apalachee feel welcome, even suggesting several times that the Apalachee clan would be doing them a service by living among them and helping with the work. There was no mention of the food the newcomers would need the first year and the extra lodges to be built. All had been in favor until the last speaker rose.

He spoke harshly. "Let the Apalachee talk. Let him tell us why he came to attack us instead of coming to make peace. Can he hear our women and children mourning for their dead? Can he hear their cries? If they wish to live in peace, why did they come to make war?"

All turned to the Apalachee. He rose to his feet.

"We have not known peace for twelve full seasons. It was in your time of turning leaves when a tribe from the north swooped down upon our encampment and burned and stole and killed. We had warm lodges and bountiful fields. Crops were harvested and stored away: corn, beans, squash.

"There were goodly numbers of us. When the attackers finished, our crops were gone, our homes were gone, numerous people had been stolen or were dead. Still, there were a lot left. We mourned our dead and missing and we ate what the land gave us. It was enough. Some of our young men tried to rescue those forcibly taken and followed the raiders north, but we never saw the trackers again except one. He had been tethered to a tree by his own entrails and made to walk around it unwinding his intestines. Our enemies are merciless.

"The next season of planting, white men came from the east, and they drove us from the land. A few of our people stayed behind but I think they are now dead; there was much sickness from the white ones.

"The white ones steal our people and ship them away into slavery on islands somewhere. We have been hiding for many seasons. We plant our crops in a different place each season. We have nothing that we cannot carry. Now, just before the new growth of crops, we were attacked yet again by whites in scarlet uniforms the color of blood. They came before the sun, while we still slept. This time they took nothing. They killed and scalped and burned. They wish to separate us from Mother Earth forever.

"It was then we decided to come to the mountains. We hid our women and children. There are no men with them, only young boys. All the rest came to make a place in the mountains. We came . . . to eliminate you in turn, the ones living in the mountains, so that we could have a place again, far from the white ones and the warring tribes. We did not come to talk peace. We had forgotten how. Perhaps you can teach us to know again."

The Apalachee sat down and stared grimly into the small fire smoldering in the center of the lodge.

Racing Fox spoke. "Will we war against children and women?

Will we chase and burn and steal as the white ones do? Or the warring tribes? Will we destroy the seed of an entire tribe? Will we kill these people who have asked us for help? Or will we bring them to work beside us in our fields? To become part of us? The men to help bring down the buffalo and the bear, and the women to nourish the children and the plants that feed us. Who among you wishes to witness the vanishing of these people from the face of Mother Earth?"

The gathering was silent, then they all began speaking at once. Racing Fox once more raised his hand and quieted the group.

"We will decide now," he said. "Does anyone else wish to speak before we vote?"

No one spoke. The vote was taken, and for the third time that day the Tuscarora unanimously decided to adopt. When the Apalachee heard the tally, the weariness fell away from him and the grimness left his face. He leapt and shouted and threw his arms in the air in celebration. All the tired warriors watched and laughed at him.

The council was over. Racing Fox took the Apalachee to his own lodge. The rest of the warriors wandered home to prepare for their sweat baths and the return-from-battle ceremony that would be held later in the evening.

Runs With The Wind stopped Billips, who was on his way to Lydia.

"We go. Find sacks. Lydia's chickens."

"When Lydia is better. Perhaps then."

"Takime come with us?"

"Yes. If he is not needed here, Jackson—Takime—can come with us if we go." Billips smiled at the Indian boy's enthusiasm. "Thank you, Runs With The Wind. I know how sorry you are that Lydia is sick."

When Billips entered Oak Leaf's lodge he found Sassy sitting by her mother's side. "How is she?" he asked.

"The same, Poppy. Only a little better."

He laid his hand on Sassy's head. "Thank you, Sunshine, for taking care of her while I was gone. If she improves, I will leave tomorrow to try and find our sacks. Will you look after her for me?"

"Yes, Poppy. I will never leave her side."

Billips smiled. "You must sometimes. You have White Cloud to look after and you need to help in the fields. You have to practice shooting, too. You can take turns with the other women caring for your mother."

Sassy's eyes flashed. *The other women.* Poppy thought of her as a woman. Well, she would prove him right. She would take her turn along with the other women and she would listen carefully and do everything just right. Poppy was going to be so proud of her.

Billips ran his hand across Lydia's cheek. She still felt warm. To Sassy he said, "Go get your little brother and play with him a while. Get him something to eat. We must spend more time with him while your mother is sick or he is going to forget who he belongs to."

Sassy's heart was singing as she skipped into Nightfall's lodge. She stopped when she saw White Cloud sitting on the floor. He was dressed in soft buckskin with fringes across the shoulders and sleeves, with dyed porcupine quills woven onto the design.

"Oh, Nightfall. It is beautiful, truly beautiful. Where did you get it?" She picked up White Cloud and turned him around and around, trying to see everything at once. "Did you make it?"

Nightfall rescued the baby from Sassy and put him back down on the floor. "Yes," she said.

"Will you show me how to make one?"

"Yes. Here, skins for you." Nightfall handed Sassy skins. Then she said, "More," and handed her an awl for punching holes in the leather, some hemp and sinew and fine leather strips for sewing.

"And these." Sassy pointed to the porcupine quills. "Do you have more of these?"

"Yes. Come back after eating."

Satisfied, Sassy carried White Cloud home with her. As soon as they entered the lodge, she pulled the little dresslike outfit over White Cloud's head and sat him down on the earthen floor. He batted at the sunlight streaming through the door while Sassy examined the shift more closely. She turned it wrong side out then right side again. She ran her fingers over the fringe and the quills and the seams. She could hardly wait for Nightfall to show her how to create one. Although her mother made her practice sewing and she had actually completed a thing or two, this was the first time she had ever really wanted to sew something.

That evening, Sassy cooked supper for her father and brothers. It was tolerable and all went well. She rushed through the cleaning up to hurry over to Nightfall's lodge for her lesson. Just as she was ready to leave, Billips gently stopped her.

"Nightfall is probably very busy. You know, there is a big ceremony tonight. Try not to be disappointed if she does not have a lot of time to spend with you. Anyway, come back early. You have to help me get dressed."

"Poppy! Are you in the ceremony? Is Takime?" she asked excitedly.

"Yes, now that we have been adopted into the tribe. The girls will probably expect you to dance with them tonight, too."

Sassy was torn between helping her father and brother get ready for the ceremony and making a dress for herself.

"I will hurry home," she called over her shoulder as she ran out.

She stopped to look in on her mother and found Lydia peacefully sleeping. Sassy tiptoed over and kissed her on the forehead. Oak Leaf, in the shadows, was wrapping small bundles of medicine.

Sassy flew across the compound to Nightfall's lodge. Nightfall handed her several soft and beautiful skins, as well as a small bone awl and a woven container of quills. "Next sun, we dye quills. Too busy now."

Sassy looked up, disappointed. Nightfall stood before her holding the most beautiful dress.

"For Sassy," Nightfall said.

"Oh, it is wonderful. I will cherish it."

Sassy held the dress up and spun around. Nightfall and her son,

Bright Eyes, laughed at her, pleased that Sassy was so happy with their gift.

"Sassy dance tonight," Nightfall said, "in her new dress."

Sassy hugged Bright Eyes and Nightfall. She picked up her hides and folded the dress across her arm. For once, her abundant energy deserted her. She thanked Nightfall again and sedately departed.

When Sassy entered her lodge, she broke into gales of laughter. The funniest sight was before her.

Jackson Billips stood dressed in only a breechclout. His long skinny white legs looked out of place, protruding from beneath the brown leather swatch. She was not used to seeing his pale, under-developed chest. He seemed so much bigger in regular clothing. Bristling at her laughter, he stood straight and glowered.

"What are you laughing at?"

"Nothing," she said, and sat on the edge of the bed and laughed some more until she fell backward onto the bed.

In one stride, her brother made it to the bed and pulled her up. With a hand behind her head and the other over her mouth, he began shaking her.

Skinny or not, she felt his strength. Her quills spilled all over the floor. He shook her until the anger he felt at her laughter left him. He stopped just as Billips entered.

"What happened here?" their father asked. Both children were red faced.

Sassy smiled as best she could. "Nothing, Poppy. I tripped and dropped my things."

Her father, too, was wearing nothing but a loincloth. She thought he looked almost as funny as Jackson, but after the shaking, she did not dare laugh anymore.

Her father was just as white as Jackson. His legs were muscular and his chest, thick and hairy. She bent to pick up the quills.

Billips turned again to Sassy. "Help us finish up here. We need a few pretties."

Sassy nodded. She pulled a few skins from above her bed. "Cut some pieces to put around your heads," she said. "Long enough to tie in the back and leave long strips hanging down."

While Billips cut the head strips, Sassy handed long scraps of skins to Jackson. "Cut two wide ones for new thongs around your breechclouts. See, like this." Sassy showed him how wide she wanted them.

She had him cut the center front and center back to match the one he was wearing. She pointed at the very wide strips left for the sides. "Now, cut very thin fringe strips out of these all along the sides."

The head strips complete, Billips cut the second wide strip for his breechclout and fringed it the way Sassy showed them.

The fringes did not make their outfits elaborate, as they knew the other costumes would be, but both Billips and his son were satisfied.

John Billips was more nervous than Jackson when they entered the council house. Billips felt totally inadequate. He could plant and hunt and fight and take care of his family, but he could not dance. He also felt an aversion to smearing himself all over with greasy paints.

To gain the respect of his adopted brothers, he would have to go through with this ceremony. Nor was it just dancing and singing to them. All their songs were sacred songs, and their dances meaningful.

There were no words for religion in their language. Every day and every experience was sacred to them. Their very existence was a religion. Tonight, they would thank the Great Spirit for its help in battle and they would reenact it on the arena floor, singing songs for the dead and for the living. And they would test their endurance. They would dance all night.

Some braves would leave in the morning to find Many Arrows. Others would repair the shelters and build new lodges. The women would work the fields as usual, although exhausted from dancing and singing all night.

As they entered the huge chamber, Blackbird handed them small containers of paint. Jackson dipped into the pots and drew two yellow lines across his face. Billips watched in fascination. The boy was doing all right. When Jackson was finished, he found his father nodding at him with satisfaction.

"Good work, Takime," Billips said, hesitating, however, to paint his own body and face.

"Sit down, Poppy. I will get you started." Once the boy began on his father's face and body, he did not quit until all was finished. A brave stopped to watch. The boy was good at this.

Billips could not see himself, but he could tell by the others' reactions that he looked impressive in their eyes. The boy had a talent for drawing, always copying something, even when he was very small. He painted on anything he could find, using berry juices or tree roots or black walnut shells soaked in water for paints.

The beginning beats of the ceremonial drum broke the quiet. Billips picked up his bow and arrows and followed the other men outside to the arena. They leaped out the door onto the hard-packed earth and began the first round of the ritual.

As Billips skipped around the inner circle, he searched the faces of the women and children standing in a half-circle along the side. They stood in place, keeping time with their feet, their dark hair shining in the firelight. They were dressed in their finest attire and many layers of jewelry.

The entire village was present except for the very sick and disabled. They came to honor the returned warriors and mourn the dead and missing.

He caught sight of Sassy's golden head. She was standing behind several women, holding White Cloud and keeping time to the drums. Her eyes sparkled and she had a wide smile on her face. He felt better just knowing where all of his children were.

Sassy watched the warriors dancing by. Her brother looked authentic somehow—he fit right in. Her father, she could tell, felt ill at ease. His long legs and arms jerked awkwardly as he moved about the arena. She could not help but laugh. She watched a while longer and then took White Cloud to visit their mother.

In the dark, Sassy carefully made her way to Oak Leaf's lodge. It took a little while for her eyes to adjust from bright firelight to total darkness. She did not want to stumble while carrying White Cloud.

She entered the lodge and stood a moment in the doorway, once again adjusting her eyes to the dimness. A small fire was burning but it gave little heat or light. When she could finally see her mother clearly, she gasped. She looked completely different from when Sassy had last seen her.

Lydia was bathed and her hair freshly washed. In the dimness, Sassy could just barely see the intricate designs sewn into the white doeskin dress Oak Leaf had put on Lydia. There was fringe across the bodice and sleeves and along the bottom. Lydia's long auburn hair was caught at each side of her head and entwined with soft white leather strips. Her white leather moccasins were decorated with porcupine quills. Sassy had never seen her mother look as lovely. She leaned over the bed and pressed her lips to Lydia's forehead.

"Mommy, if only you could see yourself," she whispered. "You are the most beautiful."

"Sassy," Lydia whispered.

The child was startled. She stared hard at her mother to see if she had opened her eyes. She had not.

"I brought White Cloud to see you."

Lydia smiled and Sassy knew her mother had heard her and had understood. Then she saw her mother's face ease. Lydia had slipped back into deep sleep.

Sassy held the baby and sat on the floor for a long time. She hoped her mother would rouse again, but she did not. But it did not matter. She would get well. She *would* get well.

The evening was pleasant and cool. Billips was thankful for that as he danced. He was all arms and legs. He had not felt so clumsy since courting Lydia. The warriors crept and leaped all around him. He tried to imitate their movements, but no two men danced the same way. Each told his own story in dance and each chanted his own song. Every now and then he caught sight of Jackson. Except for the whiteness of his skin gleaming in the firelight, he looked just like the others.

Young boys were allowed to enter the arena during most of the dances, but the girls and women could only join in special dances. Mostly, they danced outside the circle of men. Now and then he glimpsed Sassy along the edges of the circle. Unlike the rest, she would sometimes suddenly pirouette. He was amused to see several children doing Sassy's little dance.

As the night wore on, Billips tired. Although the air was even cooler than earlier, sweat ran into his eyes. Seldom were the men allowed to rest. Just when he thought he was going to have to stop, the drums quit. A man of great height and abundant flesh spoke.

Billips sat down at the edge of the crowd. He was much too tired to try and make sense out of the young warrior's speech. He was aware that some of the men were leaving the sidelines and approaching the speaker and then sitting down again. He relaxed until he felt someone nudging him. The man motioned for Billips to approach the speaker at the end of the arena just as the other men had done.

Billips stood and walked toward the man. The warrior held his hands out to Billips. They held an eagle feather.

"For our Tuscarora brother," the speaker said to the crowd, "for bravery in battle, I present the sacred eagle feather to be worn with honor." He paused. "Let it never touch the earth."

TWO

7

For years Blackbird's words kept away the French traders and the English settlers and the temptations they laid before the people. But lately, he was growing feeble and seldom spoke out. He did not always seem aware of what was around him. Now and then a startled look of recognition would suddenly appear on his creased old face and his eyes would once again sparkle with intelligence. Just as quickly as it came, the comprehension would pass and he returned to the other world that was holding him closer each day.

Blackbird had gathered the wisdom of many men into himself. His teachings and warnings helped the tribe grow and prosper through many years, and had helped them avoid the wars that plagued other tribes.

It was obvious that the last few winters had been hard on him. One day soon Blackbird would be gone from the circle. Not even he had been able to hold back time and change.

Changes, many changes, had occurred. With the adoption of the Apalachees had come horses. As the horses multiplied, some of the clan moved to the valleys below in order to graze them and protect them. Each of the People owned all of the horses. There was no individual owning of mounts, but Blackbird predicted that this would not always be so.

The People had grown somewhat lazy. Instead of walking, they wanted to ride the horses to the green corn festival and during summer hunting parties. In winter the mountain snows were too treacherous for such hunting parties, or for women and children to travel by horseback.

John Billips and his family had also instigated change. The white ones had different ways and they spoke differently and thought differently. They prayed to a strange god and taught the people about this god. Some of the people began to pray to the white god, too.

The whites formed their clothing differently as well, and many of the Tuscaroras copied their style and peculiar decoration, even as Billips and his family adopted the Tuscarora way of dressing and doing. The Tuscarora also sat around their campfires in the evenings and listened as Billips gave instruction in writing and reading to his children. They learned to speak the English language, too. Some, like Runs With The Wind, even learned to read it, and a few of the younger Tuscaroras learned to write the foreign words.

Often, when all their chores were done, the people gathered in small groups and sang songs and told each other stories. The elders were startled by the children singing English ballads or hopping one-legged through circles drawn in the dirt as they played strange games they had learned from the Billipses.

The sound of laughter floated through the snowy forest. Lydia squinted against the bright glare and cocked her head to determine the direction it came from. There were three different places that she knew of where the children liked to slide down the hills in the snow. She decided that the sound emanated from Runny Drop Creek. Since it was late in the winter and this might be the last snow, she wanted to watch them for a while.

White Cloud was nearly six years old. He loved sliding down the hills on the sled his father made for him. He could not keep up with some of the older children, but his friend Bright Eyes was usually beside him, keeping him company and seeing that no harm came to him.

As Lydia passed by the newest of three recently erected lodges, Yellow Bird hailed her and they walked toward the sound of the children together. Lydia and her family had made many friends among the tribe, including the small band of Apalachees who had arrived with Many Arrows five winters ago. During the passing years, however, the two women had become especially close.

Yellow Bird said, "Bear Paw and Great Hawk are already there. They left right after the children."

Lydia laughed. If Billips had been home, he would be there, too, competing against the other men and spurring on the youngsters. But he and Lame Crow were hunting. They might be home tomorrow or they might return next week. There was no reason for haste. Game was not scarce this winter, but the Tuscarora did not hunt close to the camp—not unless they were snowed in and could not travel far. There was no reason to kill off nearby game unless crops were being molested.

The women moved along quickly in their snowshoes. The cold sun hit the snow and bounced back into their eyes. The brightness was dazzling.

The day was crisp and beautiful. They wore only buckskin leggings under their knee-length tops and short cloaks of rabbit fur. It was not cold enough for heavier clothing.

As they moved closer to Runny Drop Creek, they could hear the soft chatter of Sassy and Rainy Days surrounded by the boisterous voices of the young men. Rainy Days was from the Apalachee band. Sassy had liked her immediately and the two had become inseparable.

When the women arrived at the small clearing on the bank of the creek, the first youngster they saw was White Cloud running in and out among the group, carrying his tiny sled with its wooden runners.

He threw it on the ground at the edge of a small hill, jumped on top, and sped down the hill. Right behind him came Bright Eyes on his sled.

Takime stood not too far away at the top of a steep incline, Runs With The Wind beside him. The boys had bent greenwood in circles and stretched skins across them. Sitting atop these, they slid down the incline side by side.

As the sleds sped downhill, the race became more interesting. The children had very little control over their conveyances. As soon as they hit the hard-packed snow, they began to spin and their laughter filled the forest.

Not far behind the boys, Bear Paw and Great Hawk threw their makeshift sleds into the snow and followed the older youths down the steepest part of the hill.

Lydia could see White Cloud and Bright Eyes laboring back up their part of the rise. Her heart filled with contentment. Her children were healthy and happy. Life among the Tuscarora was good.

The better she had gotten to know them the less "heathen" they seemed to her. On the contrary, they raised no children as thieves or murderers. A person could leave his possessions strung out across the mountains and valleys and not a soul would touch them. And they were not a violent people, as she had been led to believe. They became angry sometimes, but when they did, they would usually walk away and take time to think things over.

They were a generous and sharing people. If one ate, they all ate. If one starved, they all starved. But best of all, they had accepted her and her family. Completely. She had no fear of letting Priscilla or White Cloud travel anywhere with any of the families. Priscilla had only recently returned from a long hunt with the clan of Rainy Days and Lydia had experienced not a worry about her safety while she was gone.

On thinking it over, Lydia realized that she had accepted the Tuscarora a long time ago, during her recuperation from the loss of her baby. They had saved her life and helped her back to health.

Yellow Bird was speaking to her: "See, see. Here it comes again."

Lydia looked where Yellow Bird was pointing. White Cloud was sitting alone under a huge leafless oak, coaxing a raccoon down the tree trunk with a bit of something held in his outstretched hand. No one else in the group noticed except for Bright Eyes, who stood motionless nearby. The raccoon continued to move ahead little by little. It suddenly lurched forward, grabbed the tidbit from White Cloud's hand, and ran back up the tree. White Cloud stamped his foot and laughed.

His laughter had a strange, high-pitched sound to it. He threw his head back and watched the retreating raccoon. He loved all the animals. He was not afraid of them and, oddly enough, many creatures did not fear him either.

Bright Eyes put his arm around White Cloud's shoulder and they moved back toward their sledding hill.

"If Bear Paw was watching," Yellow Bird said, "he would wager something on that. He is always betting White Cloud can call an animal to him. Most of the time he wins."

The women continued walking until they reached Sassy and Rainy Days.

"Mommy, take mine down," Sassy said, pointing to her circular sled leaning against a tree. "And Yellow Bird can take Rainy's." Seeing Lydia's hesitation, she added, "It could be the last time this year."

"I will in a little while. First, let me rest," Lydia said as she bent to remove her snowshoes. She just wanted to sit for a few moments and enjoy the day. As much as she loved the summertime, she hated to see winter pass. She had spent many of her days hunting alongside John and the others and her evenings sewing and making extra moccasins. It had been the best winter yet of the five they had spent among the Tuscarora and she was in no hurry for it to end.

It had been such a quiet, peaceful time. The tribe had had no births or deaths, although several women were almost ready to deliver babies. There was no hunger and very little sickness. Old Leather Face seemed to be gently fading away and Blackbird was not always self-aware, but other than that, everyone was well.

"Race you to the bottom, Mommy," Takime suddenly interrupted. "Hurry, before Bear Paw gets here. He wants to sled down with you." He pulled her into a standing position and handed her a sled just as Bear Paw came into view.

"Wait!" Bear Paw shouted, but he was too late. Takime and Lydia were already skittering down the hill. "I wager Lydia wins!" Bear Paw called over his shoulder to Great Hawk. "My walking stick for yours. Takime is going to spill."

"You have a wager," Great Hawk agreed. He had nothing much to lose—just his old stick—and a great deal to win: Bear Paw's intricately carved walking stick, with the beautiful head of a fox. Bear Paw cherished that stick.

Great Hawk caught up to Bear Paw in time to see Takime pitch onto his side and slide into a tangle of brush, just as Lydia slid past him. She was frantically trying to keep her sled upright. Suddenly it shot out from under her and she was on her back, sliding with her legs in the air. She came to rest on a little knoll, laughing.

Before the approaching dusk urged them home for the evening, Bear Paw had lost and regained his walking stick twice more.

The men walked ahead as the women straggled behind to talk. White Cloud brought up the rear. He trudged along on his tiny snowshoes, turning his head first one way and then another. His sled dragged behind him. He heard nothing. But he saw everything. Hardly a winter-hardened leaf fluttered to the ground without his noticing.

Sometimes he would move his mouth and sounds came out. The sounds meant nothing. He was only mimicking what he saw others do. On occasion, he could follow the lips of the others. He could mimic the names of people on others' lips. *Mommy.* That was the first one he learned. Sassy kept pointing and saying, "Mommy." Not long afterwards, it began to dawn on him: each thing had certain mouth movements connected with it.

He watched closely and learned some of these. Other times, he pointed to things and Bright Eyes would say the words. Sometimes he understood and sometimes he did not. When it was very confusing, he wanted to get away from everyone for a while and would just go into the woods, find a good place, and lie down to sleep.

Now, suddenly, he was alert. There was a change in the people ahead. He hurried to catch up. When he came alongside Lydia, he grabbed her hand and looked up into her face. He saw a certain shining there and he knew that his father was home.

When they arrived at the lodges, Billips and Lame Crow were waiting for them. They had tossed their game against the side of the first lodge and were excitedly talking to those gathered about them.

"Six of them," Lame Crow was saying. "We saw at least six. There were two women with them. One has seen many winters, the other has not. They have built a lodge just two easy days' walk from here. On the trail we met the Lenni Lenape brave called Sky Turns Dark. He was watching them, too. He had been to Elk Eye's clans far to the south and was on his way home to the north. He warns us to be careful. He says that the white man is striding across the face of Mother Earth spreading evil, killing and burning and stealing. Except for those led by the white named Penn, the rest destroy the game and kidnap the People and are once again selling them to slavers. Anyplace they can reach in their boats is in danger. They spread like poison along the rivers. He said, 'You were wise to take to the mountains when you did.'"

Lame Crow acknowledged the sledding group, and continued excitedly: "Sky Turns Dark said that they have no honor and cannot be trusted. The Maryland Englishmen and the Carolinas whites lied to our brothers in the south, and we, too, are no longer safe. The white man does not want our mountains but he does not want us to live in them. Once the English and the French were mortal enemies. Now they league together against us. It has been said that they intend to rid Mother Earth of all natural men."

Lame Crow looked toward Billips for confirmation of what he was saying. Billips nodded and Lame Crow went on.

"Sky Turns Dark says that soon we must send all the warriors that we can spare to Elk Eye. He says that we cannot turn our backs on our brothers in the lowlands. We have been safe here for many years but we are no longer. It is known among our red enemies and our white enemies that our clan lives on the mountain that reaches for the sky. Penn has no influence beyond his own territory. We will all be made victims if we do not fight back now."

Lame Crow lowered his voice, as though someone who should not be listening was listening. "It is suspected that white ones have lived among us. The wind has carried the sound of our women singing the strange words of the white man. Some of us were seen bowing our heads in prayer to the white man's food god. We did not listen to Blackbird's warnings. We allowed traders to come to our village and they have spoken to others of what they have seen and heard."

Great Hawk protested: "The traders have given us many things that we needed. If it were not for the traders we would not have carbines and shot." He shrugged. "It is of little consequence now. If war comes to Elk Eye, it will come to all the Tuscarora. And if it were not for the Apalachees bringing their brood mares to our village, we would not have ponies. If there is war we will need carbines and ponies. These things will be useful in the low country."

Billips said, "We will need plenty more shot and carbines. We will need to do some serious trading quickly. We will probably need more horses, too. How will we get them?"

The Indians remained silent for a moment. They were pondering the question of additional horses but they were also noting that Billips intended to fight alongside them. Each in his own way was uncertain as to what Billips would do in battle. After all, he was a white man and might be called upon to kill another.

Great Hawk smiled broadly and placed his arm around Billips's shoulder. "Did the settlers you were watching have horses?"

"Yes, there was a small herd of horses and of cattle."

"Then there is your answer," Great Hawk said. "Six white men and two white women with horses and cattle—they must have carbines. Men and women with carbines must have shot and gun powder."

Great Hawk stooped to sit on his haunches. The other men did the same. "We will visit these settlers and help ourselves," Great Hawk said. "The People are in trouble and we have a greater need of these things than the settlers do."

"We must be very careful," Billips said. "Careful not to get hurt and careful not to injure anyone else if we can help it. These people have done no wrong to us."

"Agreed," said Great Hawk.

"We must have a plan," Billips said.

The Tuscarora believed that Billips had a great talent for making plans. Over time, the Tuscaroras had grown used to Billips's strategies. Sometimes they saw logic in them, other times they did not. Usually, they humored him until the moment to put the particular plan into effect. Then they did as they pleased, totally ignoring Billips's scheme.

The situation was similar to Billips's praying before eating his meals. His closest friends sometimes went along with the observance to please him, but they all knew that the real time for a praying man to pray was before catching his meals—while the bow was drawn tight and the prey was still free.

"Yes, make us a plan," Great Hawk agreed, "while we prepare our weapons. We *must* make haste. Gather the women. They must decide what they want to do. If it were not for the children, they could come with us. They must stay with the children and protect them because we will need all of the men." His glance included Runs With The Wind and Takime.

Just before dark, they all met again at the fire.

"We have decided," Yellow Bird announced. She had been chosen

95

to speak for the women and children. "We will trek toward the highest mountain village early tomorrow. You are not to worry about us. You will have the horses and can follow the valley floor. We will transport the children and the furs on the toboggans."

Sassy and Rainy Days sat among the women, listening to the subdued voices laying down the plan for their departure. Now and then their gaze would stray toward Runs With The Wind and Takime.

Rainy Days' eyes lit up every time Takime glanced her way. Although he was very thin, he was the tallest among them, taller even than his father. He sat with the other men around the evening fire, earnestly listening to the talk. His face flushed with the excitement of the sudden turn of events and with the knowledge that Rainy Days was watching. They had spent a lot of time together sliding down the hills on their spin sleds and toboggans, and on short hunting trips with the others. He would make her proud of him. His father's voice penetrated his thoughts.

"Takime and Runs With The Wind will guard the white women," Billips was saying. "And do not take it lightly," he added, looking at the youths. "These women might know how to shoot the carbines. If you keep that in mind they will be less likely to get hurt.

"If they are inside their cabin or an outbuilding, keep them standing in an open spot so they cannot reach any weapons. If they are outside, keep them against a wall or tree so they cannot run. Keep them from alerting the men. Take extra rawhide to tie up their hands."

"There are six men," Billips continued. "Likely, they will be outside. Most of them anyway. Before we seize them, we must know where each man is. Each one of us will take a man. That leaves one of us to gather the horses. After we each tie our man up, we will gather the carbines, shot, and horses, then leave. It will not be as easy as all that, but that is the way we want it to happen. If it can. Take plenty of rawhide. We will need it for the horses as well."

The older brother of Rainy Days, a half-breed named Skylook, spoke up. "I helped to drive the horses through the low country into the mountains. I have great knowledge of horses and will gather and lead them for you." No one objected, for what he said was true.

Skylook was so named because of the color of his eyes on a hazy day. His mother, Speaks Softly, had been raped by white men when she had barely reached her thirteenth winter. Speaks Softly had never forgotten her terrible thirteenth year and the awful day along the Ocilla River.

Once Skylook's proposal was accepted, he left the group to plan his capture of the horses, working out all the problems he thought he might encounter. The only problem he would not be able to deal with was if there were no horses at all. He smiled for having thought of such a thing.

Great Hawk held up his hand for silence. "Some of you are sleeping while sitting up," he said. "This is a time for listening, not dreaming. We are like the bear and the panther of the shifting-water lands. We are diminishing. It is a time for big thoughts, big actions, not for slumber."

He turned his attention to Takime, Skylook, and Runs With The Wind. "Young braves, tomorrow night there will be much dancing and storytelling among The People of the Mountains. We of many winters will be proud to share the same ground as the brave young warriors who seize rifles and horses from the white man.

"If there is something else to say, speak." He glanced encouragingly toward Long Feather, an adopted Apalachee brother. He had shown up on the mountain several months after the main body of Apalachees arrived, bringing horses with him.

Long Feather seldom said much. He never gave advice or took any. He rarely laughed. Mostly he hunted alone and always brought back game. It was thought that he had once tried to track his lost family, who had been stolen by the colonists and taken to a place called the Province of Pennsylvania.

Long Feather was not long in the village when he began to leave the kill from his hunts at the door of the lodge where Speaks Softly lived.

There were times when he would take Skylook hunting with him, but these times were rare. As surely and quietly as he did everything else, he courted Speaks Softly. She seemed happy and content with him; he lived for her.

The remaining man in the group was Great Hawk's second son and Bear Paw's brother, Snake. Snake could be counted on to do what was needed.

Receiving no further answers from Long Feather or any of the others, Great Hawk concluded the gathering: "We leave now."

The people went their separate ways. Takime quietly slipped alongside Rainy Days and pressed something into her hand and continued on his way as though nothing had taken place.

Rainy Days felt the smooth, rounded edges of whatever it was that Takime had placed in her hand. She turned and walked. She knelt in the snow by her mother's small fire, bending forward and holding the object close to the embers to see it more clearly.

Takime had fashioned a wooden medallion, perfectly round, smoothed with sand and bear fat. It was highly polished and glistened. Upon its surface he had delicately carved the faces of a maiden and a brave. Her face and his.

She had never seen anything like it. None of her people had. Her heart filled with pride. When the sun came up tomorrow, she would be wearing it around her neck. She would wear it until the sun went down upon her forever.

Sassy sat in stunned silence. She had seen the passing of the object and the change in her friend. A sadness came over Sassy. Something was different now, something between her and Rainy. Rainy was changed. Rainy was not hers alone anymore. Sassy could not bear the thought.

Then a happy idea came to her. Takime was not old enough to take a wife. It would be some time yet before he could build a lodge for Rainy. One year, at least. Maybe two. No need to worry yet. Meanwhile, she would have plenty to tease him about. She laughed a little to herself. Takime never could take teasing. She would say something to him right away.

Sassy was smiling with anticipation when she entered the lodge. "Takime?"

Takime was not there. He had already gone. Sassy suddenly felt forsaken and alone.

Reaching under the furs on her bed, she pulled out her old cracked doll. She took comfort from its familiar staring eyes and frozen smile. It was the one Runs With The Wind had hidden in the pack so many years ago. The dress it once wore had been long since replaced with soft skins. She held the little doll close and rocked back and forth. Just before she fell asleep, she brushed its forehead with her lips.

8

It was easy traveling in the dark with the snow covering the ground and the bright moon shining through the leafless trees. Runs With The Wind had lost his fear of the night a long time ago, back when he and Billips hunted down the Apalachee who stole Sassy and White Cloud. It was more difficult for his grandfather. Old beliefs die hard. Great Hawk was beyond his sixtieth winter and had seen many things in his time.

Great Hawk feared no living man or creature but he hesitated in all things that might distress the spirits. For the spirits had no bounds in which to perform their mischief. It was his hope that his small party would not offend the night spirits. He knew that the white man carried no such belief.

Great Hawk had been told that the white man sometimes used the nights the same way he used the days. If the white man was to be his enemy, Great Hawk would have to learn his ways in order to conquer him. So Great Hawk led his men as though they were marching under the noonday sun. He was a very brave man.

After several hours of travel, the men slept the two hours before dawn while Snake and Skylook kept watch. They lay down and slept again for several hours in the late afternoon while Billips and Bear Paw kept watch. These little sleepings were part of Billips's plan, as was the abundance of food they had brought along.

Upon waking after the second sleep, each commenced to put on his war paint and the mood changed. Faces became serious and footsteps lighter. Billips and Takime could no longer be distinguished as white men. Their eyes were hidden among stripes and patches of black and yellow and their long hair was caught up and feathered. They were a full day from their destination.

The warriors arrived in the middle of the second night. They were still half a mile from the cabin. Billips's plan was to scout the area and then have one more little sleep before dawn. No man among them would sleep while in fresh war paint, a fact each of the Indians knew. Still, they let him proceed as if they would rest as planned. To contradict him would have been rude.

"The family should be rising around dawn," Billips said. "Some of the men will feed and milk the cattle while the women cook breakfast. After breakfast, most likely all of the men will turn to outside chores. It would be best to attack when all or most of the men are outside. One marksman holed up in the cabin could keep us at bay for a long time."

Lame Crow volunteered to search the vicinity of the cabin because he was familiar with the area. He carefully selected his route and slipped toward the edge of the clearing. He had not reached it when dogs began barking. He slunk along the ground then lay still. Dogs at the cabin? Where could they have been when he and Billips first observed the cabin days earlier? He was certain they had not been there before. Maybe the whites had traded for them or bought them since. Maybe someone else had brought them and was there now. The dogs did not seem to be coming any closer. It sounded like no more than two of them. They must be tied.

Lame Crow did not move. The dogs still barked. Just as he was deciding to slowly back away, a shot rang out in his direction. He was too far away for any bullet to reach him from the cabin, but not from the edge of the snowy clearing. He would be in great trouble if whoever fired the shot set the dogs loose and followed them.

He had no alternative but to withdraw. Hastily he checked his weapons and adornments, making certain that he left nothing behind for the white men or dogs to find. He stood and quietly slipped through the forest. He had not gone far when he heard a change in the voices of the dogs.

They were running free.

He veered away from the direction of the other warriors. He did not want to lead the men or the dogs toward them. The place was unfamiliar but he dared not slacken his pace. The dogs were gaining.

As Lame Crow ran, he heard a shot and frantic yelps behind him, and then another shot cracked. The white men shouted to each other.

Lame Crow could not tell how many there were but he knew that they had fired in a direction different from the route he was running. Someone else must have wounded one of the dogs. There was little doubt that it was one of the warriors.

But the second dog was still in pursuit and getting closer. Lame Crow stopped and prepared. The dog would catch up to him. When it came into view, it ran directly toward him and jumped for his throat. Lame Crow shielded his face with one hand and ran his knife up into the dog's stomach with the other, slitting it from groin to rib cage. It dropped with a thud and whined horribly.

Without even glancing at it, Lame Crow veered toward the right, trotted thirty paces, then turned back the way he had come, running parallel with his original course. It was his intention to get between the white men and the cabin. No more dogs were barking but he could still hear the white men thrashing about and calling for the guard dogs.

He heard a commotion and stopped. Someone shouted, "Samuel, back up! Mason is down." Lame Crow stayed in place.

Someone said, "It's Indians. Just like I thought. Look. He has a tomahawk in his back! Creeping Jesus, we better get out of here. . . . Samuel! Christ and b' Jesus, *answer* me! Where did you go?" All the man heard for an answer was a scuffle behind him.

The second white man was being dragged off deeper into the woods. The last white man ran. He was headed for the clearing. Lame Crow stepped out from behind a tree. The white man unsheathed his knife and advanced. Lame Crow struck him on the side of the head with the flat of his tomahawk. The man wavered. Lame Crow hit him again, on the shoulder, knocking him into the snow. The man was limp. Lame Crow made short work of tieing the white's hands and feet and stuffing a small square of leather in his mouth. He quickly bound him to a tree, picked up the man's carbine, and disappeared into the woods, going several hundred feet before stopping again.

He stood quietly for minutes, listening. He heard no dogs or stumbling white men. A woods quail called and he knew the warriors were nearby. Lame Crow headed toward the signal.

Soon he came upon a downed man with a tomahawk in his back. Long Feather silently appeared beside him, bent over the still living man, and quickly scalped him.

Long Feather secured the scalp with his belt alongside another trophy glistening with blood. He picked up the white man's carbine and motioned for Lame Crow to follow.

Along the way, Long Feather retrieved another carbine left leaning against a tree.

Lame Crow silently followed Long Feather until they came upon the rest of the warriors crouched beneath a huge elm tree, waiting. Lame Crow scanned the group. Skylook and Runs With The Wind were missing. Shots erupted from the direction of the cabin.

Without a word said, the Tuscarora moved in unison toward the clearing. When they arrived at the edge of the forest, they saw people rushing about near the cabin, carrying lanterns and shouting. A woman stopped in the lighted doorway of the cabin, screaming words that they could not understand. The sound of horses galloping was plainly heard above everything else.

Great Hawk went ahead to scout. Returning quickly, he gave the sign that all was finished here. He had seen the white men return to their cabin, close the door, and put out the lanterns. It appeared that the white men were not going to follow Skylook and Runs With The Wind, who had made off with the horses. Great Hawk led his men away.

The warriors moved quietly through the night, following the captured horses' hoof prints. They could tell by the tracks that there were eight of them.

Although he said nothing, Billips was greatly shaken at the turn of events. The two scalps dangling at Long Feather's side were a vivid reminder of the price of eight horses and three carbines. They had not gotten any powder for the carbines.

Perhaps Great Hawk was right, Billips thought. One should not disturb the night spirits if one wished to keep well-laid plans from going astray. Like Lame Crow, he too wondered where the dogs had come from. The moment the dogs began to bark, all of Billips's plans had broken down. Each warrior had taken it upon himself to act independently. The young men had run for the horses, the rest went after Lame Crow. For some reason, Takime had stayed with Billips.

The warriors strode with an even gait. Dawn broke. By the new day's pale light they could see where Skylook and Runs With The Wind had crossed a creek with the horses. They made no attempt to follow, but veered off in a slightly different direction. If, with the approach of daylight, the white men chose to come after them, the pursuers would either have to split up at this point or choose a trail to follow, the warriors on foot or the stolen horses. There was no way to hide the tracks of either in the snow.

During the morning hours, Great Hawk glanced periodically at Long Feather with his swinging scalps and his face of stone. Great

Hawk's heart swelled with pride at the success of their raid. Three carbines, eight horses, and two scalps! What a mighty warrior is Long Feather, he thought. Skylook and Runs With The Wind are masterful horse gatherers, and Billips a distinguished maker of plans. And I, Great Hawk, am a powerful leader of raids. Upon our return to the village, Great Hawk thought, we will have much feasting and celebration.

The uneasiness he had felt for transgressing the world of the night spirits lifted. The vague pains from aging that had settled in various parts of his body over the past decade seemed to disappear. I live, and I am strong, he mused, and the leader of brave and valiant men. I have much cause for celebration.

Great Hawk led his men across the valley floor toward a well-worn path through the mountains. As they traveled, the path narrowed and the men fell into single file. They moved all day. A little before dark they finally stopped and finished their remaining rations. Great Hawk spoke to Snake and Takime.

"Go back toward the white man's cabin. See if we are being pursued and how many follow. When you know, Takime, find Sky-look and Runs With The Wind and tell them. They will not go to the village until they know they are not being followed. Snake, we will wait for you. Do not search for us. We will find you."

Takime glanced at his father. Billips nodded farewell, and Takime and Snake left. When the pair arrived at the creek again, Snake motioned for Takime to cross to the other side, saying, "See if white men come after horses. I will see if white men follow us. We will meet at the place where the horses entered the creek."

Takime stepped into the cold running water and struggled to the other side. The wet hardly penetrated his fur-lined, knee-high boots. Before he went in search of the horses' tracks, he lifted his bow to Snake to let him know that everything was as it should be on his side.

Although the Tuscarora were a tall people, Takime stood an inch or two above the tallest braves. His body had filled out during the last few years, but he was still on the lean side. His face was close shaven because he did not like to look different from his friends in the village who did not have facial hair. It simply never grew. His maturing beard was therefore a constant nuisance but he took great pride in his dark, shiny auburn hair. He usually wore it hanging free, swinging halfway down his back, but for the raid he had secured it tightly behind his neck and laced it with rawhide and feathers.

He wore a cape of beaver fur over his buckskin shirt and leggings. It draped across his shoulders and fell to below his knees. Two slits in the side allowed him to put his arms through. His mother had labored over the skins for many days. He was glad to have it with him now, because as the nights grew old the weather grew colder.

He walked for some time before he spotted the horse tracks. He examined them closely by the light of the moon. There were no other tracks but those of the eight horses. If anyone had followed, they had not reached this point yet. Just to be sure, he examined both sides of the tracks for a short distance. No signs of human prints.

Before morning he reached the location where the horses had exited the creek. He crossed to the other side and saw Snake approach from the shadows of the trees.

"No sign of anyone tracking the horses," Takime told Snake.

"No sign of men following us either," Snake said. "We may as well stay together for a while. When the valley widens, we will split up."

They walked on without speaking until they reached the place where the valley opened. Snake took to the creek side and Takime, the forest's edge. Takime was exhausted. Only the importance of his mission and the excitement of what he might find further on kept him from veering into the woods for a quick sleep.

Thoughts of Rainy Days crept into his head even though he had purposely stopped thinking of her. His passion for her had grown during the winter months; in the loneliness of the nights, he remembered her and lost himself in her beauty. He liked to imagine the fragrance of her heavy hair.

Takime smiled. Words of love and faithfulness flitted through his mind. Some day he would say them to her.

Snake was motioning to him. They were again near the woods where they had encountered the settlers. The cabin was about a mile on the other side of a stand of trees.

"Let us stay together," Snake said, "and examine the places of death first."

Takime nodded. Snake, being much older, assumed the authority to decide. Takime was under no obligation to heed him, but he trusted Snake's judgment and saw no reason to object.

They entered the woods and stealthily made their way back to where the white men had shot at Lame Crow. The ground was still frozen and they could tell exactly what had happened there. They came to the place of death of the one called Samuel. There were many marks on the snow, some turning a dull orange from blood.

"Women." Takime pointed to two sets of small prints. "And at least three men. That is where the dogs came from. One other joined them . . . at least one. Others could have stayed behind in the cabin."

They inspected the ground closely. "They wrapped this man in something and two carried him away," Takime said. "The rest went over toward the one they called Mason."

They followed the tracks to where Mason's body had lain. On their way, they passed a dead dog lying in the snow, its carcass only slightly disturbed by woods animals.

Takime whispered: "There must have been too much activity here for the night animals to really scavenge the dog."

When they reached Lame Crow's place of battle, Takime said, "They left him for a while and ran to the one he tied up. They must have heard the injured man while they were examining Mason. They all came back here in the morning, wrapped Mason's body in something, and carried him off. This Mason was alive when we left him in the night. He died—here. They were probably afraid to come back out after him in the dark and he bled to death."

Snake said, "These are last sun's tracks. We will check the cabin and see what they are doing now. We must be cautious, Takime.

There could be at least five men and two women and maybe more. We must live to reach Great Hawk with our story."

On their way to the cabin they passed the second dead dog and crept to the edge of the woods from where they could clearly watch the cabin. Small wisps of smoke wafted from the chimney and a great deal of activity was going on. Two men were standing guard with carbines while the women carted the contents of the cabin outside and wrapped them in cloth.

There were two strange travoises beside the door, each with two large wheels attached to the sides. What was probably a chest strap was connected to the front of each. The body of a dead man lay on each one, wrapped tightly in a blanket. Strapped to the sides and above and below the dead men were all manner of household goods. The remains of a stripped-down and useless wagon lay collapsed beside the cabin. The settlers had used the wheels from this to make the travoises.

"They are leaving," Takime whispered. "They are going back down the mountain."

The last thing the whites did was release two cows from the lean-to. Each woman took one to lead.

A young man called out: "Should we set the place afire? So no damned Indians can pick through the leftovers?"

The younger of the women called back, "Please, Jake. Leave everything the way it is. Indians would not want it. Some passing settler might make use of it one day."

That seemed to satisfy the man, and he closed the door of the cabin and joined the rest of his party. Takime and Snake watched them struggling through the snow with their heavy burdens until they were well out of sight. Then Takime and Snake quickly made their way to the cabin. All that was left was crude furniture and broken bits and pieces of dishes and a few odds and ends.

Snake stirred the ashes in the remaining fire and added bits of kindling. He succeeded in making a few flame up and methodically began setting the cabin on fire.

Once they were sure the fire would destroy the cabin, they went outside and investigated the lean-to before it too burned. The only useful things they found were several horse bridles and saddles. These they quickly gathered and dragged off into the woods.

They busied themselves hiding the bridles and saddles. There would be time enough later to retrieve them.

Takime and Snake were totally exhausted by the time they finished. There was nothing they could do to hide their own tracks in the snow and so they decided to look for a place to rest for a while.

They set off and traveled several hours back in the direction from which they had come before finding a safe place to sleep, hidden from enemies and a bitter wind that was rising.

They awoke to the sight and sound of an oncoming blizzard. Both men's first thoughts were of the women and children traveling toward the village. The villagers were probably still one day from home. Snake and Takime hoped they would not tempt this weather but would find a protected place.

"I hope all is well with the women and the little ones," Snake remarked. "Great Hawk is much closer to them than we are. There is nothing we can do until this storm is over. Come, we will find a better shelter where we can sit through its fury." He picked up his pace. "Hurry. Before it is too late."

They left the valley and trudged up the mountainside, looking for just the right rock outcropping or tree formation to protect them from the wind side of the storm. The snow was building up fast and there was an urgency in their search. They came across a double shelving of rock high enough for a man to sit upright in and deep enough into the mountain to get completely out of the blowing snow. Each knew at a glance that this was the place where they would wait out the storm.

As Snake climbed toward the shelving, a startled deer leaped into the air and ran. Takime shot it twice before it had gone fifteen strides. He pulled his arrows from the deer's body as Snake stood by, ready to help gut and carry it to their shelter. They would not want for food for a while and the deer hide would help block the wind-driven snow.

While Takime skinned the deer, Snake gathered firewood. There was an abundance of dead fir branches still attached to the trees and protected from the snow by overhanging branches that remained green. Snake gathered as many of these as he could carry. He started a fire and Takime finished skinning and butchering the deer. After a section of deer was put across the fire to cook, both of them foraged for firewood to stack in back of the shelter.

Later, stuffed with deer meat, Takime lay down to enjoy the glow of the flames and listen to the winds pushing the snow before them. His thoughts turned to Rainy Days again, and the warmth inside his body rose up to match the heat of the fire on his face.

They started to fall asleep. Takime heard Snake say, "White ones do not know how to survive a blizzard. They are probably still trying to gain ground instead of finding shelter."

When Takime did not answer, Snake went on. "They do not know how to build a fire or protect themselves in this snow. The women will probably freeze first." He shook his head sadly. "They cannot go back to the cabin. I burned it down. They know that. The smoke could be seen for a great distance."

The fate of the little group bothered Takime, too, but he had not realized that Snake was also concerned. It seemed odd to be worrying about these people. After all, the warriors had killed two of them.

"We cannot go back and find them," Takime said. "No need for us to follow the horses anymore. The tracks are obliterated now."

Takime yawned and turned in. Snake sat by the fire a while longer, staring into its flames and letting the heat seep into his bones. Then he lay down too, and slept.

They awoke to absolute stillness. Neither the sound of any bird singing nor the movement of any creature broke the silence. Snake looked out across the land and saw that its spirit was at peace. It would be a good time for traveling.

They built up the fire and cooked their breakfast, then packed the meat they wanted and threw the rest down the hillside for the animals to find and feed upon. It was midmorning before they started out for the village.

The crisp coldness held all day, making travel easy for them. Trekking steadily, they came upon the tracks of Great Hawk. The women and children were with him. Still, they did not follow Great Hawk's tracks exactly, and as a precaution, kept many strides away from them.

When Snake and Takime arrived at the village, they found the people in an unusually excited state. Before reaching their lodges they heard someone calling them. "Snake, Takime. Come to the council house. There is much that is new. We have decisions to make."

It was not uncommon for Snake to be called to the council house, but Takime had never been singled out for the initial meeting about an important decision. His part in the raid must have swayed them.

The meeting began after the two young men entered the council house. The people had sent runners to look for the pair and the runners had reported their approach.

Takime took his place at the fire. It felt good to be home again, to see all the faces. His father sat across from him, Snake sat on his left, and Skylook on his right.

The pipe was being lit. The men sat mute until the pipe was passed among them all. Old Blackbird was in his usual place, but wore an extra fur draped about his shoulders.

When the pipe was smoked and all were settled, Many Arrows rose to speak.

"We have gathered together to celebrate the increase of our horses by eight and our carbines by three. Above the door of Long Feather's lodge hang two scalps, the first such scalps seized in the memory of most of you.

"We are also gathered to honor Long Feather for his bravery and success in battle. I have been told that our warriors meant to conduct this raid without any bloodshed, but that was not possible. Since the bloodshed could not be prevented, let us be glad that it was the white man's and not the blood of the People."

Many Arrows paused. The warriors around the fire grunted in agreement.

"This most successful raid was led by Great Hawk, planned by Billips, and carried out by them and Bear Paw, Snake, Long Feather, Lame Crow, Skylook, Runs With The Wind, and Takime."

The warriors were filled with pride when their names were mentioned. It was a great honor to have one's name spoken in such a way at council.

"Our women and children were brave enough to travel back toward the village alone in order to release the men for this raid. Let us listen now as the men tell us of their exploits."

Many Arrows sat down and Great Hawk stood up. Great Hawk's tale of the raid held spellbound those sitting in the circle of the fire. Each person involved in the raid was called upon to tell his part, and each did so with gusto and expressive gestures.

Later, during the celebration dance, the women would hear the stories and see them acted out. Although most of the women already knew the details, the tale would be told over and over in dance and song and passed along by word of mouth. Only the particulars of the adventures of Snake and Takime after they had left the main party were unknown to the women.

There was still a bit of daylight when the men left the council house and returned to their lodges. The sweat baths were prepared. There would be a cleansing of mind and body.

9

Old Blackbird was slowly making his way toward his lodge when White Cloud spied him. As usual, Bright Eyes was not far behind the boy. White Cloud ran after the shaman and put his chubby child's hand in Blackbird's bony and gnarled one.

Hands clasped, they walked through the lodge door and the little boy ran to the fire in the center and stirred it up. He placed a few pieces of wood on the flames and tried to pull Blackbird down beside it. Bright Eyes peeked in. The old shaman's wood stack was running low so he went out to retrieve enough from the neighbors to keep him warm through the night.

White Cloud signed to Blackbird that he wished a story. The old man gave no indication of understanding. He only sat and stared into the little fire, shivering beneath his blankets. White Cloud saw that his friend was cold and tired. He took the old man's hand again and tried to pull him toward the bed. Blackbird refused to move from the fire. White Cloud was too small to force him to bed. He went behind Blackbird and pulled his shoulders backwards and down. This time the boy was successful and Blackbird went gently down to the floor with his feet toward the fire.

This done, White Cloud searched the lodge for another fur blanket. He found one and covered the old man with it. But White Cloud saw that deep down in the furs, the old man was still shaking.

White Cloud unwrapped the furs, and lowered himself into them, carefully replacing them around himself and Blackbird. He wrapped his legs around Blackbird's thighs, threw his arm across Blackbird's chest, and placed his head on his shoulder.

White Cloud made a promise to himself that he would stay wrapped around his friend until Blackbird was warmed and stopped shivering—even if it took many moons.

White Cloud did not move when he heard Bright Eyes return and dump a load of wood in the corner. He did not move when Bright Eyes unwrapped the furs to peek at him, but he did smile when Bright Eyes climbed beneath the furs on the other side of Blackbird.

It was not long before the heat from the bodies of the two boys warmed the bones of the old man. In a little while, Blackbird stopped trembling and the three fell into a deep sleep.

Many looked in on them during the evening but no one disturbed them. The three did not awaken until the beating of drums marked the beginning of the celebration of the raid.

Sidelong glances were cast at Takime, and eyes followed Rainy Days everywhere. It was common knowledge that she wore a new necklace beneath her buckskin dress. She never acknowledged that she had it, not even to her mother or Sassy. Until Rainy Days mentioned it first, no one else would refer to it.

It was the custom of the people to display all of their jewelry at celebrations. Rainy Days was wearing hers, yet she hid it. Speaks Softly suspected that Takime had given the necklace to her daughter. She had mentioned this suspicion to only one other woman but that woman told everyone she met. Consequently, as many observed the shy young boy and girl as they did the dancing, prancing warriors.

Rainy Days could not take her gaze from Takime while he told and retold his part in the raid, making his way around the arena time and again. As he performed his dances and sang his songs, his heart was with the girl who followed him so intently.

He knew that the women of the tribe were watching them. They were not even trying to hide their interest. They would laugh and talk behind their hands and nod at him or Rainy Days.

Even so, all he wanted to do was grab the girl and run away for a little while to some place quiet where they could be alone. He already knew the place. He had prepared it well ahead of time.

Priscilla Billips stood at the edge of the crowd. She watched it all: the looks exchanged between Rainy Days and her brother, the women smirking, and the pageant of the warriors on the ceremonial grounds. She was glad that Rainy Days and Takime were getting all the attention. It gave her more time to study Runs With The Wind without being noticed. He was too busy to pick her out of the crowd and she studied him at leisure.

As he did for all ceremonial occasions, Runs With The Wind wore around his ankles the teeth of the big mountain cat that he had slain last year. He used to wear them around his neck, but that was before he killed the huge black bear. Now the bear's teeth encircled his neck and its claws were attached to the bottom of his tunic. The claws swayed and clacked as he danced around the circle of tamped down snow.

Runs With The Wind's face was painted yellow and black. The black covered his eyes like the black strip across the eyes of a raccoon. His hair hung loose and fell just above his waist, except for a strip along the top that was cut short. He wore two notched eagle feathers just above the left ear. Through the years that Sassy had known him, he had grown tall and straight and perfect. And Sassy loved him.

She sighed as he made his way around the circle. He would soon pass by the place where she was standing. He raised his weapons high in the air and made a grunting sound from somewhere deep in his chest. Then he bent over as though tracking some ferocious animal in the snow.

Runs With The Wind finally came alongside Sassy He quickly faced her and jumped high into the air with arms and legs spread wide. He yelled, "Iiieeeea," as loud as he could. The unexpected sound and movement frightened Sassy. She screamed and jumped back. A grin flashed across his face just as he turned and resumed stalking the unseen beast around the circle.

The people standing closest to Sassy hid their mouths and laughed aloud at her fear of nothing but a ceremonial posture.

At first, Sassy was embarrassed enough to melt into the ground. Then she thought, I will get even with Runs With The Wind if it is the last thing I ever do. But as the thought raced out of her mind, she, too, began to laugh. That was one of the reasons she loved him and not any of the others. He could best her when no one else could. She was strong willed, but he was spontaneous and disarming.

She stood in the last reaches of the firelight, laughing at herself. She did not hide her mirth. Now and again the glow of the fire caught her golden hair. Little sparks of light bounced from the flames to her eyes, half-shut with laughter.

Sassy's girlish glee floated toward the circle and many turned their heads to look, the women, too. Takime took advantage of the distraction and nodded at Rainy Days to follow him as he left the arena.

Rainy Days quietly disappeared into the crowd and reemerged near the place she had seen him go. He was at her elbow in an instant, guiding her between the lodges and down toward the trail leading to the berry bushes.

The snow-laden path was narrow and steep and was usually tread in single file. Takime pulled Rainy Days close to him so they could walk side by side. Along the way, they stumbled on roots and slippery rocks. Takime silently thanked each impediment for nudging her closer. He held her a little more firmly each time she tripped. When they arrived at the spot he had marked off in his memory, he pulled her from the path. Another twenty strides and they reached the place.

They entered a small clearing, no bigger than the space of one lodge. There was only one way in or out—the path on which they had come. They stood, holding each other and catching their breath.

Takime folded his arms around her and lay his cheek upon her hair. He closed his eyes. The smell of her hair and the feel of her body engulfed him. He had stood this way with her many times in his dreams. Their legs lost their strength and their bodies swayed back and forth.

He said, "I have waited so long just to have your hair surround me."

Rainy Days looked up into his eyes and pushed away from him. She slowly removed the rawhide and little shells that held her hair in place. She bent down and placed the shells in a pile at their feet. Standing up, she ran both hands through her hair, fanning it out as far as it would go. She drew his face to hers, spreading her arms and her hair all around him.

He had only meant to speak with her. To hold her. To ask her if someday soon she would be his mate. He did not mean to take her body. Not yet. But there was a fire in him and a blackness behind his eyes and he could not stop. She would not let him stop. Clumsily they removed their clothes. He ran his hands across her body and pulled her down onto the cold ground beside him.

They would not return to the ceremonial fire. Instead, Takime would gather his things from his mother's lodge and find Blackbird. He would ask the elder to perform the marriage ceremony. And Rainy Days would go to Speaks Softly's fire and ask her mother for permission to enter the lodge as man and wife.

"We will share our life together," he said, shivering from the cold and the passion.

"I know," she said, and put her hand on the wooden necklace that lay between her breasts.

10

Two travelers arrived in the village. One was Sky Turns Dark, the Lenni Lenape warrior some of the clan had met during a winter hunt at the-place-where-the-cliff-hangs-over. He brought a friend: Crooked Arm.

The day of their arrival was bright and sunny. Most of the villagers were outside, enjoying the changed weather. As always, the children danced and skipped around the visitors. Lame Crow shooed them away, rescuing the men and leading them to Great Hawk's lodge. Great Hawk conducted formal greetings, and ordered food placed before the guests. The visitors filled their stomachs and puffed contentedly on the pipe Great Hawk proffered.

The formalities over, the visitors announced that they had an important message.

Sky Turns Dark said, "I prefer that only the wisest of the men of the village come forward to hear it. When they have heard what we say, then bring your young men and your old men, your women and children, for what you hear will affect them all."

Great Hawk called upon Blackbird, Many Arrows, Billips, Long

Feather, Leather Face, Racing Fox, Bear Paw, Snake, and several others whose wisdom and bravery he held in high esteem. When the pipe was smoked by all and all eyes were upon him, Sky Turns Dark stood.

"I have come to ask a great thing of you," he said. "You know of the wrongs done by the white men to the People in the Southlands. The Tuscarora towns are plundered and torched, the people killed or captured. Crops are destroyed. They are chased from the riversides and never allowed to return."

Sky Turns Dark gazed into each face turned toward him. "And the Apalachee?" he said. "Some live among you and are absorbed into you as the rain is into the thirsty ground. They are no longer a nation. Their land was the land of the long sun, but now the weak and cold winter sun beats down upon the few that remain. Many were taught by the Spanish ones to walk the path of the white god. But where was this white god when the Apalachee were attacked again and again by the English settlers? Where is he now? He is with the white man.

"And our brothers to the east? They lost their homes and hunting grounds long ago. My people? My people once lived in the east and now we are scattered to the four corners. The bones of our fathers and mothers are no longer among us. We do not know what is happening to them in the spirit world. The white man has no respect for the bones of our fathers and mothers. He molests and destroys the most sacred of the sacred."

Sky Turns Dark stopped for a moment to study the faces of his listeners. "Have you all heard of these goings-on?"

The men solemnly nodded and Sky Turns Dark continued.

"Many lies have come from the mouths of the white men. Dangerous lies. Our brothers to the south no longer listen to these lies. Too many have been told.

"You who live in the mountains have avoided contact with the English settlers." Sky Turns Dark raised his arms to include everyone in the room. "But the time is coming when you will be asked to leave these mountains and fight the enemy alongside your brothers."

The faces around the council fire were creased in thought as Sky Turns Dark spoke of war—not a darting raid but an all-consuming war. Nation against nation. And not in the homeland but deep in the lands to the south.

The voice of Sky Turns Dark filled the council house. "Let me tell you of a proposal made by the peace men of several nations. Among these are the Conestoga and Shawnee. They request that you join them, along with the other Tuscarora towns, in once more presenting the grievances and desires of our nations to the white men.

"We are told that there are fair and just white men in the place called Pennsylvania. Our people want at least one representative from your village to help take your concerns to them. There will be other men in the final party from other Tuscarora communities. I will need to know your answer when I return by the next moon. If your answer is yes, your chosen one must accompany me on the journey to Pennsylvania."

Sky Turns Dark stood silent for a moment. The People absorbed his words.

"As a token of friendship and trust, the people of Elk Eye have decided to make a belt of peace to send to the wise white men of Pennsylvania. Some other Tuscarora towns and villages are doing the same. I know what they have chosen to say and I will tell you. Then you must decide if your village wants to address the wise white men of Pennsylvania."

The discussions in Many Arrows' lodge went on for a long time. Many subjects were touched upon, but the final decision of the message of the belt of peace would be left for the entire tribe to resolve.

By midafternoon, the village council house was filled with men, women, and children. The purpose of the peace belt was explained and put to a vote. All were in favor of it.

"The people of the village of Elk Eye," Sky Turns Dark said, "have

chosen to ask the Pennsylvania men for a peace without end in order
that all nations may walk the forest trails safely and unharmed. The
women of the Pine Forest People are making a belt of peace seeking
the friendship of all Christian ones in order to live each day in a safe
and friendly manner."

Blackbird, in a rare lucid moment, was on his feet. "Let Racing Fox
take our message to the peace men of this place called Pennsylvania,"
he said in a slow and halting voice.

All eyes turned to Blackbird. It was a good sign that the old
shaman was rousing himself from his inner world and joining in the
council discussions.

Racing Fox was the most pleased of all to hear the old man's
rasping voice, and to be picked from all the others to deliver this most
important message to the strangers of the far eastern lands.

"And let the message be for our children yet unborn," Blackbird
said, focusing his old eyes on several young women in the crowd.
Their bodies were swollen with new life. He searched the faces of
women holding newborns or firmly clutching the hands of toddlers.

"And let the message be for our children born," he said. "Let the
message on the peace belt from The People of the Mountains be for
the children. All the children. Those born and those yet to be born."

When the last words escaped his lips, the air seemed to leave his
body and he sat back down with a clumsy thump. He closed his eyes
and swayed back and forth. When he opened his eyes again, the
shining light was gone from them. He had reentered the world of
near-spirits.

No one spoke. Blackbird's simple words were still in the air around
them. Yes, that would be their message. The vote was taken and it was
unanimous. All that remained was to decide who should be responsible for making the belt.

Nightfall was chosen to oversee the work. Such an honor was not to
be lightly taken and she would spend most of the next thirty days
devoted to its completion.

The council decided to hold off on discussions of a possible war with the colonists until the results of the peace delegation were known. During the last several seasons, the training of the younger children and the women in the use of arms had stopped. There did not seem to be a need. With this new talk of war, it was decided that the training would begin anew. Billips, the maker of plans, was once again called upon to oversee the practice.

The council ended. Sky Turns Dark and Crooked Arm left The People Of The Mountains and continued their mission of enlisting different tribes and clans in a last attempt to gain the white man's cooperation in a peaceful coexistence with the red man.

The next morning, right after mealtime, Nightfall brought several women into her lodge. Although he was not asked to leave, Little Badger called his son to him. They gathered their bows and arrows and went for a walk. They did not want to be present in the lodge while the women conducted their business.

"We will bring back the wood to make the loom," Little Badger said as he left.

The women sat cross-legged around the small fire and discussed the best way of going about making a belt of peace.

"First," Nightfall said, "we should take an inventory and find out how many wampum beads we have on hand. We will ask every household. We will need many, many white strings of shells for the background. We will use the purple ones for our message. We must have the best and most perfect beads."

"We will find out how many quahog and whelk shells are available," said Oak Leaf. "Once we have the beads and the shells, we can decide how many more beads can be made in time for the weaving of the belt. There is no way that we can trade for more beads or shells. We do not have enough time for that. There is very little time for the men to grind the shells."

"We cannot decide on the exact design until the estimate is finished," Nightfall added. "We have at least three men skilled in making beads, but time is short, even for them."

"I will start the inventory," Yellow Bird volunteered.

"And I will help Yellow Bird with the tally," Lydia said. Lydia knew that she was not as talented as the others in beadwork. But she was willing to serve in any way she could.

Nightfall nodded at them and the two women left.

After the others were gone, Nightfall spoke to Oak Leaf. "We will ask Sassy and some of the other young girls to do the cooking until the belt of peace is finished. Let us meet again as soon as we have spoken to the girls and the inventory has been completed."

The days went quickly by. The women were busy from sunup until well into the night. The belt of peace was finished in time for the return of Sky Turns Dark. Racing Fox chose one other man to accompany him on the journey.

The people held a special ceremony in honor of the undertaking. They were in good spirits and had high hopes for the success of their belt. Their spirits remained high long after the shadow of the little group headed for Pennsylvania had left their mountain.

Time passed. The land turned green again. The season of planting was at hand. The men cleaned the fields for the new planting and the women and children began the laying down of seed.

There were several different locations for fields. Those living in the valleys below needed fields of their own. In the past, they had used new fields only when the land was depleted of its energy. But with the coming of the Apalachee and the birth of many babies and the marriages of many young people, the tribe had greatly expanded.

While the women planted the first seeds of spring, the men patched up the lodges and built any new ones that were needed. When these things were done, they turned their attention to repairing old weapons or fashioning new ones. Spring hunting parties came and went.

Instead of building his own lodge, Takime lengthened Speaks Softly's to accommodate himself and Rainy Days. Takime expanded the structure with the help of Billips and Runs With The Wind.

Rainy Days preferred living with her mother rather than in an abode of her own.

Rainy Days was behaving very strangely lately and Takime did everything she wanted done. Although she did not mention it, Takime was sure that she was carrying their child.

The days grew longer and the rains came. The seeds sprouted and all was as it should be with The People of the Mountains. Even old Blackbird rallied as the sun grew hotter and its heat reached down into his bones. He was often seen with his little companions, White Cloud and Bright Eyes, roaming among the lodges and through the nearby woods. His lodge was once again frequented by those in need of advice and they were not disappointed in his recommendations.

The signs of summer were very encouraging and they were taken as an indication that Racing Fox's mission with the belt of peace would be a success. Thoughts of war receded.

The only worry of the people was that they might lose their medicine man, Leather Face. He had been ailing for some time. No matter what Oak Leaf did for him or he tried to do for himself, he did not get better. Although Oak Leaf was well schooled in the art of healing and setting bones and the mysteries of life, she was a woman. A man was needed to treat warriors. The elders gathered to discuss this and to choose someone to eventually assume the healer's work.

Most of the villagers knew all about human skeletal structure. Their instruction began when they were children. They watched their mothers cutting up animals for meals. They watched their fathers, uncles, and older brothers. Anyone finding an injured bird or creature quite often brought it home and tried to help it.

In the spring and summer, there were usually half a dozen tame birds of all kinds around the lodges. The young children especially liked to try their hand at taming them. The birds were not kept in cages or restrained in any way. They flew and hopped among the lodges at will until they decided to leave. Some departed as soon as they were able. Others stayed for years.

Small game, such as squirrel and rabbit, was seldom hunted by the adults. Consequently, creatures were abundant around the village. The children would form little groups and hunt them with their bows and arrows.

Animals that were only wounded were often nursed back to health and set free again. The children took almost as much pride in their healing arts as they did in their hunting skills. The animals that they killed were taken home to their mothers, who proudly added them to the pot for the evening meal.

Sometimes, at an early age, one or two among them showed unusual talents in the mysteries of life. White Cloud was such a one. He was already, at the age of six, being trained to become a medicine man. But, of course, he in no way could take the place of either Leather Face or Blackbird. He was only six. That he could not hear made no difference at all and was, in fact, considered favorable.

Runs With The Wind was a candidate for a time. He spent much of his day with Leather Face and Blackbird. He knew almost every plant that grew and all of their varied uses. He could set a bone or treat a fever. He could read the signs in the skies and on the ground. He could read the thoughts in a man's head. But the elders believed that he was too good at too many things to be channeled solely in the direction of becoming a medicine man. He was also a fierce warrior and hunter, and so it was thought that one day Runs With The Wind might become war chief. Candidates were chosen by the women and elected by consensus of the men. Runs With The Wind was held in high regard by the males and females alike. And so he was passed over for the honor of medicine man. A man of thirty winters was chosen instead to follow Leather Face. He, too, knew the art of healing, and his name was Leaning Tree.

Leaning Tree moved into the lodge of Leather Face and spent every waking moment with him. His job was to learn the secrets known only to the few healers of the tribe. For many months he would remove himself from the company of the villagers, spending all of his time either alone or with Leather Face.

Once the problem of who would take the place of Leather Face was solved, there was no need for the elders to meet again for many days, and the early summer passed in peace.

The men went on extra hunting forays for furs to trade. The women wove extra baskets for the same reason. Old Blackbird watched these dealings with a saddened eye, but his tongue was silent. He had spoken many times in the past against trading with the white men, but now, in his old age, he was overruled. The time had come for him to accept the changes.

When traders made their visits to the village, the Billips family kept well hidden. It was rumored that a white family lived with the Tuscarora, but solid proof was missing. No one among the Indians wanted warring whites to come to the rescue of an imagined captive family.

The morning was bright and sunny. After breakfast, Sassy asked Billips, "Would it be all right if just Mommy and I went to gather oak saplings? We could chop them and drag them by ourselves."

A shadow of worry crossed her father's face.

She said, "I want to make a basket for Rainy Days, for when the baby comes. She will need a place to store things."

Billips looked at his daughter and shook his head slightly. "You must wait until I can send someone with you. I don't think any strangers are around but we must be careful. Anyway, you wouldn't be able to drag the saplings up the mountain."

Sassy lowered her eyes. A small pout appeared at the corners of her mouth.

"Sassy, when you marry, your husband is always going to know when you are disappointed. Your face will show it," her father teased.

Sassy ignored her father's remark. "Mommy and I *can* drag the saplings." She lifted her eyes to stare directly into her father's.

"Priscilla, I wish you were not always so impatient. It will be a long while before the baby comes. You'll have plenty of time for making baskets." Upon reflection, he added, "Is that what you were doing yesterday when I saw you coming from the woods? I *thought* I saw you carrying black walnut root. Was it for the dye?"

"Yes, Poppy."

"Did you go to gather it alone?"

"Yes, Poppy. And I do not need anyone to go with me! I have my bow and arrows and I can shoot as well as anyone. I am not afraid. I can take care of Mommy, too."

Billips sighed. He was afraid that the girl would sneak off and go by herself again if he did not find someone to go with her. She was much too strong willed.

"Wait a little while. I will find someone to go with you. I cannot do it myself today. Or tomorrow. And, of course, you would not wait three days, would you?"

"No, Poppy."

Her honesty was sometimes unnerving. "All right, Sunshine. There must be someone who will volunteer to go. Please wait until I find that person. I will be back as soon as I can."

Billips left. Not long afterward, Runs With The Wind showed up at the lodge door. He wore a big grin on his face. "So," he said, "today turns out to be basket-making day and the women have no escort? Runs With The Wind will be your escort. Runs With The Wind will protect you with his life."

Another shadow fell across the doorway—Yellow Bird's. "And I am going to protect Runs With The Wind," she said, giving him a playful tap on the shoulder.

Runs With The Wind laughed and stepped aside to let his mother enter. Lydia was quite pleased that Yellow Bird was coming along. It was going to be a pleasant outing.

They gathered up tools and rawhide. Runs With The Wind packed the supplies on one of the horses. He brought along another to help carry the young trees.

News of the outing got around the village and several of the people joined them along the way. It was midmorning before they found their first stand of young oaks. The trees were situated just the way they preferred—close together, yet tall and straight. They started hacking on the oaks about a hand span above the ground. After the trees were downed, they were dragged to the side of the trail and left there while the search for others continued.

In the early afternoon everyone took a long rest. Most of the trees they needed were already down. They would carry or drag the ones that could not be packed on the horses.

No one had brought anything to eat so no one mentioned being hungry. They rested in little groups, spread out here and there in the woods.

Lydia and Yellow Bird rested with their backs up against a huge old tree. Sassy and Runs With The Wind were sitting not too far away with their heads close together, talking.

"They look as different as the blue jay and the crow but they go well together," Yellow Bird commented.

The young man's hair was as black as the crow's wing and Sassy's was as bright as leaves of gold in the time of the falling leaves.

Lydia had often felt when looking into Runs With The Wind's deep, dark brown eyes as though she had come up against the wisdom of the ages. By contrast, Sassy's bright blue eyes held an innocence and mischievousness that were sometimes worrisome. She feared for her daughter's future. The girl was too unruly. She was too full of life and vulnerable.

Lydia realized with a start that Sassy was of an age to marry. All trace of childishness had long since faded from her body. She had the carriage and look of a young woman.

The old guilt rose up to haunt Lydia. Was this all she could offer her children—a life in the forest? They knew little else. They were not prepared for anything else. It was far too late to change the direction of their lives. Even if it were possible to go back to a coastal settlement, they would be outcasts among their own kind.

Then she thought about Takime and his happiness and she began to feel a little better. She thought of her grandchild, stirring in the womb of Rainy Days, of her and John's contentment here, among the People. Perhaps everything was for the best.

Her eyes returned to the two young people before her. They certainly looked good together. With a rush of comprehension she accepted what everyone else had known for some time. These two were always going to be together.

Why had she not seen this before? Sassy had always been taken by Runs With The Wind, smitten when she was just a little girl. But Lydia had not realized until now that the feeling had grown into love.

She stared hard at the two of them.

Yes, there was definitely a closeness that Sassy did not share with other young men. It probably would not be long before Runs With The Wind asked her to marry. What would Sassy say? Lydia knew without question that Sassy would pledge herself.

With this realization came acceptance. Everything would be all right. And, if there was to be a wedding, she would also have a basket or two to make. Sassy would be needing her own things. As well as a wedding dress.

She must begin now. Sassy would have a dress like no other ever seen in these mountains. Rainy Days had gotten married so quickly that there had been no time for special dresses and extra baskets. For Sassy it would be different. There was plenty of time. She would start today. Even before a wedding was decided upon.

The People did not make a great to-do over weddings. A few words were spoken over the couple, friends and relatives quietly dropped gifts at their closed door, but little else was said or done. Lydia would miss the big wedding celebration that she had known, but she could still see to it that everything was as nice as it could be. She began planning for her only daughter's wedding.

She would use the white doeskins she was saving. There were enough of them for a dress. She would decorate it with the blue trader beads. She had a store of red and white beads, too, but only the blue ones would do, to match the color of Sassy's eyes.

She would make a soft pair of moccasins out of the white doeskin, too, and cover them with the blue beads. But how was she going to get all of this done in secret, with Sassy always underfoot? Yellow Bird could help with some of it. And she herself, could send Sassy to the riverbank for cane for more baskets. Perfect. The cane patch was far enough away that they usually spent several days gathering cane there.

Lydia leaned back against the tree trunk with a satisfied smile. It could all be done. She would be ready when Sassy broke the news of impending marriage.

Lydia leaned toward Yellow Bird to speak of her newly made plans, then hesitated, wondering if Yellow Bird disapproved of Sassy as a wife for her son.

"Yellow Bird," Lydia whispered, "you say they look so good together." She nodded toward the two young people. "What do you think of their spending their lives together? It has just occurred to me that they expect to do so."

"I am glad that you have finally thought of this," Yellow Bird laughed. "I have always thought so but I was afraid to speak of it. In answer to your question, I would be proud to have your daughter as my daughter." Yellow Bird lowered her voice. "I have been wondering when Runs With The Wind will approach her. And you and Billips. I feel sure that he will ask very soon. See how he cannot keep his eyes from her."

Lydia sighed with relief. "I see that. And it is the same with Sassy."

The women sat, watching Sassy and Runs With The Wind. The two were so engrossed that they took no notice of being watched.

"I was sitting here making plans in my mind," Lydia said and told Yellow Bird of her schemes. Soon they were conspiring.

Sassy glanced over at the two women. She and Runs With The Wind were having a wonderful time and she wondered if her mother was going to do or say something that would spoil the day for her.

It was unusual for the elder women to allow young people of their ages so much freedom together. She turned once again to meet Runs With The Wind's direct gaze. Her heart lurched inside of her chest as it always did when he was so close and looking directly at her.

The feeling was almost more than she could contain. She wanted to jump up and dance around him and run and shout. But instead she returned his look with a long and steady gaze.

The sudden movement of those around them interrupted their absorption. As if with one mind, the oak gatherers had decided the rest was over and it was time to finish their work. With a final effort they completed their labors and set off.

Tired and hungry, they arrived back at the village well before dark. Runs With The Wind relieved the dray horse of his burden, dropping trees at different lodge doors as he went. Others arrived a little later to drag trees away.

After they had eaten, the women began removing the bark from the trees and slicing long strips of oak to be woven into baskets. It was necessary to work the wood before it dried out.

Lydia was good at basket weaving, but Sassy was a master. Lydia's great talent lay in her sewing techniques. Both women, along with most of the other villagers, were making additional garments to swap with traders for beads and cloth and pots and pans. The traders visited with ever greater frequency.

Most of the women stayed up late the night of the oak gathering, boiling the strips in black walnut root or bloodroot. They would get up early in the morning and remoisten the splits before weaving their baskets. Not all of the strips would be colored, only those used in making designs. The main color of the baskets was the soft oak itself. The girls helped their mothers strip the saplings and boil the strips. Some of the younger girls started the actual weaving of their first baskets.

Sassy stood beneath the bright light of the moon, stirring her strips while, in her mind, she conjured up Runs With The Wind's face. A smile played around her lips and her usually bright eyes wore a vacant look. She was totally lost in thought and the peacefulness of the evening.

A pleasant night breeze rustled through the village and cooled the women at their fires. The men sat in small groups here and there about the lodges, telling stories or softly singing. The younger children slipped into sleep out-of-doors, nestled among tree roots or on soft skins thrown down for that purpose. The older boys sat close by the men, quietly listening to the tales and songs, too respectful to interrupt or ask questions, but sometimes joining in with the singing.

Sassy appeared to be in some other world, devoid of time or space. Lydia only hoped that everyone else was too busy at their own fires to notice the silly look on her daughter's face. God knows, she could still remember having the same feelings for John. She grinned to think that she could have worn that same ethereal look. She probably had. Most young folks in love did.

John! She suddenly remembered that she must share all this with John.

Lydia slipped away to check on White Cloud and then went to Yellow Bird's fire.

"I was hoping you would visit tonight," Yellow Bird said. "We can finish our talk about our children. I have not mentioned anything to Bear Paw. He would not understand our haste. But I am excited and I would like to begin making something special for Runs With The Wind, too."

Lydia thought for a moment. "Why, we could match them up. We could put nearly the same design on his tunic as on Sassy's dress. And we could do the same thing with their moccasins. Takime might even carve matching necklaces. Not so fancy as the one he did for Rainy Days. That would take too long. But something nice. I am sure he would do it."

The two women were all abuzz for the next hour. Yellow Bird had never heard of such a fuss being made over a marriage, but she was pleased about it. It was exciting.

They worked everything out and even spoke with Takime and got his promise to make the necklaces. On her way back to the lodge, Lydia rounded up White Cloud and shooed him off to bed. She waited by the fire until John came home, then she told him of her suspicions and of all her and Yellow Bird's plans.

"I think you're right," he said, "about their intentions. And it will not be much longer, either. I've seen them together many times. But you cannot make too much of this. It's not the way of the People."

"I know. But it is our way. And Sassy is our daughter. We will not have a big celebration or anything. We will just make the two of them the finest clothes we can. Takime will give them the jewelry. That is all. Nothing else. Yellow Bird wants to do it, too. She will mention it to Bear Paw as soon as she works up the nerve."

"I know you, Lydia," John said. "You will want to fix a big meal and invite guests. We cannot do that. The new clothes are fine. Even the necklaces are acceptable. But nothing else. Step lightly or you may find yourself insulting someone. Their customs are too old and too sacred to be changed." John looked Lydia straight in the eye. "Promise me you will not do anything else."

"I promise. But it would be so nice if we could."

John put his arm around his wife of almost twenty years. "I can only hope that they will be as happy as we have been. Don't despair for lack of a wedding celebration. They are Tuscarora. Neither of them knows anything of bridesmaids and garters and guest lists. They have what they need—each other."

11

Racing Fox returned from his mission to Pennsylvania and the news he brought with him was not good.

He told the elders that the colonists of Pennsylvania had refused to accept the conditions presented by the Tuscarora. Their great leader, Penn, had not been there. Many believed things would have been different had he been present. Racing Fox made it known to the council that the settlers continued to attack and kill the People wherever they found them. The news he had brought was unsettling. All through the summer and deep into autumn, runners brought dire news from North Carolina. Rape, pillage, murder—there were no limits to the violence against the lowland Tuscarora. The whites wanted the land at any cost.

It was full summer when Sky Turns Dark appeared in the village carrying a tomahawk painted red. He had been sent up from Elk Eye in the Carolinas to tell The People Of The Mountains that war was imminent.

Sky Turns Dark asked them to join all the other Tuscarora towns and villages in fighting the settlers in the south. Warriors from many nations would join together and drive the white men back beyond the ceaseless waters forever.

A council was called to see if The People Of The Mountains would pick up the red tomahawk or leave it in the hands of Sky Turns Dark.

Racing Fox opened the council, saying, "Racing Fox, peace man of The People Of The Mountains, calls this council to speak to you of war. Racing Fox has heard the words of the white man, and the words were flung at Racing Fox like a cold and angry rain. And as they spoke to him, he looked into the hearts of the white men and found only heavy stones resting there.

"Racing Fox was sent for by the white men to speak of peace, yet he was not welcome in the white man's home. His words, and the words of all the people, did not move them."

Racing Fox gazed above the heads of the seated warriors as though reliving the scenes he had witnessed in Pennsylvania. A pained look crossed his face. "Our people are slaves to the white men. They are separated, one from the other, and they die of loneliness. The dogs of the white man's village are treated with more respect than our people.

"Even so, we were willing to forgive the past and begin all over but the great men of Pennsylvania would make no promises of value. They will not stop attacking our people. Mother Earth is profaned by the seeping of our blood into her belly.

"There is no place to run that the greedy ones will not follow. They attack the forest with weapons stronger than the oak, and the forest lies down before them. The forest dies from their onslaught. On land that once gave us our food and our clothes, they build their towns and put down their seeds. The animals die because they have no place live. If any survive, the whites kill them without reason. When the animals die, we die. We are left without food or clothing. Our people starve and are naked and cold."

Racing Fox shook his head in bewilderment. "They are ugly and evil and I do not understand why their mysteries are so strong. These are my last words today. It is difficult for me, a man of peace, to advise you to fight. But if we are to live, we must fight. And we must win."

As Racing Fox sat down, the warriors nodded in agreement. Sky Turns Dark stood up to have his turn.

"The time for talking with the white men is finished," he said. "We offer peace no more. The elders of Elk Eye have sent messengers across the land carrying the tomahawk of war, gathering warriors for battle. Those of you who choose to come with me will leave in four suns. We will travel to the Neuse River and await warriors from other tribes. When we are strong and our warriors are many, we will attack the white interlopers and we will drive them away from our lands for all time."

There was much talk among the men, but in the end, the red tomahawk of war was picked up and passed from hand to hand, and once again, the women of the Tuscarora heard the high-pitched cry of war coming from the council house.

In silent resignation, they laid out clothing and pots of paint for their husbands and fathers and their sons. Oak Leaf was called to the council house and informed of all their decisions. She hurried from lodge to lodge to tell the women there would be a great ceremony that very night and that there would be only four more days of life as they had always known it.

Sassy sat cross-legged on the ground. Her staring eyes were bloodshot and her face was haggard. It was almost midmorning and the warriors were still dancing. Some of the women were shuffling around in the outside circle, too tired to do more. They had danced all night and they were exhausted. Children lay wherever they had fallen asleep.

Sassy could not believe that it was true: her father and Takime, leaving the village. They would be gone for many months.

This was no hunting party. They would trek to places they had never been before and go farther than they had ever been. And Runs With The Wind! What was she to do? How could she bear life without him? Suppose he found a bride in some distant tribe. Suppose he never came back. Suppose he forgot her. Her heart was heavy with these thoughts when someone lightly touched her on the shoulder.

She looked up to see Runs With The Wind. He had left the dance arena and had slipped up behind her. He motioned for her to follow and quickly led her to Blackbird's lodge. Once inside, they stood apart and gazed searchingly into each other's eyes. She was so overcome that she swayed. He did not receive her into his arms, but reached out his hand to steady her.

With his hand still on her shoulder, burning its print into her flesh, he said, "I leave soon." His hand dropped to his side. "I cannot ask you to wait."

Sassy's heart plummeted at the sound of his words. Did he not want her? She had never been sure, but now she knew. He only teased. He did not really want her. Sassy's heart sank, but her pride surged. She lifted her head.

"I have no intention of waiting for you," she lied.

Her words pelted him like so many hard-flung pebbles. Looking into his face, she saw that it was without expression. His mouth was set like stone. His eyes showed no emotion.

In a voice that frightened her, he said, "Sunshine, this day I am asking you to share your life and your fire until the breath leaves my body. We do not have much time. If your answer is yes, I will go to your mother and father and ask permission. If your answer is no, I will leave right now for the south path to battle."

For an instant, Sassy did not comprehend what he had said. It seemed to be the reverse of what she thought he was going to say. He had called her "Sunshine," her father's special name for her. Others seldom used it. He wanted to marry her—now!

"Oh, Lordy, yes. Oh, Lordy, yes," she said. "Yes! Yes! Yes!" Before he could speak, she jumped up on him, wrapping her legs around his waist and her arms around his neck. "Yes, yes, yes," she exclaimed, swinging from left to right with her head thrown back. "Now, right now. We will be married, right now!"

In spite of all the dignity and reserve that Runs With The Wind had put into his proposal, he could not help but succumb to her exuberance. He howled with elation. The sound reverberated, startling the remaining dancers outside. Old Blackbird lifted his head and turned in the direction of his lodge. He paused a moment as he heard the sound again. Then he slowly trudged home. He was sure that the howling noise had come from his own lodge.

Just before he reached his door, Runs With The Wind and Sassy passed by. They looked strange to the old man. Runs With The Wind's war paint was smeared. Sassy sported smudges of yellow and red and black all over her face and arms. Blackbird giggled a little. The two young people did not speak but walked past with a dignified step.

All activity stopped as Sassy and Runs With The Wind passed the different lodges. No one hailed them. Instead, the Tuscarora quietly looked piercingly at them and noted their condition. The women smiled behind their hands. One young girl ran to tell Yellow Bird that it had finally happened: Runs With The Wind was asking for Sassy in marriage.

Lydia came to the doorway in answer to his call. She took one look at her daughter and said, "John, come quick. It's Priscilla."

John arrived at the entry breathless. Runs With The Wind said, "John Billips, I have come to ask for your daughter." His voice was unnaturally high in pitch. "I offer you in exchange the hickory bow that I used to kill the mountain bear. It is a sacred bow, for I was on a sacred mission from my vision when I killed the bear. I have not used it again since that day."

John Billips stared at his daughter; he had never seen her so disheveled.

"I have made a new quiver and many arrows." Runs With The Wind sounded like he was speaking through a hollow log. Billips had to strain to grasp what he was saying.

"They will also be yours," Runs With The Wind said in a high falsetto. "I offer them. In addition, I will give you two buffalo robes. And I have a fan of eagle feathers for Lydia. John Billips . . . will you accept these gifts in exchange for your daughter?"

John Billips understood. He was staring intently at his daughter.

Lydia poked John in the side and he realized that it was his turn to speak.

"I accept the sacred bow that you killed the mountain bear with, in exchange for my daughter, Sassy," John said. He added, "I have heard many men say how mighty a bow it is and that strong medicine lives in the grain of its wood. I accept the quiver and arrows that you have made. You are known for the strength of your arrows that always shoot true. I know the quiver is well made and will last me many moons.

"I accept the two buffalo hides. They will keep Lydia and me warm through the coldest nights. And for my wife, I accept the fan of eagle feathers, for we have nothing like it in our lodge. Your proposal for my daughter is accepted and you are welcome to join our lodge if you wish to."

It was done. A great sigh escaped from Sassy. They would be married. None other would have him now. He would be hers, and she his, forever.

Runs With The Wind said, "Blackbird is feeling well today. I have seen him. He will speak for us. I go to bring you my offerings. Then I will prepare for the marriage ceremony. It is best that I stay in your lodge. It is best that Sassy lives with her mother and brother while we are gone on the south path."

Before Runs With The Wind was fully out of sight, Lydia pulled her daughter inside the lodge. "Wait here," she said. "I will see that the baths are prepared for you in the women's lodge. Bear Paw will take care of Runs With The Wind."

Lydia was ecstatic. She ran to Oak Leaf's lodge and asked her help in carrying water and heating stones. Oak Leaf would know just the right leaves and ointments for Sassy and the correct washing of her hair.

Next, she hurried to Day Star with the same request. Surely Runs With The Wind had told his parents, so she rushed to Yellow Bird's lodge and asked for her help, then to Speaks Softly's lodge to enlist Rainy Days and Speaks Softly. With all the women assisting, Lydia would be free to attend to Sassy's toilet.

Her last call was to Lame Crow and Wananada. She was going to ask them for the biggest favor of all. Wananada was alone. Lame Crow had already gone to help the men with the nuptial preparations.

"Wananada, could Runs With The Wind and Priscilla spend one day in your lodge while you and Lame Crow stay with us for that one day? As you know, they will be married this afternoon. Just one day," Lydia pleaded.

Wananada laughed at Lydia's pathetic pleading. "Yes. We could not ask for better company than you and Billips. Our gift to them will be this lodge for one day."

After Lydia did everything she could think of, she returned to her lodge to get Sassy and prepare her for the ritual. Sassy and Runs With The Wind would only have a few days together. How long would it be before he returned?

Sassy was sitting on her bed when Lydia came in. She had made no attempt to clean her face or comb her hair.

Lydia took a long look at her. "Child, you are exhausted."

Lydia went to her own bed and pulled the long basket out from beneath it. She removed the lid and lifted out the exquisite doeskin dress and laid it across the bed. She took out the moccasins and the necklace Takime had made for his sister.

Sassy got up and peered over Lydia's shoulder.

"Oh, Mommy, when did you make this? It is the most beautiful—"

"Sassy, you are going to look like one of God's angels."

"And these moccasins! This necklace! Did Takime make this?"

"Yes."

Sassy held it toward the light. Takime had carved the head of a bear circled by the sun. Sassy thought for a moment. "This sun— 'Sunshine'—is for me and the bear is for Runs With The Wind's new name—'Standing Bear.' I will never call him that," Sassy said. "How can people keep changing their names all the time and expect you to remember the new ones?"

Yellow Bird had slipped in unnoticed. She said, "Runs With The Wind's name changed when he saw his vision. It is our custom. He no longer carries his little-boy name. He is a young man now and he carries a young man's name. His name may change again. Perhaps with some feat in battle. A new name would indicate a special act of bravery. Or maybe a dream that will not go away. It is possible for his name to change many times. Even if you never use the names you must remember them all. It is how others may identify or describe him. This is one way of tracing each person's special history."

Yellow Bird lay her hand on Sassy's arm and began to lead her toward the women's lodge. "Little daughter, you may call my son by any name. He will always answer you. Now come. The bath is ready."

Once Sassy entered the women's lodge, she was pounced upon from all sides. She could not stop the women, and gave herself over to them entirely.

They scrubbed her skin until she thought it would come off. They oiled her body and removed the oil, and then yet another oil was put on and removed.

They washed her hair and rinsed it in some sweet-smelling water, then dripped the remaining water all over her body. They gave her a drink that was unfamiliar to her. After drinking it, she became alert and the tired feeling, with her since early morning, left.

They vigorously rubbed her hair and body dry. While Lydia tightly braided her hair in two long braids, Yellow Bird presented her with a beautifully beaded headband that matched her dress and moccasins.

"Oh, thank you," Sassy exclaimed. "When did you make this? How did you all know? When did you know we would marry? You must have been preparing for weeks and I just found out today!"

"I know my daughter," Lydia said.

"I know my son," said Yellow Bird. "He tries very hard to treat everyone the same, but he always behaved differently around you, Sassy. It was easy to see."

Sassy laughed. "Sometimes I thought so, too. But only sometimes. Other times, I thought he was teasing me just like he teases everyone."

"Finished," Lydia said, and stood back to admire her child's hair.

Sassy stood in the middle of the floor, thoroughly scrubbed and completely naked. The only part of her that was dressed was her hair. Lydia had woven into it a strip of white leather with blue beads and tiny white shells.

The contrast between Sassy's tanned torso and the rest of her body was quite noticeable. The faint line of the old scar on her neck would not tan. It led to a small scarred circle where long ago the Apalachee warrior, Lone Runner, had tied a vine around her neck.

Like the other girls and women, Sassy removed her blouse and went about unclothed from the waist up during times when the sun was hot and unbearable. But she seldom exposed the rest of her body to the sun, only when bathing or swimming.

Her small hips and shapely legs had never looked so white before, especially contrasted to her brown upper torso, arms, and face. Her little mound of pubic hair shone with golden highlights, even in the dimness of the lodge. The women glanced at one another and smiled.

Oak Leaf said, "Runs With The Wind is getting himself a half-Indian, half-white girl. No one who has seen her can deny that. And the halves are split right through the middle."

The women laughed, including Sassy.

"We can give you a new name now," Yellow Bird added. "On your wedding day I name you 'Split-Through-The-Middle.' Do you think your new husband can remember to call you that?"

Laughter again.

"Please. No!" Sassy pleaded. "*Please* don't ever call me that."

Rainy Days saw Sassy was getting upset so she held the wedding dress up to the girl and said, "It is almost time. Get ready. No one will ever call you Split-Through-The-Middle unless they are joking. And you can not stop the People from joking, Sassy. So say nothing and pretend you do not hear them."

"Good advice," Oak Leaf said.

Sassy slipped the dress over her head and then the necklace. Lydia patted Sassy's hair into place one last time and stood back to admire her daughter. Sassy was busy squirming her feet into her moccasins.

Lydia smiled. "An angel. You look like an angel. Just like I thought you would."

"*Angel?* What does this word mean?" Yellow Bird said.

Lydia was speaking the Tuscarora language until she got to the word *angel*. There was no word for *angel* in Tuscarora.

"Angel. It means, 'God's helper.' Usually a very beautiful person who helps God give messages to those on earth."

The women said nothing. Sassy certainly did look beautiful. But as for Sassy being a helper to the white god, they were not so sure.

"Ahh," Oak Leaf said. "And what is the beautiful one who makes mischief for the white god called?"

With that remark they erupted—hooting and giggling.

The women enveloped Sassy as they escorted her to Blackbird's lodge. Runs With The Wind was coming toward them from a different direction. He was alone. He walked ahead of them to call Blackbird outside. Billips, Bear Paw, Takime, Lame Crow and White Cloud were already waiting beside Blackbird's door.

Blackbird appeared. He walked solemnly through the small crowd to Lydia's fire. The rest followed a little behind. Runs With The Wind walked beside Sassy. The young couple did not look at or speak to one another. When they all reached Lydia's fire, Blackbird spoke to Sassy. "Sassy, child of the sunshine, will you build the fire that never goes out? The fire that will cook the food that will nourish your husband and the children you bear."

Sassy picked up the implements that had been placed there by her mother. In unhurried fashion, she twirled wood against wood and fanned the smoky results with her breath until a small fire was started. When the fire was going well, she carefully pushed it over into her mother's fire. Should she ever leave her mother's home for one of her own, she would just as carefully remove a symbolic portion of her mother's fire and carry it to her next abode.

Blackbird turned once again to Sassy. "The fire having been made, where is the food you will place upon it?"

Sassy entered her mother's lodge and retrieved a cooking pot and some of the corn from the field she had worked. She poured water into the pot and hung it over the fire, then added corn to the water.

Blackbird faced Runs With The Wind. "Standing Bear, hunter and warrior of The People Of The Mountains, what have you to offer to this meal?"

Runs With The Wind left the group and went to his mother's lodge. He returned with a small piece of venison from his last kill and placed it in the pot alongside Sassy's corn.

Blackbird stirred the soup and tasted it.

He nodded toward Sassy. "You do well as a nourisher of the people. And you," he said to Runs With The Wind, "do well as a provider." He placed the large wooden spoon in the pot and slowly shuffled away to his lodge.

The wedding ceremony was over.

Sassy and Runs With The Wind walked toward Wananada's lodge, feigning calm. They entered sedately and dropped the skin curtain in place. There was no need to secure the entry. They would not be disturbed. Minutes went by. Then a deep, guttural sound erupted. It ended in a kind of howling, followed immediately by a high, feminine yipping.

"John," Lydia said.

Billips turned to Lydia. "Runs With The Wind is howling and Sassy is answering him."

The little group standing with them was gleeful. Then they began to scatter. Lame Crow and Wananada stayed on as arranged. At suppertime, they pretended that the feast put before them was everyday fare. In truth, Lydia outdid herself for the wedding supper in which Sassy and Runs With The Wind would not partake.

She had used her special supply of maple sugar and added cornmeal and nuts and fresh berries and made a wedding sweet of sorts. She had also laid out smoked meat and grilled meat and stewed chicken.

When Lydia had first come to the mountains, she had brought many seeds with her, including dandelion. From early spring through summer, she always kept a crop of the little yellow flowers growing on the hillside. Now she mixed the fresh young leaves and flower heads with poke and lightly fried it all as a side dish. She served this along with dandelion root coffee. She made a mixture of beans and corn, in addition to vegetable and chicken stew, and boiled at least a dozen eggs.

It was much too much for the four of them. Lydia nodded to passersby to stop and have a bite, as if the small feast was just a happy coincidence. There was really nothing that Billips could fault her with, and no one seemed to mind a little additional food, so he held his peace and said nothing.

The evening passed in lazy conversation. Every once in a while, someone would place a gift at Lydia's door for the newly married couple. It had been exciting but exhausting. Billips and Lydia went to bed early. Lame Crow and Wananada followed not long afterwards.

The night passed. There was no sign of Sassy or Runs With The Wind the next morning. Wananada waited until after noon and then went to her lodge and pushed aside the curtain. The huge space was empty. Everything was clean and in its place but there was no sign of the newlyweds. Wananada rushed to tell Lydia. But Lydia just smiled.

"I'm not worried about them," she said. "They just want to be alone for a while longer. They are somewhere in these mountains, close by."

They had caught two of the clan's mares and ridden along the path to the swimming creek. No one was about. They tied the mares and shed their clothes and swam around below the little dam. They held hands and leapt up then fell back into the water as they had done as children. They howled and played until they were tired and then they floated around on their backs for a while.

When they tired of the water, they got out and dressed again, except for their moccasins, which they tied to their belts with their provisions, and waded further down the creek, leading the horses along. The day was mild and the mountain creek water cold and invigorating. They spied a secluded spot shaded by willows that billowed down from the high bank. They scrambled up the slope and entered a little glen.

There they lay side by side, staring up at the sky. Runs With The Wind reached for Sassy.

"Your eyes always remind me of the blue jay's wing," he said.

Their love was made even sweeter by the knowledge of the little time left to them. Two more days. Days had never mattered before. Now each moment was precious.

"Runs With The Wind, please, let us not go back tonight. It will be a hot night. We can stay out alone. We have plenty to eat and if not, we can always find something.

"Can we just keep riding until we are ready for the night? I have never been in this direction before. Tomorrow we will have all day to ride back. We will stay with my mother tomorrow night. We will visit your mother and then, and then . . ."

And then he would leave.

"Yes, we can do those things," he said. "I will show you a valley the buffalo come to. It is not far. I have heard it said that in the land where the sun sleeps there are more buffalo than a man can count. They say it has always been so. Someday I hope to go there and see for myself."

"We will see it together," she said.

He smiled broadly at her. "Yes, we will see it together." It was good to have such a willing companion. "While I am gone you must become the best rider. It will not be so hard to travel such a distance on horseback."

"I thought the warriors were taking all the horses down the south path to battle."

"No. We are leaving a small herd for the people. Mostly mares that have been mated and will drop foal in the time of budding leaves. You will have enough to pick from. Many Arrows has decided that the horse each man rides away on will become his own. That way, each warrior will take very good care of his mount. If he loses his horse along the way or in battle, he will have to walk or trade for another one or steal one from the enemy."

Sassy said, "How is it that Blackbird knows almost everything? He said that one day the horses would no longer be owned by all the people."

"He is a man of uncommon judgment. The words that come to him in the silence are true words. The dreams he dreams in the day and in the night sometimes become real. He knows the difference. Often, when he touches a person, he can see his tomorrows. But he is old and not well. And there is no one to take his place. You must be born with these gifts. You cannot learn them."

Sassy hung her head and would not look at Runs With The Wind. "Has he said how many warriors will come back from the south?"

Runs With The Wind took her head between his hands and lifted her face to him. "I am coming back."

He lifted her up from the grass and stood her on her feet. He gave her a slight shove on the shoulders. "Go! We have miles to ride to the buffalo ground."

The valleys wound around and around between the mountains, seeming to have neither beginning nor end. They rode steadily until they arrived at a place where the valley widened considerably and intersected a different range of mountains. The little creek they were following emptied into a shallow but wide river.

The meadow was waist high in grass. He said, "We will sleep here. If the buffalo come, we will not sleep very well." He shrugged playfully. "They usually come from there." He pointed across the river.

"We can make our fire by that big flat rock." Sassy motioned toward a low outcropping. "If they come, we can get on the rocks."

Runs With The Wind chuckled softly. "Yes, if they come, we will need those rocks. But if they do approach, you will hear them a long time before you see them."

After they watered and tethered the horses, Runs With The Wind went looking for small game while Sassy explored among the rocks. Although the boulders looked solid from the outside, she found a wide crevice between them big enough to walk through. On the other side of the crevice was a perfect room with four walls of stone. Of course, there was no roof.

She surveyed the area. It would be easy enough to climb out if there were any trouble, or she could go back through the crevice. She decided to surprise Runs With The Wind and make their bed and build their fire inside the room of stone. If she had wanted, she could even have brought the horses in.

Runs With The Wind found her easily when he returned, following the drag marks from the pine boughs she was using for bedding. He handed her the turkey he had shot for their supper.

"This is our first home," she said. "The first one that really belongs to us. I wish we could stay longer."

They spent the evening in total harmony. She cooked for him as he watched her. He liked the way she used the back of her hand to brush her hair away from her face. He always had. The golden waves were continually escaping the bondage of her tightly woven braids. She was as quick and competent at her chores as any of the women. He was very proud. And to him, she was the most beautiful creature.

After supper, they turned the horses loose to graze while they walked along the riverbank. When it was dark and the stars appeared in the sky Sassy pointed up at them.

"Look. The stars have come out in a perfect night. It is the right ending to a perfect day. I will never forget this day and night."

"I will always remember, too. But most of all, I will remember how the stars appeared in your eyes and you sent them back to the sky." He pulled her close to him and they walked back to their room of stone.

12

In the late afternoon the village was filled with activity. The women were cooking extra food for the coming journey of their men. They were also hurriedly finishing clothing for them.

The men were taking horses; they could carry extra provisions. It was to be a long journey and deciding what to bring and what to leave behind was difficult. There was no ceremony. All the songs had been sung and the dances danced the day they decided to take up the red tomahawk. The intervening time had been spent in preparation.

Most of the families ate a quiet supper together and went to bed early. They would rise before dawn. The horses had been brought up the mountain the night before. A meeting place had already been arranged with the warriors who lived in the valley below.

Even before first light the men ate a hastily prepared breakfast and packed their horses. A light rain began. It was time for them to take their leave. The women stood in the drizzle in dry-eyed silence and watched them go.

Lydia returned to the lodge and sat hunched on her bed. A great fear entered her mind. What if John and Takime never returned? She shook her head to clear her thinking. Why did she always think first of the dark side of things? She wished she could be more like Sassy, an optimist.

Sassy! Sassy had not come in from the rain yet. Lydia glanced at White Cloud, asleep on his pallet. Then she went to look for her daughter. She did not go far.

The girl was still standing where she had stood last—beside the tall oak that guarded the entrance to the cornfield. The oak tree was as far as the women had followed their men. Sassy was staring off into the shimmering drizzle. The men were nowhere in sight.

Lydia reached out her hand. "Sassy. Come home now. They're gone. He would not want you standing here making a spectacle of yourself. Be brave. He would want you preparing for your new life together. Come now." She tugged gently on Sassy's arm.

Without a word, Sassy followed her mother to the lodge. Her face was composed but when she spoke it was with quiet sadness. "I just want to sleep for a while, mother. I feel so very tired."

Sassy went to bed. She did not get up until almost noon. The first thing she noticed when she awoke was the sound of rain. Good, she thought. It is raining and I will not have to go out and face the other women and pretend that nothing is wrong. She looked around for White Cloud but he was not there.

Lydia placed food before Sassy but she ate very little. Afterward, she circled the room listlessly, looking for something to do.

"Here." Lydia handed Sassy several finished skins. "I have been saving these for something special. Make your husband a shirt. There is enough leather here to make it in the old way that your father wears."

Sassy's face lit up. "Yes. I will do that. Thank you, Mother. You always know how to cheer me."

For the rest of the day Sassy busied herself making the new shirt. She glanced at her mother from time to time and realized by the look on her mother's face that she, too, was stricken by the turn of events. With a surge of understanding for her mother's feelings, Sassy felt ashamed that her own sadness had only added to her mother's worries. She vowed not to let Lydia see her pain again.

The rain stopped. Sassy put down her sewing and said, "There is no sense in staying cooped up in here forever. We can visit Rainy Days and Speaks Softly for a while. We can pick up White Cloud along the way."

Lydia was agreeable so they spent a pleasant evening chatting with the other women.

The next day was sunny. The women and younger children worked in the fields. The older boys and men crafted new weapons and restored their old ones. They hunted small game and did minor repairs around the lodges. Several days passed and village life fell into the old patterns. But there was a quietude that had never been there before. Existence had changed. Their futures now were something unknowable.

Sassy did not tell Lydia of her plans because she knew Lydia would object to her going alone. So she packed her gear the night before and left it out, in back of the lodge, so as not to wake anyone in the morning as she left.

Sassy woke before dawn and slipped quietly into her clothes. Just after full light, she went to the valley of the horses and stood before a little black-and-white mare.

The young boy watching over the horses said, "She is a good one. Bright and alert. She will make you a fine companion for the day."

"Yes, I like her. Hand me the bridle."

Sassy jumped onto the horse and rode her around the field a few times. The horse had a lot of energy but was fairly easy to handle. She would spend the entire day riding, maybe even try to hunt from astride the horse.

"I should be back before dark," Sassy said and rode off. She went in the direction of the stone room. She probably could not get there and back in one day and practice hunting, too, but it was as good a destination as any to head toward.

As she passed the places she and Runs With The Wind had been in their nuptial days together, her heart grew heavy.

It was a long while before she remembered to try shooting from the horse. She was making too much noise to surprise any game, so she decided to make a target and shoot at that instead.

She stopped in a narrow valley with a stream on one side, gathered dry wood, and bound it with old fox grape vine. Shoved in among some rocks, this made a two-foot-high target. That would do for a beginner. There was plenty of room to ride by it on either side.

She rode the horse up and down the valley, becoming accustomed to its gait. Then she trotted a hundred feet from the target and turned. Approaching it at a slow trot, she realized that she was going to need a lot of cooperation from the little mare. She could only control the horse with her knees, using her hands to pull the bowstring and sight the arrow as she had been taught.

She missed the target completely on her first try, but it was not the mare's fault. The little black and white kept a steady pace right on past the bundle of wood. She would have gone on for miles, but Sassy caught the reins and pulled her up. It was Sassy's clumsiness that caused the miss. She hit the mare's side and her own knees with the end of the bow.

The pressure of her knees would make the mare stop and turn as needed. Then she must learn how to draw the arrow and angle the bow in one smooth motion. By her husband's return she would be skilled and together they might head west.

Sassy spent an hour just galloping up and down along the creek, teaching the mare to start and stop and turn at the pressure of her knees. The little horse learned quickly. Sassy jumped off her back and scratched the black and white's ears and rubbed the soft face. She turned the mare loose for a while to graze while she sat down to eat and take a rest. Then they resumed their work.

The shadows grew longer. Sassy was hitting the target on a regular basis. She hid the target but there was no way to hide the path the mare had worn in the ground on both sides of the holding stones.

Two days later, Sassy returned and put her target up for practice. The following day, she set off again, but she had finally told Lydia where she was going and why. Lydia protested but Sassy insisted. She felt closest to Runs With The Wind when she was off on the trails alone. She did not know how to explain this. Alone and far away, she remembered their time together as wife and husband and the memories were the only thing that brought her peace.

By her fourth trip out, she could ride at a full gallop and hit the target every time. She was confident enough now to go in search of a moving target but decided to rest first.

She staked the mare and lay down in the shade of the rocks and slept. Her dreams were unsettling and she awoke to the pressure of hands forcing her to the ground and two of the bluest eyes she had ever seen.

13

The man cocked his head to one side. "Or is she a half-breed?" He was speaking excitedly to someone standing just over his shoulder.

"She's different from the Indian women I've seen," said the second man.

"Help me get her up, then bring that mare over here," said the blue-eyed one, holding her down. "She's scared. She'll probably fight."

The man eased off to let her up. Sassy jumped away. She tried to run but the man caught and held her. She fought. The other joined in.

She scratched and bit and pulled the blue-eyed man's hair. She kicked and slapped at both. They struggled with her and wrestled her back down. She was on her back on the ground.

"Turn her over, Jake, and hold on tight. She's a wildcat," the second man said.

Jake turned Sassy over onto her stomach. He pressed her head into the earth while the second man sat on the back of her legs and secured her wrists behind her back.

"Did you see the mark on her neck?" said blue-eyed Jake. "Looks like rope burn."

"A pretty little thing if she was cleaned up," the other man remarked. "I wonder if she knows any English?"

Both men stood, towering over Sassy. She lay still. She must not let them know that she could speak or understand until she found out what they wanted.

"Get her up," the second man said.

"You get the horse, Paul. Then we will see what we have here."

Jake reached down to pull Sassy up. Sassy quickly rolled away and struggled to rise by herself. Edging her back along the rock, she pushed up onto her feet.

Jake reached for her again. Sassy arched away. She spat and berated him in Tuscarora. Paul was laughing.

"Regular wildcat," he said, as he led the black and white over to Jake. "Here, hold the horse while I take a look."

Paul passed the bridled horse to Jake and stepped toward Sassy. There was no chance of escape. She did not try. She stepped away from the rock. When Paul came close enough, she kicked him hard in the shin. Paul howled and danced around in pain. It was Jake's turn to laugh.

"Better leave her alone for a while," he said. "Until she gets used to us. What are we going to do with her anyway? If she was an Indian, we could sell her. But look at that hair. She's a white girl. We can't sell a white girl." He shook his head in consternation. "And we can't let her go back to the savages. Maybe we should have just left her sleeping. We might have to keep her and eventually take her east."

Paul was still limping around, holding his shin. His face was grim.

"*You* keep her. I don't want her. Better still, just leave the wildcat here."

"Hey, little brother, I thought you came with me to find adventure." Jake pointed toward Sassy, who stood glaring at them. "Well, here it is."

Paul pouted. "I would rather take a bear home than that girl! Mother would probably like a bear better, too."

Jake snickered. "Go get our horses. Then help me put her on hers. We still have a job to do and we have to get on with it."

Jake squatted in front of her and waited for his brother. Paul reappeared with three horses. One was loaded down with supplies. The other two were saddled.

The men approached Sassy. She knew that they wanted to put her up on the little black and white but she pretended she did not understand. She kicked and screamed and tried to wriggle away.

Jake yelled, "If you keep this up I'm going to put you in a sack and throw you up on that beast."

Sassy calmed herself. She did not want Jake to know that she understood him but she certainly did not want to be put in a sack.

Jake lifted her on. "I guess I will have to lead this horse until we feel safe enough to untie her hands."

Paul packed Sassy's gear onto the horse and Jake led the mare as they headed northwest. They spoke of the place where Racing Fox had gone with the belt of peace. It was a bad place. It was the place where they treated dogs better than they treated Indians. It was the place where Indians were sold as slaves. Long Feather's wife and family had been taken there long ago and had not been seen or heard from since.

A cold fear cupped her heart. She would try to behave so they would untie her hands. When the chance came, she would escape. She relaxed a little. These men could not keep her.

They rode on. One side of her—hair, face, clothing—was caked with dirt. The rest of her appeared clean.

They spoke very little. Sassy tried to remember the route. They were not going toward the stone house. She had never been in this place before.

The hours went by. Sassy's shoulders and back ached. It was agonizing to ride with your hands tied behind your back while trying to keep your balance on a horse solely by using your knees and thighs.

She needed to relieve herself but did not know how to tell the men. The tops of her legs hurt from pressing into the horse's flanks. She decided to try stopping the little mare and gave the signal with her knees, then pulled back with her knees and thighs.

It worked. The mare halted. Without even looking, Jake pulled on the lead to get the mare moving forward. After a few steps, Sassy stopped her mount again. Jake pulled again. The third time, Jake turned around to see what was happening.

"I think the girl needs to rest or eat or relieve herself or something," Paul said. "How are we going to handle that without untying her?"

"We do not untie her. She is still too close to where we found her. She could probably find her way back if she got free. We'll tie her hands in front for a while. We can't waste too much time, either. There's a ways to go before dark."

Jake pulled Sassy down from the horse. He released her hands and retied them in front of her, then pushed her gently toward a stand of dense bushes. Sassy was too tired and sore to fight him and her bladder hurt from holding herself so long. She went into the bushes. When she reemerged, the brothers were patiently waiting by her mare to help her up. She obediently let them lift her on.

The men made camp just before the dark. Sassy sat at the base of a great oak tree and watched with intense interest as they unpacked the extra horse, made a fire out of the first available wood they came across, and put some food on to cook. The fire burned too hot and made too much smoke. She hoped enemies were not lurking anywhere near. If so, they would be sure to see the fire or smell the smoke.

They turned the horses out to graze and Paul spread three dirty blankets on the ground. He did not gather leaves or branches to stuff beneath them for comfort. She wished he would. She was very sore and tired and would have liked a nice, soft pallet.

Jake was mixing some kind of paste with water from a nearby

stream. He put the mixture in an iron pan and placed it directly on the flames.

Jake set Sassy between himself and Paul and untied her hands so that she could feed herself. They were eating their meal of pan bread and bacon with beans when a voice startled them: "Hail, the camp. Hail, the camp."

Jake grabbed his gun and dragged Sassy away from the firelight. Paul was not far behind.

A bulky man stepped into the light with his hands held aloft. "Be calm, friends," he said. "I have not seen a kind face in a long time. I saw the fire and tied my horses a ways back and came on by myself. I am alone."

Jake stayed back with their captive while Paul stepped forward. "What is your name, sir? And what keeps you in these parts?"

"Why, they call me Zeke and most of the time I live in these parts. Got me a little squaw woman and a passel of half-breeds further north. I do trading and my woman does a little crop raising. We make out just fine."

The odd-shaped man stood motionless in the firelight, waiting for a response. He was the ugliest man Sassy had ever seen. There was a gaping hole where his top front teeth should have been. He was bald on top, with long stringy hair growing everywhere else. His beard was heavy and dirty, his nose huge, and his skin pitted. She caught the stench of him, even across the smoke-filled encampment.

When no one responded, Zeke said, "I would sure be pleasured for some company on a night like this. A white man stays lonesome up here. I ate my supper a while ago, but I can add some fresh meat to breakfast. Got two turkeys laying across my packhorse right now."

"Welcome to spend the night," Jake said, much to Sassy's dismay. Things were bad enough for her without the addition of this stinking stranger.

"Well, thank you, sir. I will just go get my horses and bring them in first. There is a little something in the side bags that is much better than turkey." He smiled his toothless smile at Jake and sauntered off to fetch his earthly possessions.

Supper was finished and everything cleared up by the time he returned. He had three horses with him, two of them heavily packed for trading. He hobbled the horses and retrieved something from a bag. Lumbering over to the fire, he pulled the stopper out of the container he was holding. A strange, sharp odor floated across the fire to Sassy.

"Whiskey. I got us some of the best whiskey you ever want to taste."

Sassy knew about whiskey. Her father had told her many times and Blackbird spoke against it. But Jake was smiling, his blue eyes crinkled with pleasure, and holding out his hand for it.

"No, no." Zeke shook his head. "Let your little lady have a turn at it first." He shoved the whiskey toward her.

Jake grabbed it instead. "No. This lady does not drink whiskey." He took a short gulp and passed it to his brother.

The men sat and drank and talked while the fire died down. Sassy watched them getting drunker as the night wore on. She was amazed at the changes the whiskey made.

Paul's face grew slack and a trickle of saliva gathered at the corner of his mouth. Jake talked and talked. Zeke's eyes were small and naturally half-hidden, but they seemed to get smaller and shinier.

The men appeared to have forgotten all about Sassy. She edged away from the embers of the fire toward the night shadows. She considered making a run for the woods. Zeke glanced her way. "Your friend is awfully quiet. A taste of this good whiskey would loosen her a bit. The last drop is about gone."

Jake realized right away what she was up to. He jumped up, grabbing her tightly by the arm. "Paul," he said, "get the rope. We better tie her feet, too, this time, or she'll try to get away in the night."

Intuition told Sassy not to fight as Jake and Paul hobbled her. The drunken men were behaving very differently from the way they had earlier in the day. She cringed. Jake put her on a blanket and dragged it thirty feet away, then took another blanket, threw it over her, and returned to the fire.

"Who is she? I thought she was your woman." Zeke was full of questions.

"No. Just saw her for the first time today," Jake said. "She was off by herself, riding a horse and practicing with a bow. She was good at it. We watched for a while and when she fell asleep, we got her."

"Just came across her accidentally like?" Zeke asked.

"Well," Paul said, "my horse heard her first. When he nickered we thought there was another horse around. So we tied ours and went searching. We found her before long. She was making a lot of noise."

Zeke yawned. "Seems like a right pretty little thing. How much would you take for her?"

"What?" Jake was indignant. "She is a white woman. I would not sell a white woman."

"No need to get your hackles up. My woman could use some extra help with the crops and all. What do you intend to do with her?" Zeke stood up and sauntered toward the big bay.

"Can't rightly say." Jake's words followed him. "But we will do the Christian thing by her. Probably take her home with us. If my mother does not want to care for her, there are charities in Philadelphia."

Zeke came back carrying another precious bottle of whiskey. He had only meant to share one container with the strangers, but . . . He handed it to Jake. "How old do you think she is?"

"Oh, maybe fourteen or fifteen," Jake said.

"Well, don't you think those savages have probably had a go at her already? What white man would want her then? Certainly not you or me. Am I right?" Zeke raised his eyebrows.

"She does not look to be abused." Jake yawned. His head swam. He was not used to drink. Paul was hardly listening to the conversation: his nodding head hung down on his chest.

. . .

Sassy lay under her dirty blanket, feigning sleep. If only she had not ventured so far. The boy guarding the mares would be sleeping now. He would not realize until morning that she had not returned. Probably no one was out looking for her yet. There was no one to spare. The men were either too young or too old to track her.

She could not depend on any one searching for her so she must think of a plan of escape. Most of all, she must lull them into leaving her untied. Lydia would be beside herself. She closed her eyes and tried to sleep.

"I have had enough," she heard Jake say. "Need to sleep now." In a short while they were all asleep. But someone stirred—the largest man, Zeke. The other two snored as if they might never wake.

Zeke's footsteps approached. He squatted down and quickly stuffed a cloth in her mouth, roughly tieing it behind her head.

He rolled Sassy tightly in the blankets, scooping her up and carrying her into the woods. He carted her a long way until he found a small clearing, then dumped her on the ground. She landed on the side of her head and shoulder. Pain shot across her jaw and down her chest.

Zeke unrolled the blankets, spilling her out. He stood gazing down at her frightened face, then reached behind his back and unsheathed his knife. He cut the cord that belted his filthy pants, and the rawhide that bound her ankles. Calmly he drew back his fist and struck her hard blows across the cheek and nose. When he judged her subdued, he drove the blade of his knife into the earth beside her head and pushed back her clothing. In the way she had learned from the Tuscarora, she willed her body to be still, to not feel the pain in her jaw or nose. At least she could no longer smell the filth of the man. As he tried to mount her, she ripped the knife from the earth.

14

Paul took one direction and Jake another. They circled the area over and over in ever-widening arcs until they finally came across the body.

"Look what she did to him," Jake said, standing over Zeke's corpse. He had been stabbed five or six times, once directly in the heart. His abdomen was deeply sliced in an almost perfect V-shaped wound. An incision around the back of the head looked like she might have tried scalping him for good measure. Paul did not want to think further on that possibility.

"Was she trying to rip his face off?" Jake said.

"I do not care about what she did to him. Look what he has done to her. Here. Help me drag her into the shade." Paul carried the blankets over to where Sassy lay. "Be careful. She may have broken bones."

Paul was the healer of the two. Jake knew nothing of fevers and bruises. Like most men on the frontier, he could set a broken bone but little else.

She lay on her back, her dress split in half, body exposed, bruises all over. The face was hardly recognizable. Both eyes were turning black. Blood was everywhere.

A carved wooden necklace was wrapped around her wrist. She was breathing and moaned when Paul spoke to her.

Jake picked up the knife. "Cover her up with something."

Paul took off his shirt and draped it over Sassy.

Jake said, "She looks bad. What are we going to do? We can't stay around much longer. We still have country to map out and trade to set up. It may be too late to save the girl anyway. I mean, even if she survives, what will we do with her? She is more savage than white. Look what she did to him. How can we even safely lay ourselves down to sleep with her around?"

Paul knelt next to her. "What *she* did to him? Look what we did to her. You. And me. We tied her up and she couldn't protect herself. Then we brought a stranger in camp and got drunk with him. The only time she fought us was when we first caught her. You would have fought, too. We owe her, Jake. We owe her a lot. She was better off with the savages. She was young and beautiful and unharmed. Now look. And we are responsible."

Jake saw the truth of his brother's words but he did not know exactly what to do about it. In resignation he said, "What do we do?"

"We can't exactly toss her back, can we? You will have to go on and I will have to stay and take care of her."

Jake nodded. "I suppose you are right. It will be three or four weeks before I get back. But then what?"

"Then we will just have to take her home with us."

"I will bury Zeke," Jake said.

"I think the three horses and all his supplies and trade goods should be hers," Paul said. "She can use them to pay her way until she finds her people."

"If that is the way you want it." Jake turned to go get a shovel. He threw his hands up in the air.

"We will nurse her back to health, we will give her the horses and goods. We may even take her home."

A sound startled them. She had mumbled.

Paul bent down close. She moaned again.

"There. She said it again. You heard her." He stood up smiling. "That proves it. She is a Christian girl and we must treat her accordingly. Somewhere deep in her she remembers. How terrible life has been to her. The savages must have captured her when she was very young."

The men diligently went about their chores and by nightfall had built a rough shelter of pine boughs not too far from the creek. It was a good mile from their previous campsite and well off the trail. Jake left early the next morning.

Sassy lay in the shelter staring up at the makeshift roof. She could hear someone moving about not too far away. Though much of the last twenty-four hours was hazy, she had awakened with a clear head. She remembered what she had done to the brute. Her lips were cracked and swollen, her body bruised. But her spirit was unburdened. She need never hang her head in shame; she was avenged. She had avenged herself. She had done it as well as any warrior. Runs With The Wind would be proud of her.

Paul appeared in the shelter's opening. Sassy stared unblinkingly at him. Her eyes were like two slits in her swollen face. Her hair was tangled and dirty and underneath the filthy blanket, she still wore the split doeskin dress. Paul stooped and wiped the blood off her face and arms. She was in need of a warm bath. She wouldn't understand but he would speak to her anyway. He hoped his tone might soothe.

"Please, do not be afraid of me. I am going to bathe you as best I can. I have some clean clothes for you, too. They are mine but they will do for now." He reached for her and she kicked at him.

"Oh, no," Paul said. "I am not going to fight you. You can just stay dirty. It's okay."

Sassy pushed herself up into a sitting position. He helped her a little; she actually let him. She pointed to the pan of water and then to herself.

"Oh. You think you can do it by yourself?"

She pointed to the little pile of clothing he had laid nearby. He brought the clothes and the bath preparations closer. She shooed him away and painfully washed her face and then bared her chest to wash her torso.

"I will take a little walk," he said.

Sassy ignored him. She sat on the old blanket in the early morning sunshine and washed herself. She could not cleanse her hair. She needed to get in the creek to wash her hair and she was not up to that. She loosened the braids and combed her hair with her fingers. It was the best she could do. Then she put on Paul's cotton shirt and his pants, which she had to fold over at the waist and at the ankles.

She was exhausted by the time she finished. But there was one more thing she must do. She got to her feet and moved away from the smelly old blankets. She was not going to lie down in those again. Not until they were cleaned. She let out a high, shrill whistle and Paul came running.

He felt like laughing when he saw her. She was holding up the pants with one hand and pointing at the blankets with the other. Her damaged face was partly hidden by her hair, which hung down to her waist. The face looked unreal—like some kind of mask, puffed and discolored.

Paul picked up the blankets. She motioned toward the creek and he understood immediately: wash the blankets. He felt a bit embarrassed. They stank. He and Jake had never thought to wash them.

Taking them down to the water's edge, he plunged the blankets into the cold creek over and over again, and scrubbed them on rocks. He spent a good deal of time at this and then laid them out in the sun to dry. When he looked around for Sassy, he saw her curled up in a ball at the edge of the woods. She was sound asleep.

Her legs held so Sassy took a little walk around the clearing and along the creek. Paul nervously kept his eye on her just in case.

He had hobbled the horses a little further down the creek. Sassy approached her black-and-white mare and called out. The mare nickered. They had missed one another. Sassy hugged her around the neck and murmured, "Dear Friend." The smell of its mane brought memories of home.

"I will try to keep you with me always, Dear Friend," she whispered. "One day soon, we will go back together."

Sassy ate breakfast. She nodded at Paul appreciatively for the food.

He sat down beside her. "Poor little orphan," he said. "I will not let anything else happen to you."

She clutched her blankets and eased closer to the crackling fire. Paul took up her torn doeskin dress and began punching holes in the leather along the side of the tear. He finished one side, punched holes in the other, and began fastening it together with thin strips of rawhide. When he was done, he took the garment to the creek and washed it. And all the while he kept up a running one-sided conversation with Sassy, even though he thought she could not follow any of it. "You will feel better in your own clothes," he said finally. "They were loose enough on you to take the stitching and still fit."

Sassy lay in the sun, watching. She never knew a man to sew on a woman's clothes before. Or wash them. This Paul was strange but also kind. How could such a man steal her in the first place? What did he want?

Paul glanced at her. "My, you look better sitting there in the sunshine. After a while, we'll go through the packs that Zeke left. Maybe there will be things we can use. Maybe something to put in your hair. There is a bolt of cotton. I saw it. And beads. Many beads. You probably like beads." Paul stared at Sassy. She was humming. The tune was vaguely familiar. It did not sound Indian.

Sassy realized her mistake and stopped humming. It was too late. Paul said, "What was that? What were you humming?"

Sassy stared back at him steadily and said nothing.

"Who knows? Maybe I'm hearing things."

Paul went back to the dress and pressed as much water as he could out of it and hung it on a tree branch to dry. Then he went beyond the edge of the woods to where he had stored the packs and dragged them over.

"These are yours," he said. "They all belong to you. And the horses, too. Let's see what you have. I saw some of it but I did not have time to look at all of it."

He untied a package and let the contents spill out. Small packages of red and white and blue beads lay on the ground. Sassy was entranced. Tiny mirrors lay strewn about. Sewing needles in little containers and spools of sewing thread were among the treasures. Buttons . . .

Paul untied another package but Sassy stopped him, putting her hand on his shoulder. She picked up each item and examined it carefully. She even studied each needle although there was very little difference between them. She was fascinated with the miniature containers. She pulled on the spool and bit the thread, testing it for strength. It did not seem very strong.

The beads she saved for last. They were of different sizes and colors. She would share them with all her friends. Rainy Days could decorate her first baby clothes with them. Her mother and Yellow Bird and Nightfall and all of the women would be overjoyed. The second package held knives. She reached for one in a tooled leather sheath.

Paul firmly took her wrist. "No. I cannot let you have a knife. Not yet, anyway."

Sassy stiffened and turned her back on him but Paul was having none of it.

"This pack is not so good, huh? Well, we will get a better one." He shoved everything back into the pack and brought her another, containing three bolts of bright cotton material. In spite of her resolve to be angry with Paul, Sassy could not keep her hands from the fabric.

She stood up and wrapped the cloth around her. It was patterned with flowers in shades of blue, from very light to very dark. Even with the changing hues of her many bruises, the color brought out the deep blue of her eyes and the brightness of her hair.

"Well, I can see what you will be doing for the rest of this week—making yourself a dress." He pantomimed sewing.

Sassy nodded. Paul put the rest of the things away, except for the sewing equipment. He let out a sigh of relief. He had found something to keep the girl busy for a while.

Days went by quickly. Sassy improved dramatically. The swelling receded and the bruises yellowed. She took a dip in the creek and washed her hair until it was clean.

With these improvements came an added alertness. She was watching Paul's every move and he was aware of it. She was biding her time, waiting for a chance to escape. Paul was never more than a few feet away, and he carried weapons. She had none.

Sassy worked feverishly on her dress, placing tiny, tight stitches all along the seams, just the way her mother had taught her. Paul meanwhile pondered the problem of food. They needed fresh meat. He was going to have to hunt, yet could not leave Sassy behind. There was little likelihood of bagging anything with her along but he had no choice. If he left her, she would probably run away. She would most likely take the horses, too. His only other choice was to tie her up and he had made up his mind never to do that again. He would have to take her.

Paul tapped her on her shoulder. He wished he knew her name. It would be nice to call her something. She turned and gazed at him questioningly with that unwavering look she sometimes gave him. He was struck by her shining beauty. Shining was the word. Her face shone, her eyes sparkled, and her hair reflected the sun.

"We need fresh meat. I must hunt. I will have to take you, so be very quiet." He pantomimed it.

She smiled and nodded and made motions of shooting an arrow.

"No. No." He shook his head. "You cannot hunt. Only me, and I am taking the rifle."

She stood up and folded her arms and stomped one foot on the ground. Then she turned her back on him determinedly.

"Oh, well. What am I going to do? If I drag you along you certainly are not going to keep quiet." Paul was thinking about letting her take her little bow along. What harm could she do with that? As an afterthought he said out loud, "Kill me, that is what she could do with those arrows." But somehow he did not really believe that she would try to harm him. They had been together now for days, and he saw nothing in her to make him believe that she would try to hurt him.

He knew she wanted to get away. That was obvious. But she was not a cruel or dangerous person. She spoke to the wild birds and small animals that sometimes came in close to the camp. She took excellent care of the horses and always spoke softly to the little black-and-white mare. And sometimes, when she did not know that he was watching her, she looked upon him with the gentlest expression.

"All right." He nodded yes to her and drew a make-believe bow. "All right. You can take your bow if it makes you feel better."

Sassy was delighted. She was tired of the food and the camp. And maybe, while they were out, she could even find a chance to run away. Maybe not. She promised Dear Friend that she would take her, too. She did not want to leave the mare behind.

Her mood changed immediately. She clapped her hands and did her old tippy-toe dance for Paul.

Paul was fascinated. How resilient she was. After all she had been through, it took so little to make her happy. He felt ashamed that he had ever thought she could harm him. He laughed at her antics and motioned for her to follow him, leading her to a spot in the woods where he had hidden her bow and arrows and some other weapons.

She picked up her bow and caressed it as though it were an infant. Runs With The Wind had made it for her. A small piece of his spirit was locked within its wood. The same was true of the arrows. Having them in her hands made her feel whole again. She could feel her strength returning. She could fight any battle now, even the battle of loneliness that lay before her.

Paul saw a change come over her when she touched the bow. Her face took on the maturity of a woman. A calmness settled over her.

"How many people are wrapped up inside of you?" he asked. "Every time I look at you, you are different." He shook his head. "Come, girl." He motioned for her to stay in front of him.

They went deeper into the woods. She moved just as he imagined she would. Like an Indian.

She made almost no noise. Not once did she turn to see if he was following. He stopped when she suddenly paused. He admired the smooth flow of her arm as she raised the bow and set the arrow. The arrow flew and he heard a thrashing sound up ahead. Sassy was already running with another arrow at the ready. By the time Paul caught up, the doe she had shot was dead.

Sassy pulled two arrows from the carcass. She wiped the blood from them with leaves from an overhanging tree and slipped them back in their quiver. She turned to Paul and reached for his skinning knife but he backed away. She followed, determined that she was going to skin her own deer.

"No. I am sorry. You cannot have it."

Sassy was furious. It was her deer. It belonged to her. She was perfectly willing to share it but it was her duty to skin and dress it. The hide belonged to her. She was not going to give up the hide.

Paul did not know how to handle her. He did not want to face the angry girl and he could not give up his knife. He turned his back and strode away.

"*Paul! You come back!*" she shouted.

Paul spun around. She had spoken. She knew his name.

"Lordy, Lordy," she muttered.

"You could speak all along," he accused. "All this time you knew what I was saying. And Jake, too." He raised his voice. "*Why* did you keep it a secret?"

"Because you stole me. You tied me up."

"If you had spoken up, we might not have tied you."

"Why are you here? What makes you think you can come to the mountains and steal people?"

Paul softened. "We did not come to steal people. We came to make maps and set up trade for some business men back east. Maybe scout out some land for settlers. Jake and my sister and her husband, Mason, came out last year. They brought Mason's mother and his brother, and a hired man named Samuel. Built a small cabin. They meant to settle in the little piece of wilderness they found. It was a long way from here or anywhere.

"Jake was going to help them and then he was planning to go back home. But Indians killed Mason and the hired man. They stole weapons and all of the horses. Later, after the rest of the family left, they burned the cabin."

A dark anger crossed Paul's face. "We will recognize the horses and the weapons if we see them. Mason did not harm anyone. Those thieving Indians killed him for a few horses. We are looking for those Indians. If we find them, we will kill all we can. If some survive, we will bring back other men to finish the job."

"How do you expect to find them?" Sassy said.

"We know the horses, the gear, the weapons. And Indians talk. They seem to know everything that goes on everywhere. We will find one who knows something about this."

Paul stretched, flexing his legs. "They had a hard time getting back. It was the wrong time of year for traveling. They almost froze to death in a blizzard not long after they started out. Anyway, when Jake came looking this time he asked me to come with him. We were exploring and mapping and reconnoitering trade routes for weeks before we saw you." Paul shrugged. "What about you? Where did you come from? I mean, where were you born? Who are your parents?"

Sassy knew she could never tell the truth—that her brother and father were among the raiders when the two whites were killed. Her husband, too. Some of the horses could still be in the valley. The gear could be anywhere. She must never let them know where she lived.

And they must never find her mother. They might even bring soldiers if they knew another white woman was up in the mountains.

"Where did I come from?" she repeated. "I have no memories of where I came from. I have been with the Indians since I was little."

"Do you have a name?"

"Sassy. I have been called Sassy."

"Well, Sassy, why is it you speak so well? If you were taken when you were little, how come you remember so many words and speak so well?" Paul had been tricked by her. He had never once thought that she could speak English. Now he was unsure whether to trust her.

"There was an old woman in my village," Sassy lied. "She spoke the language. I looked upon her as my mother. She was white. She died when the last snows came. She taught me sums and to write my name. A little reading, too. She taught me many things."

"Why did they allow this?" Paul was curious.

"Because she was married to a very respected man of the tribe. He died, too."

"How were you treated?"

"I have always been treated well."

"Poor thing." Paul believed her. "You have been orphaned twice." When he saw a strange look come over her face, he thought it was because he had suggested her real parents were also dead.

"I do not mean your real parents are dead," he said. "I only meant that you are without them. Just be glad that we have found you. We will take you back east where people are civilized." He swung his arm toward the deer carcass, indicating that her killing of the deer was not a civilized act. "And maybe one day you will find your real parents again." He paused. "Where was your village?" he said.

Sassy was tired of the whole conversation. Any more and she might let the wrong words slip out again. The less she lied, the less lies she would have to remember. She put her hands on her hips and stared him in the eye. "I am finished talking. Now I would have the skinning knife so I can skin my deer." She held out her hand.

Paul handed it to her and Sassy went about her work. Now and then she would grunt from exertion and the strain on her still aching body. There was no longer any swelling in her face and only slight signs of the old bruises. When Paul tried to help, she almost snarled at him. He jumped back in alarm. Even though she is white, sometimes she is like a wild animal, he thought.

Sassy gutted and skinned the deer and sliced off the choice parts for them to carry back to camp. She told Paul to put the remains in the crook of a tree. If they needed it, they would come back for it later. If not, the meat was hung low enough that, with a little effort, other animals could feast on it. She did not consider meat wasted if the forest animals ate it. Paul did.

During the following week, Sassy saw several opportunities to escape. She took none. Her fear was that Paul, in trying to track her, would find the valley of the horses or the main village. She set her mind to protecting the village.

Paul was aware that she could have fled on several occasions. He thought that the reason she did not leave was because she wanted to return to civilization. One morning he woke to find her wearing Zeke's tooled sheath and skinning knife. She could have easily killed him in his sleep. He never mentioned the weapon and she wore it as part of her daily dress.

Paul had never known a woman to work harder than she did. She was always up at dawn and worked steadily until dusk. Her cotton dress was finished and the first deerskin was almost completely tanned. She was working on a second one. She made a little tent of the hides and built a fire inside to smoke out the skins.

Along with all that, she was making a shirt for Paul out of the same cotton as her dress. Paul was pleased and she knew it. Sassy was working very hard. It helped to ease the pain of being kept from so much of her life. Everyone she had known was gone from her. Only Dear Friend remained.

When the shirt was finished and she gave it to Paul he thanked her and said, "You have been working much too hard. It is time you had a little fun. We will celebrate this afternoon. Let us get all cleaned up and you put on your new dress and I will wear my new shirt. I will teach you a dance that is being done back home."

"Oh, yes. Yes." Sassy was ecstatic. She had not worn her dress. Now there was a reason. He would teach her a dance and she loved dancing. She gathered her things and went around a bend in the creek to take her bath.

Paul was as excited as Sassy. They would have a real social. Just the two of them. Back home, he was known for his steps and his singing voice. He could play the piano a little bit, too. But when the family left Philadelphia for the backwoods, they had sold a few things, the piano among them, and bought a small herd of cows.

Paul bathed in the creek within sight of the camp. He took his time and splashed around a bit. He washed his hair and beard twice. His face and neck were deeply tanned as were his hands and arms up to the elbow. The rest of him was as white as the day he was born.

His light brown hair was sun streaked, his beard a shade or two darker. He ran his hand across his mustache and beard and decided they could use a trimming. He got out of the creek and dried off. The creek waters ran too fast to work as a mirror. He would just have to trim them by feel. He worked at it until he was satisfied. He trimmed up the mustache so at least it did not hang over his mouth anymore, and he put on his new shirt. He felt good.

Sassy sashayed around the bend just as Paul buttoned his shirt. They stopped and stared at one another, each amazed at the change in the other. They did not look like the same two people.

Paul held out his hand to Sassy and she took it. He bowed and kissed her hand. "May I say that you are looking lovely today, Miss Sassy?" he said with exaggerated politeness.

"You may," she said.

"You are supposed to curtsy now."

"I am supposed to what?"

"Curtsy. Here. I'll show you." He curtsied in an exaggerated manner.

"I remember," she said, and gave him a deep curtsy.

"Perfect, my lady. Now watch. I will show you the newest dance steps."

Paul hummed a tune and pretended he was holding her and showed her the dance. Sassy tried it a few times.

"That's it. I think you are ready." He stood behind her and held her hands, left to left and right to right. Sassy picked up the steps and the tune quickly, and soon they were humming and dancing.

Paul turned Sassy around to face him and showed her more steps. She mastered them, too, and they started from the beginning and included the new steps.

They spent the hour dancing. When they rested, Paul taught Sassy the words to a tune popular in Philadelphia. Paul was surprised: their voices blended so well. He delighted in the girl's talents. With the right clothes and a few well-taken suggestions, she would fit again into society, albeit his Quaker friends disapproved of dancing.

Suddenly she sang a savage chant. It sounded somewhere between the bleating of a sheep and the nasal howling of a dog. He could not understand any of it but it seemed she was repeating the same phrases over and over.

"What are you singing?" he said.

She stopped. "I am singing about the end of the long sun days and how many, many moons will pass before they come again."

He sensed unhappiness in her voice. "Does it make you sad?"

"Yes. It always is when the long sun days leave. And they are leaving now." She swept her arm toward the skyline.

"Well, we can't have that today. Today is for celebration. You have sung my songs and danced my dances and now it's my turn. Teach me one of your songs or a dance, but not a sad one." He waited for an answer, hoping her mood would change.

"Yes. First we can do the running buck dance." She loped to the edge of the woods and broke off two small tree branches, the leaves still attached. She brought one to Paul and kept one for herself. She had him hold it behind his head like antlers.

"I have a better idea," he said. "We can add these to hats." He picked up his hat and attached her branch to it with rope. Then he retrieved an old beat-up hat from his saddlebags and fastened his own branch to it. Sassy's eyes sparkled with anticipation.

"Is this your favorite dance?" he said. "Is that why you are so excited?"

Sassy laughed. "No. It's not my favorite. I was never allowed to dance it. It is only for the men. But I practiced when no one was around. It is fun to have someone to dance it with. We must have a fire, though. We cannot dance without a fire."

Paul built a small one. They were ready. She said, "You bend down like this and keep very still." She placed her hands on the ground. "You are a buck in hiding until a warrior comes along." She stayed crouched, remaining perfectly still. Slowly her body tensed. She lifted her head and sniffed the air. She stood. She moved her head from side to side with a majestic attitude. She pawed the ground, then bounded away, around the fire, head up, with a high-stepping gait. She circled the fire several times and stopped. She stood very straight and searched the ground with her eyes, then bent slightly forward and danced again, this time with different steps and threatening postures. She swooped low, searching, cocking her head from side to side, listening.

"Oh, I see," he said. "You are the warrior instead of the deer."

She stopped. "Yes. And now you must dance with me. Sticks will make the music for you." She left the fire and retrieved two sticks, stripping the bark as she walked. She beat them a couple of times and resumed her own dance. Paul assumed a stooped position and began to dance to the clack of sticks. They danced with abandon, spinning and twirling, yelping, calling out unintelligible sounds.

Finally Paul cried, "Enough! I need to rest. A cold drink of water. Something." He removed his antlered hat. "I have never had so much fun," he said. "No wonder the savages keep this up all night." He saw the sudden frown cross her face. "I'm sorry I said that. I did not— please forgive me. This has been too good a day to be spoiled by my foolish tongue."

"Forgiven," she said. "I enjoyed the day, too."

They walked to the creek and took a long drink. The shade of the trees beside the water felt good after all their exertions.

"We can rest here a while," he said, and leaned back against a tree trunk.

Sassy lay flat on her back with her eyes closed, enjoying a breeze. Paul looked at her. He smiled, he felt so content. He wanted to talk to her but was afraid to.

She said, "How many brothers and sisters do you have?"

"One sister—Mary Ann—and three brothers. Jake is the oldest, then me, then Mary, then Prescott. Richard is the youngest. There were two more, both younger, but they died before they were a year old. Mother had a stillborn baby between Mary and Prescott. So there would have been eight of us but there are only five."

She tilted her head slightly, no longer listening to him. A scent, a sound—she wasn't sure which—had come to her. They were not alone.

15

Jake stood at the edge of the woods. He did not mean to spy. It just happened. The two young people he was watching were so absorbed with one another that they had not heard his approach.

Jake was stunned. The girl lying in the meadow grass did not look like the same sorry creature he had left behind. Even at a distance, he could see the soft loveliness of her hair spread out about her and the gentle swell of her body under the thin dress. His brother looked all spit-shined and was behaving the way he sometimes did in the best parlors of Philadelphia.

Paul stood and reached down to the girl, helping her to her feet. They walked across the meadow toward their camp. Paul put his arm around Sassy's waist. She did not pull away.

"The very idea," Jake muttered. "Acting like a moon-sick cow."

He shook his head in exasperation. Things had greatly changed. He should have taken Paul with him. As it was, he thought he'd better hello the camp before the two got into something more serious.

Jake stepped out of the woods, pulling his horses behind him. He

THE LONG SUN

dropped the reins of the lead horse and cupped his mouth to call across the meadow.

Paul turned at the sound. Sassy also, a frown flitting across her face. She had grown used to Paul and even trusted him a little.

"Jake is back," Paul said.

"I can see that for myself." Sassy could not keep the irritation out of her voice. Sneaking away and finding her route back home would have been easier with only Paul around. With the two of them, there would be small chance of permanent escape. There was nothing to be done about it but accept the fact that Jake had returned and soon they would be on their way east again.

The two brothers slapped each other on the back and shook hands as though they had not met for years. Sassy stood where she was and watched.

"Well, it is good to see your old face again, big brother," Paul said.

Jake looked closely at Paul's new shirt, his freshly shaved face, and newly cut hair. "And you are looking fresh as a newborn calf. Where did you get that shirt?"

"Oh, this." Paul hooked his thumbs under his armpits and pranced around. "Sassy made this. Made it just for me."

"Sassy?" Jake said.

"Sassy. That's her given name." said Paul.

"Yes. A good name for her. She sure is sassy all right. No wonder you were mooning over her."

"I did not pick the name. Her mother did. It's her Christian name. And what do you mean—'mooning over her'?" Paul looked perturbed.

"I saw you," Jake said. "I saw the simple look on your face when you were talking to her. What were you talking about, anyway? She can't understand anything you say."

"You were spying! You stood in the woods and spied on me!"

"Do not accuse me. I was coming into camp when I saw you two. I just could not believe what I was seeing. You, playing moony-eye in the middle of the woods with a savage." Jake shook his fist. "You had better come to your senses before we get home or I will knock some into you."

179

"Calm down. You don't know what you're talking about, Jake." Paul sighed. "She speaks English, Jake. Speaks it well."

"Yes, well, remember that she knifes men, Paul. Knifes them very well. Try not to be her next victim."

"You seem to have forgotten why she did it. Or maybe you do not care to remember that it was our fault." Paul drew a deep breath. "Maybe we should take her back up the mountain."

Jake shook his head. "Wouldn't be safe. The Indians are on a rampage." He stared at the ground, reflecting on Paul's remarks. There was no denying it. The fault was his. He was the eldest and he was in charge of things. He had made some bad decisions and then gotten drunk. How could he have been so stupid? It was his duty to see that the girl was well taken care of. He so seldom made wrong decisions. He did not know how to own up to his mistakes. Already he could imagine the hurt and disappointment in his mother's eyes when she found out.

"Okay," Jake said. "I am tired and hungry. The fight is all gone out of me. Either you or the girl make us some supper while I take care of the packs and the horses. I will tell you all about my trip after we eat. Then you can tell me about this."

Sassy decided that she would make the meal. The last thing she wanted was the two brothers fighting because of her. Jake just did not seem to like her. Well, she would try to impress him with her cooking.

All through the meal, Sassy could feel Jake's eyes on her. The food was good and she knew it but he made no comment. The evening was perfect though no one seemed to notice. There was a stillness in the air, hanging over the camp and enveloping the three uneasy campers.

Finally, Paul spoke: "It will storm tonight. A bad storm. Maybe we should delay our trip one more day."

"No." That was all Jake said. Paul made no comment.

Sassy cleaned up after supper and began to pack for the journey east. The brothers stayed around the fire and every once in a while Sassy caught enough of their conversation to tell that, all in all, Jake's trip had been successful. He had brought back good news for the merchants back home, news about trade deals. He had also mapped the area to his satisfaction. When they talked about the Indian uprising their voices were especially hushed and guarded. But she did overhear Jake explaining that the brunt of the fighting was in the Carolina tidelands and Maryland where the English colonists had been especially brutal in seizing Indian land.

Sassy changed into her old doeskin and packed her new blue dress with the skins she was tanning. She was aware of Jake's eyes once again and saw him staring at the new hunting knife sheathed at her waist. She was too tired to worry about it. It was almost dark and she was ready for sleep. Without a good night to either of the men, she slipped into her bed of soft pine boughs and nodded off.

Paul told Jake all about the time he had spent with Sassy. How she made the dress and shirt and killed the deer and tanned the hides and about her life with the Indians.

"You realize," Jake said, "we are taking this girl home to Mother. She will be in the midst of our family. If she is not the right sort of person, she could cause a lot of trouble. On the other hand, if Mother takes a liking to her, we will not be able to pry her out of the house with a stick."

The men laughed. It was true. Their mother was known for her remarkable loyalties. Be it a neighbor, a cow, or an orphan, Mrs. Martin was nearsighted when it came to the faults of those she loved and gave no quarter when defending their interests.

Jake said, "She is a beautiful girl. It should not be difficult for her to find a husband back home. I have no love for the savages and though you say she is white, she has the heart of a savage and nothing can change that.

"And, Paul," Jake continued, "there is no need ever to mention the incident with Zeke. No matter what happens, let's make a pact never to mention Zeke's name or what took place that night."

"Agreed," Paul said and slapped Jake's shoulder in brotherly fashion.

THREE

16

They had been on the trail for days and it was still raining. Everything was soaked. The packs on the horses were a sodden mess.

Their mounts churned up mud as they traveled the narrow track in single file. The constant rain sent a chill through each of them. There was no escaping the steady drizzle or the route.

The Indians had made the paths further back than memory. In years past, a succession of white men had tried to leave the old trails and make their own, but it never worked out right. The ancients had established the easiest and shortest routes over the rivers and mountains, and those paths were still the best. They would just have to take their chances on who they might encounter along the way.

Sassy sat as straight in her saddle as she had on the first day. Her hair was plastered to her head and face and rain trickled into her eyes. If it impaired her vision, she showed no sign of it. She ignored the harsh weather as completely as she did the men riding with her, concentrating instead on maneuvering Dear Friend around the debris, water, and winds sweeping into her path.

She had not spoken one word in three days. The men, given the circumstances under which they traveled, welcomed it. The other women they knew would have kept up a steady stream of complaints against the weather, the food, the camps. Instead of complaining, Sassy rode at an even pace and did her share when it came time to unpack the animals or make camp. At night, she used her Tuscarora ingenuity and quickly built shelters that deflected the rain and kept them all reasonably protected.

More times than he cared to admit, Jake found his eyes wandering toward her rigid back during the monotonous journey. There was a lot to be admired about the girl.

The fourth morning of their journey broke clear and bright. Heat was in the air before the second hour of daylight, hinting at a hot, humid day.

Jake was restless all through breakfast, then he suddenly announced, "We will stay here today and dry everything out. No sense going on like this."

Paul said, "Good! I was hoping you would say that. Sassy can take care of the horses and spread out the dry goods and clothes in the sun. I can clean up the rifles and pistols. You could go for fresh meat." Paul was not accustomed to giving Jake orders and when he realized that he was doing so, he sheepishly added, "If you have a mind to. Most everything we have is sodden."

Jake could find no fault with this division of the chores. He cleaned his rifle and left for the hunt. Sassy hobbled several horses, including Dear Friend, and set the others free to graze where they pleased. There was little chance of the free horses straying too far from those she had confined. In a few hours, she would switch them around. In the meantime, she spread the bright colored cloth bolts out in the sun to dry alongside the other goods.

All of the confiscated dry goods and buttons and pins were hers. So too the beads and the shiny new knives and countless other trinkets, plus Zeke's three horses and his personal rifle and guns. How proud everyone would be of her if she could just ride back to the village with her bounty. She had felled an enemy and taken the prizes due the victor.

Sassy spent a good part of the morning thinking about who she would give what to and worrying about Runs With The Wind. As the day wore on, the sour mood she'd been in since Jake's return began to dissipate.

Paul noticed the change.

"I will help you with all that stuff and the horses, too, if you will help me," he said. "There is more here than I thought."

Sassy smiled. "It is good to be together for a while again. Just the two of us. Like it was before your brother came back."

Paul nodded. "I was thinking the same thing. But do not say that to Jake or we will be on the bad side of him again."

Sassy nodded. "Before I help you, I have to take a bath and wash and dry my dress. It will only take a few minutes to dry in this sun. When I am through, I will whistle and you can come help me with the horses."

"I should have thought of that. This old self could use a good scrub down, too. You follow the stream around that bend and I will stay here by the camp. See you after." He waved her away and started toward the little stream.

Sassy headed for her part of the stream. As soon as she reached it, she shed her clothes, rinsed her dress out, and laid it on the ground to dry. Naked, she waded into the water and wasted no time in finding the deepest spot to splash around in. The water was colder than she'd expected, but she was used to mountain streams. She finished bathing and ducked under the water a few times. It reminded her of the days after her wedding and memories of Runs With The Wind came flooding back.

Impulsively she stood and stretched her arms toward the sky. "Oh, Spirit of Breath," she called out, "look kindly on me. I live. But most of me is dead."

Her dress needed more sun so she left it and ran to Dear Friend. The horse nickered at her approach. Sassy embraced her about the neck. The mare bobbed her head, rubbing Sassy's cheek with each movement.

That is how Paul found them. Sassy was standing in bright sunshine, her hair covering most of her torso. He watched as she bent down to release the horse from the confining rope, then gave the mare a slap on the rump that sent her scampering across the field. Sassy watched the horse for a moment and then turned and directly faced him.

Paul was mesmerized by her young body, her sun-darkened color in such contrast to the bleached white hips. Her pubic hair glinted with water. She shook her head to dry her hair. It bounced across her body as she walked, sometimes hiding her round, firm breasts, sometimes allowing a glimpse through the thick, damp strands. Had she no modesty?

Paul's tongue grew thick and his feet froze to the earth. He prayed for the strength to remain where he was, for his only desire was to pounce on the girl and take her right there, on the ground out in the hot sun. I am no better than Zeke, he thought, and yet he trod quietly toward her.

His heart began to race and he could feel a hot flush surging through his body. She was covered by nothing but her long, heavy hair. Standing there as brazen as day, she gazed at him.

Before he realized what he was doing, he had gathered her in his arms and was holding her tightly. Her face was pressed into his chest and he lay his chin on the top of her soft, sweet-smelling hair.

She did not resist him. Nor did she respond. She remained quiet. They stood that way for many moments.

He released her slowly and held her at arm's length, staring into her dispassionate face.

"I am truly sorry. I cannot say what came over me," he stammered.

"You have done nothing," she said and turned away, heading for the treeline. At the edge of the wood, she disappeared among the shadows.

. . .

The mornings went quietly by. Some days they stopped for lunch and other days they did not. It all depended on how much information Jake needed to record in his trail diary or if he needed to work on his maps. He was meticulous about recording all such observations, Sassy had noted.

A little after noon one day, Jake called out, "Hold up. I have some things to do. Paul, fix us a bite while she helps me with these records."

Sassy sat her horse, waiting.

Jake pursed his lips. "Well, get down, girl. I have been told that you read and write. Is that true?"

"I can do some of that," Sassy answered, not wanting him to know that she was very adept at it until she knew more about what he wanted.

"Do you think that if I spoke the words, you could write them down in this book? I need to draw on this map a little better and it takes a lot of time."

"Let me see," Sassy said and dismounted.

Jake stood beside her, showing the book half-filled with his scrawled handwriting and misspelled words. Here and there among the pages he had drawn portions of maps. The maps were of a much better quality than the words. He had drawn them carefully and exactly and marked all landmarks along the way.

"Yes. I can do this," Sassy said. She hoped her excitement at this discovery of his work was not showing. If she had access to the words and the maps, she could easily find her way home at some point. Without the maps it was unlikely either man could ever retrace his steps precisely.

"Come on then." Jake motioned to Sassy. "Paul, take care of these horses, will you? While we straighten this stuff out." Then to Sassy: "You have no idea how useful it would be to have some help with this."

Sassy made no reply as they settled themselves down among the roots of an old tree. Jake unrolled the bundle he was carrying and handed Sassy a quill and ink. He kept the measuring stick though he seldom used it, depending instead on his memory and judgment.

As Jake perfected his maps, he described the terrain and the benchmarks he could remember for Sassy to write down in the book. Sassy was surprised at the accuracy of his memory and the depth of his sharp observations of the land they had crossed that morning. He could recall whether it was an ash or an oak growing at a certain bend in the trail or whether it was a stand of junipers or long-needled pine that stood just north of the huge rock shaped like a cow's bell.

Sassy realized that she, too, noticed most of these things but did not really commit them to memory. In a day or two, she would have forgotten most of it. She made it a point to memorize as much of the information that she was writing down in the book as she could. One day, when the time was right, she would make her escape and the information in the journal would help her get back home. She hesitated for a moment after Jake spoke, closed her eyes, and relived the scenes in her mind. Then she wrote the words down, carefully entering the date atop each page—2 October 1710.

They worked in this manner until Paul called them to their meal. Time passed quickly. The morning's route was recorded in detail. Jake noticed Sassy closing her eyes before writing. Was she trying to recall the words before attempting to write them down because it had been such a long time since she had written anything?

After lunch, he did not have time to look over her work. He would do so when they stopped for the night. Then he would decide if she could carry on ciphering and mapping for him. If he could not read her work, there was no sense in her continuing.

For much of the rest of the day, Sassy caught herself transforming the vistas before her into words. It was a novel experience. Hours passed before she realized that her head was so filled with these formations that not once in the entire afternoon had she thought about Runs With The Wind or her family. She did not know whether to be saddened by this. Could she have lost touch with her life so quickly? What was happening to her?

For the first time since the journey began, the spirit seemed to go out of her. She felt queasy. Her back bent forward and her head drooped. She rode this way until they dismounted for the evening.

Jake and Paul could not help but notice the change in her, but said nothing. The girl was always moody, one minute bright and bubbly and the next, withdrawn and distracted.

Supper was uneventful. Although it was still light, Sassy and Jake stayed around the fire while Paul cleared up. They worked until well after dark on the journal and maps.

When they were finished, Sassy went walking. It was a beautiful, early fall night. The moon and stars were bright enough to see by and the air was just cool enough.

Jake read the account that Sassy had written in the trail journal. He was well pleased with her efforts. There were a few mistakes but far less than he usually made himself. He decided to let her take over the task of the writing.

"I knew you would like her if only you gave her half a chance," Paul said.

"Maybe I was afraid that I would like her." Jake turned to face his brother. "You know, my plans for the near future do not include a woman—unlike your agenda."

Paul shoved his hands in his front pockets. "You sure won that little lady's heart, giving her the journal to write on. Own up. She has managed to get through that tough skin of yours and make it all the way to your heart."

Jake looked seriously at his brother. "Your flirting with her is no longer a game, is it? You have got yourself all caught up."

Paul, caught off guard, colored.

Jake said, "By next week, we should be near Cutter's Place. There is a preacher there. He could marry her off—*if* you're serious." Jake stared into the fire. "Since Father died, I have put the family first and *my* life second. Everything I have done, I have done for Mother and all of you. I am not ready to provide for a woman and family of my own. You are. But is that what you want? She is a winning little creature, but we have Mother and others to think about."

Paul squirmed. "There is another small matter, you know."

"What is that?"

"She might not want to marry anyone."

Jake shrugged. "We cannot force her to. No parson would marry a woman who did not want to marry. But we have to try to make it as right as we can for her."

Paul struck a wistful pose. "I might think on it."

Jake gave him a sideways glance. "Watch what you say, little brother. Words have a way of living longer than they were meant to."

"I am saying this. I will be around to see that she is taken care of. So *you* watch your step."

"Is that some kind of threat?" Jake said.

Paul smiled a not entirely friendly smile. "I believe that you are just jealous. You have taken a fancy to the girl yourself. I am serious. We will take good care of her and defend her honor or there will be me to contend with."

"You whelp!" Jake said. "Who took care of you and the rest when Father died? Who moved the family and handled the finances and fought the Indians and felled the trees and farmed the land? *I* did!" Jake shouted furiously.

Paul looked nervously toward Sassy's empty pallet, although she could not hear them from wherever she had wandered off to.

"You did all that and more. I am sorry. I should have held my tongue. I have no right to make light of it." Paul fell silent for a moment. "You are right. The girl has a hold on me." Paul scrunched up his brow. "She's awfully young."

"Yes," Jake agreed. "Yes. But I've watched her close as we've traveled. . . ."

"What?" Paul said, impatient.

"For a tough Tuscarora she's been mighty woozy from riding some days." He looked at his younger brother. "She may be with child."

17

It took six another days to get there. From the hill overlooking the little valley Sassy could see the smoke rising from the chimneys of four houses at Cutter's Place. There were three more houses visible when they rounded the bend.

She was hungry. Since they expected to reach Cutter's Place in late afternoon, the men had decided not to eat lunch. They wanted to wait for what they called real food. All morning during the long ride, they praised Mrs. Cutter's abilities in the kitchen. Sassy found it hard to wait for the evening meal.

She was also worried about meeting more white people. She knew they would ask her all sorts of questions about where she came from, about the Indians. She did not want to answer any more questions. She was having enough trouble keeping up with her lies now.

Sassy's stomach rumbled as she urged Dear Friend down into the valley. When she reached the valley floor, she saw rough-hewn logs made into fencing set up all around the fields. Here and there the fencing changed to fieldstones, then back to the logs again.

Most of the crops were already harvested. A section she passed abounded with several varieties of gourds still on their vines. The gourds would be left to cure on the vine during the winter. When thoroughly dried, they would be crafted into kitchen utensils and water dippers and bowls. It was something, she realized, she had known as a very young child.

The yapping of dogs announced their arrival. The first cabin they reached was the Cutters'. The Cutters were standing in the small space that served them as a yard, awaiting their guests. The smell of oddly familiar food reached Sassy's nose and she glanced toward the open door.

Sassy was surprised by the appearance of the Cutters. The man was small and thin, hardly bigger than Sassy herself. The woman was big and hefty, at least half again as big as her husband. They looked a strange pair, standing with mouths agape and grinning foolishly. Their clothes were in need of repair and there was dust and grime on them.

"Good to see you boys again!" Cutter said. "Who is that you have with you? Where did you find such a pretty parcel out there in the far country?"

"Mr. Cutter," his wife exclaimed, "where are your manners? Let the little girl get down from that horse and breathe a spell before you go off pressing questions like that." She swung her muscled arm toward the rear of the cabin as she talked. "You boys take those horses around back and come on in and sit at table."

Mrs. Cutter stepped up to Sassy's mount and held its bridle while Sassy swung her leg over the horse's neck and softly dropped to the ground.

"Gracious, child, you are no bigger than a butternut. Look, Mr. Cutter," she pointed. "She could not weigh more than a good puff of smoke."

"Eeeh. I can see that for myself, Mrs. Cutter."

Sassy stood looking up at the powerful woman. Everything about her was huge. Her head was big and covered with thick dark hair. Her eyes were deep set and wide and generous, like her mouth. Her nose seemed enormous, her teeth straight and strong, except for one of the front ones that was broken in half. A smell came from the woman that was pleasant, a smell of the outdoors, cool and soft—a light sweat dried in the wind.

Sassy smiled at Mrs. Cutter.

"Look at those eyes, Mr. Cutter. A delight to have on earth. Why, they are the bluest eyes I have *ever* seen." Mrs. Cutter placed an arm around Sassy's shoulder. "Come, child," she said in a softer tone. "Let Mrs. Cutter put a little meat on those bones."

Sassy had not felt so safe since leaving her mother's lodge. For just a fleeting moment, she thought about confiding her plight to this horse of a woman. But then she realized that the woman's instant attachment was to her as a white girl. Affinity for the Tuscarora would not sit well. If she knew of Sassy's loyalty and ties to Indians, Mrs. Cutter might not act so caring. Instinctive caution told Sassy to wait a while before disclosing anything about her situation.

She was barely in the cabin when Mrs. Cutter began ladling a heaping serving from the iron pot hanging in the fireplace.

"Sit, child," Mrs. Cutter said as she placed the hand-carved wooden bowl in front of Sassy. Then Mrs. Cutter took a stick leaning against the fireplace wall and rummaged through the ashes beside the fire. Out rolled several baked potatoes kept warm by the still-hot ashes. She picked up one and rubbed it on her dress to get the remaining ash off.

She placed the potato on the bare-board table beside Sassy's bowl, retrieved a knife from the mantel of the fireplace, and split the potato in half.

"Got fresh berry makings." She nodded and headed toward the open lean-to attached to the side wall of the house.

Sassy blew on her stew to cool it down a bit. The wonderful smell was too much for her and she took a spoonful in her mouth. It was hot but not too hot. She sighed as she swallowed the juices and chewed the savory meat. She scrutinized the cabin and took another bite.

It was a large room. A stairway at one end led up to a loft. There were two windows, one on each end of the house. There was no glass in the windows, but each had shutters that locked from the inside. The fireplace stood opposite the door. Wooden hooks along the wall held most of the Cutters' clothing. There were no beautiful woven mats on the floor or woven baskets holding food or anything else.

Why, Sassy thought, Mother's lodge is much more impressive. Everything in here is made of wood. It was then that she saw the chamber pot. Sassy gulped down stew and ran over to examine the chamber pot more closely. It was white porcelain. There were tiny blue flowers with yellow centers all over it. The lid fit tightly and was not cracked or even chipped and it carried the same floral design as the pot.

"I will not allow anybody to use it," Mrs. Cutter said. "Been with me since I was a child. I have carried it every place I ever went."

Mrs. Cutter placed the berries on the table and went to stand beside Sassy. "I believe it is the loveliest thing I ever saw and I could never abide anyone's rear end perched above it. Mr. Cutter is a good man. He understands."

In answer to Sassy's unasked question, the big woman elaborated: "When the urge strikes us, we just head back there in the woods. Course in the middle of winter, I make do with an old pot and dried leaves I save just for the occasion."

Sassy laughed. "You must be proud to own such a chamber pot. If I could stay longer, I would show you how to weave a double basket to take its place and you would not have to run into the woods in the middle of the night."

"Where did you learn to weave such a thing, child? The Naturals are the only ones who can do that."

Before Sassy could answer, the men came through the door.

"Wife," Mr. Cutter said. "There is to be a gathering tomorrow. There will be no work. Right after we eat I will tell Reverend Lambert. Then I will ride to tell the neighbors."

Mr. Cutter's eyes were sparkling. He dearly loved a get-together.

Mrs. Cutter's face broke into a grin as she placed a huge ham on the table. "Well, child. It is your visit we'll be celebrating."

Everybody suddenly laughed at Sassy, who was breaking corn bread and dumping it into her bowl along with the stew. Jake reached over and sliced a piece of ham and laid it in front of Sassy. She turned grateful eyes toward him.

Mrs. Cutter finished setting the table. "Fall to, men. There is a lot to be done if there is to be a party tomorrow."

Jake thanked the Cutters for the fine meal and nodded toward Paul. "Guess this means I will have to take a jump in the water just so I can frolic at the same shindig with the likes of you."

"Big brother," Paul teased back, "I was meaning to tell you about that. It has been sort of hard, sitting downwind from you. I will take care of your gear, you just scrounge up some clean clothes and scrub some of the scruff off you."

Jake stretched. "I guess a man can get sort of rank when he is used to traveling alone. And, little brother, traveling with you is just like being alone. You are not very challenging company. I do not believe that you have ever had an original thought since the day you were born."

With that final insult, Jake faked a punch at Paul. Paul bent his head down like a bull and charged at Jake, catching him right around the middle, and the two of them went tumbling to the floor.

They wrestled and pretended to fight while Sassy and the Cutters stood watching in absolute delight. In all the days she had been with them, this was the first time Sassy had seen them relaxed with one another. It was all she could do to keep from joining in the melee.

Jake sprang up, his hands in the air. "Enough. I've had enough. You win. But tomorrow is another day and tomorrow things can turn out different."

Jake was the usual winner in any fight. He was tall and strong and quick and his fists always found their mark. But in a game of wrestling with Paul, he oftentimes came out the loser. Paul was shorter and stockier and, although not as fast, when he got a close-in hold on a person, he used his oxen strength to squeeze the breath out of him.

"Giving up again, huh?" Paul said. "Well, that is just like you. Quitting when everything is going my way. All right, then. I will just put that nag of yours out to pasture since you are all dragged out."

Paul headed toward the door and the horses outside but Jake stopped him.

"Hey, what about my bath? I'm going, too."

And out they went. Mr. Cutter went, too, to make the rounds of the outlying houses down the valley, inviting friends to the festivity.

Sassy and Mrs. Cutter prepared party food and cleaned dishes.

"Put the dishes there, child." She pointed to the bed in the corner. "What is wrong? You have such a look on your face."

Sassy did not answer.

"Sassy," Mrs. Cutter said. "I know it is none of my business, but if you are in some kind of trouble, you can depend on me to help. Things are not easy in this wilderness for a woman. Me and my man have been out here for five years and things are not much easier for us now than they were the day we came. Of course, there is usually plenty to eat. And the Naturals are mostly friendly. We have only had trouble with them once or twice."

At the mention of the Indians, Sassy's eyes flickered toward Mrs. Cutter, then she looked down again.

Mrs. Cutter caught the glance. "I see. It has to do with the Naturals."

Sassy looked up with tears in her eyes. This woman was shrewd but also sympathetic.

"You need not worry about me, child. I will never tell—not even Mr. Cutter. It's none of it your fault. How long were you with them?"

"I cannot remember," Sassy lied. The tears slid along her nose.

"There, there." Mrs. Cutter wrapped her arms around Sassy. "Go ahead and cry. It will do you good."

Sassy sobbed as though her heart were breaking. She had held it all in for so long and now it came bursting out. She sobbed and babbled in Tuscarora until her sorrow was spent and she could not cry anymore.

Mrs. Cutter let go of her and sat down beside her. "I have no idea what you said, but you know the Naturals' language pretty well. It is no tongue I ever heard of around here. Where did you live?"

"Please. I do not want to speak of it." Sassy moved away.

"I see. Then you shall not have to talk about it to me. I have never understood why people hold it against women captured by the Naturals. It is surely no fault of their own. Oh, my. Now, just sit and gather your thoughts while I fuss.

Mrs. Cutter talked as she busied herself around the room. From time to time she ran out to the lean-to for flour and other staples. She was making a kind of meat and vegetable pie. She placed it in a big round iron pan with a lid and put that directly into the low-burning fire. Every few minutes she took two long sticks and turned it several inches.

Sassy laid a bowl aside. "Can I help with anything?"

"Hull these nuts. Then I will crack them." Sassy pulled up the bottom of her dress and filled it full of black walnuts. "And put this cloth on your hands or you will never get the stains out."

Mr. Cutter clumped in. "Everything is ready," he announced. "Most everybody will be here tomorrow. I will put a plank table outside to hold the food."

"I meant to ask," Sassy said. "What are the marks above the door?"

The Cutters glanced at one another. Mr. Cutter said, "Oh, that. The Reverend Lambert sure took a dislike to those marks." Mr. Cutter pulled off one of his boots. "Mrs. Cutter put the marks there. She says it keeps out witches. Keeps them from messing up her stews and spoiling the food and such." He pulled off the other boot and pushed them both under the table. "I guess it works. We hardly ever have any food go bad. As long as Mrs. Cutter wants those marks above the door, that is where they will stay."

Mrs. Cutter laughed. "My mother taught me the marks. Mother belonged to the Society of Friends, but Mr. Cutter took me away from all that years ago. Out here in the wilderness, it does not make much difference where a person came from."

Sassy headed for the door.

"Where are you going?" Mrs. Cutter asked.

"Where is the closest water around here? I need to bathe and to wash my hair."

"Lord, child. That's a spring feed creek and the air is chilly. You will catch a chill out there. You cannot bathe in the creek. It is much too cold. In a few minutes I will be heating water for Mr. Cutter. When he's finished, you can use his water."

The thought of bathing in Mr. Cutter's water was not pleasing to Sassy. She did not want to slight Mrs. Cutter, but she was not going to bathe in Mr. Cutter's dirty water.

"I will just be bathing in the creek if you will show me the way. Maybe I could have that blanket to wrap in." Sassy pointed at a threadbare blanket hanging on a peg.

Mrs. Cutter was genuinely worried about the girl. She had watched many a poor soul die from lung troubles.

"If you must, you must. Here." She handed Sassy the blanket. "Wrap up tight. And here. Rub off with this." She handed Sassy an old rag of a dress from one of the pegs. "The creek is south, just below the rise." She pointed out the direction and pressed a small piece of rendered fat soap into Sassy's hand.

Sassy found the creek. She left her dress on the bank along with the blanket and Mrs. Cutter's old dress. Looking down at her mid-section, she realized she was beginning to show. There was no mistaking what her body was telling her. The creek water was not very high. She had to lie down in the water to cleanse herself. She was lying on her back, trying to rinse her long hair when she sensed she was being watched. She turned, searching the bank, frightened.

Standing just within the treeline on the far side of the creek were three Indians. They stood motionless, watching. She could just barely make out their features. Two had their hair mostly shaved off, except for a thin strip in the center and a larger thatch on top. The third had a full head of hair. Shawnee? Mahican? She had never seen them before.

Sassy raised her hand in greeting, then waded back to the bank. Without looking back, she slipped into her moccasins and threw on her doeskin dress, scooped up the blanket and Mrs. Cutter's dress, then ran up the little rise, fast.

The cold air burned her lungs. Her dripping hair and wet body drenched her dress. In her haste, she forgot to wrap up in the blanket.

From the top of the rise she looked back at the three strangers. They had not moved.

Sassy rushed into Mrs. Cutter's kitchen, dripping wet. Her eyes were too bright and her cheeks too rosy. She gasped for breath. The cold creek water had chilled her very bones.

"Mrs. Cutter," she panted. "There were Indians . . . down by the creek. Three of them. They saw me. They did not come after me."

"Good thing we have plenty to eat." Mrs. Cutter seemed undisturbed by the news. "If they find out we're having a celebration, they will bring the whole unnatural tribe."

Sassy was amazed. "You mean they come around here a lot?"

"Too much. Believe me, child. I wonder if every time I turn myself up in the woods for relief, there is some Indian out there spying. Not much goes on around here that they don't know about."

Sassy took Mrs. Cutter's old dress and dried her hair. Indians, all around, she thought. Back home in the mountains the people did not want to be anywhere near the whites. It seemed peculiar that the whites did not mind the Indians being around.

"Child," Mrs. Cutter said. "What have you done to yourself?" She stood with her hands on her large hips, looking dismayed. "Why, you never even wrapped up in the blanket, did you?"

"No. I was scared. I ran all the way back. I forgot."

"Here, let me do that." Mrs. Cutter took the dress and roughly dried Sassy's hair.

Sassy felt as though her head were being lifted from her body. "Ouch! It's dry, really." She tried to convince the big woman to stop. "It's dry."

"Now get out of that wet dress and go over there by the fire."

Sassy did as she was told, standing stark naked by the heat of the fireplace. Mrs. Cutter pulled the cover from her own bed and threw it around Sassy's shoulders.

"Gar, girl. You will be catching your death. A scalping by the Indians would be quicker."

Mrs. Cutter considered the situation. "You would be better off lying in the bed. You will only be in my way there by the fire." She pointed her chin toward the bed. "Take a rest while you dry off. Get warm; it will do you good."

Sassy nodded and lay down on the bed. She felt like a prisoner, forced to do something she did not want to do, but within a few minutes she was fast asleep.

She awoke to the soft, muted voices of the Cutters. Then she heard another noise. It was the sound of splashing water. To her amazement, Mr. Cutter was sitting in a huge round wooden tub placed in the center of the floor. Mrs. Cutter was scrubbing his back with characteristic vigor, shoving the poor man's thin shoulders first one way and then another.

"Leave the skin on. Leave the skin on me, Mrs. Cutter," Mr. Cutter whispered harshly.

Sassy stirred.

"Miss Sassy," Mr. Cutter said, "you best be turning your head toward the wall. Young women should not be watching their elders at bath."

She did as she was told and faced the wall though she could not help but laugh. She laughed until her sides ached. Finally she quieted down and felt relieved. "I feel good," she announced.

"Those Martin boys have about done you in—dragging you through the mountains without another woman to as much as look at," Mrs. Cutter said. Mr. Cutter got out of the tub, dripping dirty water all over the floor. Mrs. Cutter handed him his clothes before going on. "Of course you feel better. Rest up now. Tomorrow will be memorable."

There was food everywhere. The settlers had brought enough to feed all the guests for days. Food covered the makeshift tables outside, and the table inside was overflowing, too. Sassy did not catch everyone's name but she remembered those of Lou and Sarah Daniels and their three tow-headed boys.

The middle Daniels boy reminded Sassy of White Cloud. Her brother was the same size and of the same disposition. The boy ran around the festooned table, sticking his fingers in the food and licking them. Sarah stayed close behind him, whacking his bottom as needed. Sassy's heart ached for White Cloud and her family and her husband of two months.

The last guests to arrive were the three Indians Sassy had seen by the creek. She noted that their presence did not cause concern among the settlers. Mr. Cutter addressed the oldest of the three as "Little Gabriel."

"Why do you call him that?" Sassy asked when the Indians had stepped away. "And what tribe is he?"

Mr. Cutter said, "He is Mahican. His two friends are Shawnee. We call him Gabriel. See the flute he carries by his side? It is not the same as Gabriel's horn but he will surely blow on it before the day is over. Wherever he goes, he plays that flute."

"Mahican," Sassy repeated. "Do you trust the Mahican?"

Cutter shrugged. "We never trust any Indian. But what choice is there? They roam these woods all the time. As long as they do not give us trouble, we will not give them trouble."

Paul, who was never far from Sassy's side, pulled her away from Mr. Cutter. "It is time for the sing."

Reverend Lambert asked Sassy, "What is your full name, child?"

She had not even thought of her name in years, yet she promptly answered, "Priscilla Ann Billips."

Reverend Lambert nodded. "Would you like to sit with us for the sing?"

Sassy could feel the eyes of the three Indians on her. She nodded yes.

Everyone joined in the hymns, Mrs. Cutter's voice rising above all the others. It was rich and deep and exquisite.

Sassy was fascinated with the sound of such a voice coming from a woman—the pure beauty of it. She noticed the Indians gave full attention to Mrs. Cutter. Sassy was grateful for a few minutes' relief from the Indians' unblinking stares.

After the songs were sung and everyone had filled up on food, the soft wailing of Gabriel's flute floated across the meadow. He had left the other Indians and was standing alone. He played tolerably well, and the high, mournful notes brought a new wave of homesickness to Sassy.

The Cutters' neighbors began leaving well before dark. One by one, they shook hands and departed. Sassy felt ever so tired. Before the last guest was gone, she was yawning. They waved good-bye to Reverend Lambert, the last guest to leave. Sassy looked for the Indians but they were nowhere to be seen.

Paul walked her into the house. The Cutters were strolling down along the creek.

"Sleepy?" Paul asked.

"Yes. I have been tired lately."

"I know," he said.

Sassy said, "I hope your mother likes me. She is going to be shocked, you know. You went away on a trip with just you and Jake, and you come home with me."

"She will take you in as her own. That is the way she is," Paul said.

"So you say." Sassy sounded doubtful. "So you say."

"It will be your home, too. You must not forget that. At least, it will be yours for as long as you want it to be. Although a rich woman like you might want a place of her own," Paul teased. "Or to go into business for herself."

If only their sense of chivalry would permit them to let her go back to her true home, she thought. But Christian charity, she knew, would not allow it.

18

The air was clear and cold. Jake, Sassy, and Paul were ready for their journey an hour after sunup. Amid hugs, and handshakes, they said their good-byes to the Cutters. Just as Sassy led Dear Friend away from the cabin and onto the trail, Mrs. Cutter grabbed the horse's reins.

"A minute with you, girl," she almost shouted. She handed up her precious chamber pot to Sassy. "I want you to have it. I thought about it all night."

Sassy made no move to accept the gift.

Mrs. Cutter persisted: "Go on. Take it. Me and Mr. Cutter will never have children of our own. Who will I leave it to? I want you to have it."

"No," Sassy said. "It is the most beautiful thing I have ever seen. And I mean to see it again when I come by this way."

"You will never come this way again." Mrs. Cutter shoved the pot toward Sassy.

"There is one thing I *would* like to ask about. Are you feeling well? No one of your size is going to eat the way you eat unless . . . There

206

must be a reason for that big appetite in such a little girl, and what I think it is, is that you are carrying a child inside of you."

Sassy sighed. "Yes. I am with child."

"Paul loves you, dear. You can see it in his every glance. You are lucky. He will take care of you the same as Jake has taken care of his mother and brothers and sister. And you can trust me with your secret. I will not tell anyone about the baby."

Sassy turned in her saddle and shouted to Paul. "I am coming here again," she stated as a matter of fact. "Next summer. Or after. But I am coming."

"You can count on it," he said.

Mr. Cutter retrieved the pot from his wife's hands. "That settles it then." He tucked the pot safely under his arm. "Until next year." He took off his hat and saluted the travelers.

Mrs. Cutter knew if anybody could be depended on, it was Paul and Jake Martin. "Until after the harvest," she said.

It was two hours before sundown when Little Gabriel reached the edge of the woods by Cutter's cabin. He signaled for the braves behind him to stop. His keen eyes searched the fields. There was no movement anywhere. Smoke wafted from the chimney of the little cabin. Most likely, the Cutters were taking their evening meal. Probably they would offer him food. He was not hungry.

Inside the cabin, Mr. Cutter's new dog growled. Mr. Cutter came to the door with his rifle. As he stepped outside he called back over his shoulder to Mrs. Cutter, "It's only Little Gabriel and a few of his friends. Set out some more food."

Mr. Cutter reached back inside and propped his weapon against the wall. He ushered Little Gabriel in. The three Indians with him followed suit. The last Shawnee lifted his tomahawk and struck Mr. Cutter a stunning blow. Surprise was evident on Mr. Cutter's face as he sank toward the ground. The Indian struck another blow to the top of Mr. Cutter's head. It cracked like kindling and the sharp stone axeblade cleaved his brain.

Mrs. Cutter sensed the commotion but could not clearly see. Too many stood in between. With arms and fists, she forced her way through. They were too startled to stop her.

When she saw her husband lying dead on the porch, a terrible roar rose in her and erupted from her throat. She struck the heathen closest to her with a fist and knocked him down, wrenched the tomahawk from his hand, and swung it at the next Indian, hitting him a solid blow alongside the ear. By this time, her first victim had sprung to his feet and was wresting his tomahawk from her grip.

Mrs. Cutter fought murderously but she was outnumbered. A gash opened in the side of her cheek where a tomahawk hit. Little Gabriel landed a flat blow to the back of her head that sent her to her knees. She swayed back and forth. Little Gabriel kicked her in the back and she fell on her face and was still.

"Mine!" Little Gabriel screamed at his companions. "Mine."

Little Gabriel's eye was already swelling where Mrs. Cutter had punched him with her mighty fist. The group stepped back from the fallen woman and waited for Little Gabriel to finish her. Instead, he bent close to her to see if she was still breathing. He shook his head in satisfaction and tied her arms behind her back, then secured her feet. All but one of the group chuckled.

So the big woman would travel with them. The one who did not laugh was holding the side of his bleeding head where Mrs. Cutter had hit him with the tomahawk. His eyes had a glazed look about them and he did not know exactly where he was.

When Mrs. Cutter was trussed to his satisfaction, Little Gabriel dragged her out and along the ground. His companions set the Cutter cabin ablaze. Anything of value such as blankets, pots, and clothing lay strewn across the yard. Little Gabriel hunted among the booty for poles to wrap blankets around on which to lay Mrs. Cutter. A group of seven Shawnee approached the burning cabin. They had a blond-haired woman and three boy captives.

19

When Elena Martin was a child her mother had told her that she possessed the second sight. The passing years had proven that her mother was right. The gift was most evident when it involved her children. She could always tell when one of them was in distress. Sometimes it took her a while to figure out which one. She did not see things, as she had heard some people did. She felt things. She knew things.

It usually started in the center of her breast. She would find it hard to catch her breath. When the feeling came, there was no sense in trying to ignore it. No matter what she was doing, her mind would move away from her chores. Today, she was thinking about Jake. All week she had been thinking of Jake.

She had not been long at the fence when she sensed movement at the end of the meadow. She stared in that direction and saw a horse and rider emerge from the forest. She knew it was one of her sons, but from such a distance, she could not tell which one.

Several packhorses followed the first rider out of the forest. Then came another rider. At the sight of the second rider, Elena suddenly became wary. The second rider did not look familiar. Too small and slight to be one of her sons. She was thinking that maybe it was not her sons after all when a third rider appeared.

Oh, she thought. They have brought someone with them. A sense of foreboding came over her. She cupped her hands over her eyes, trying to distinguish the faces that were steadily moving toward her.

I will never be able to stand this waiting, she thought, this not knowing why a stranger is with them and who it is. She hitched her skirts above her knees, climbed over the fence, and walked briskly down the meadow to meet them.

"Whoa." Jake pulled back on his horse's reins. "Look. Coming to meet us."

Paul brought his horse alongside Sassy's. "The family is going to be so taken with you," he said. "Mother will put you under her wing like a hen with new chicks."

Sassy's heart plummeted at the thought. She had a family and did not need a new one. Her one desire was to be with that family, waiting for Runs With The Wind's return and the birth of her child. With narrowing eyes, she watched the approach of the woman in the distance.

"Come on," Paul urged. He was too overjoyed at being home again to notice the misery on Sassy's face.

As they cantered toward Elena, Sassy felt her old life far behind her. The wave of homesickness was overwhelming. She thought of swerving Dear Friend into the woods to escape, but she knew it was useless. The distance back was too great, the route difficult to retrace.

Jake jumped off his horse and lifted Elena up, swinging his mother in a circle. He kissed her on both cheeks then put her down firmly on her feet. Paul embraced her.

"Guess what I brought you?" he said.

"I can see what you brought me."

What a beauty she is, Elena thought. More beautiful than anyone around here. Elena stretched her arms up toward Sassy. "Get down, child. Let me have a look at you."

"Mother," said Paul, "this is Priscilla Ann Billips."

Reluctantly, Sassy slid to the ground. She stood leaning against Dear Friend for support. Paul was shocked when he glanced at her and realized that she had the same look on her face she'd had when he and Jake first captured her. It was frightening and heartrending at the same time. His eyes filled with love and pity for her.

"Everything is going to be all right," he said. "Everything."

"Why of *course* it is," Elena said. "Here. Give me the child."

Jake snorted. "She is not a child."

"Well . . . ," Elena said. The look of a hunted animal was on Sassy's face.

Elena started at a brisk clip back toward the house. She put her hand in Paul's and slipped her arm around Sassy's waist. Glancing over her shoulder, she said "What is wrong with your older brother? Why is Jake hanging back there with those horses?"

Elena squinted against the sun. Paul was the ladies' man, the smooth talker, the dancer and singer of songs. Women surrounded him during socials. Was that why he had not married? But maybe Paul would take this girl more seriously. If she knew that her boys were raising families, she would feel better. Her daughter, Mary, was still in mourning over the loss of her husband, and her sons Prescott and Richard were far too young as yet for marriage.

They reached the porch and Sassy stopped to catch her breath. The frame house was the largest she had ever seen. It had a center door with windows to either side. Chimneys grew out of the roof in all directions. The porch ran all the way across the front of the house. There was a second floor. Windows—real glass was in all the windows.

Sassy's curiosity got the best of her. She bounded up the three steps and across the porch. She fumbled with the latch. Elena came up beside her and gently turned the knob. Sassy had never seen one. Without invitation, she stepped inside and stopped.

She was in a wide center hall. A door at the other end was just like the one she had come through. Doors were closed on both sides of the hall. Candle sconces adorned the walls, some with glass covers.

Sassy pulled the cover off one and sniffed at the candle inside. She held the cover up to her eye and looked through it. It distorted her vision. She laughed.

Off to the side a stairway led to the floor above. Sassy opened the nearest door. The room within was magnificent, filled with chairs and settees and books and heavy cloth covering the windows. She turned and ran back across the hall and through the door directly opposite. It was much like the room she had just left except for the books.

Elena followed her from room to room, watching the excitement on Sassy's face. The girl picked things up, running her hands quickly across them. She bent and pressed her cheek against a chair back that looked soft and dewy. It felt like prickles on her skin and she pulled back in surprise. She poked and sniffed and stroked everything. Back in the hall, she stood looking up at a painting of Elena.

"Takime," she whispered, staring at the likeness of the woman standing beside her.

"What?" Elena said.

"Takime could make that." She pointed at the painting.

"Takime?" Elena repeated.

"Takime." Sassy's young face began to crumple as she gazed at the painting. She did not want to be there. She wanted to go home but these good Christians would never willingly let her return to the mountain. She leaned against the wall and wailed. To Elena, she sounded like a forlorn animal caught in a trap.

When Jake and Paul came in, they found the two women on the floor entwined in each other's arms.

Sassy woke in the center of a bed to a bone-chilling coldness. She was alone in a room. The bed was high but plain. Firm squared posts with round knobs on the ends held it at its four corners. The back had extra boards in the form of an upside-down half-moon. Sassy ran her hand across the glossed wood. "Like black ice," she said.

The room was as big as her mother's lodge. It was only for sleeping, Elena had said.

She pushed aside the heavy covers and rolled over. Peering down at the boards in the floor, she tried to locate her moccasins. It seemed a long way down. To fall out of this bed, she thought, could break some bones. She had climbed in last night with the help of a little stool. Now the stool was somewhere underneath the bed.

There were a small table, two chairs, and a large piece of furniture that could be opened or closed. It held clothing. Another piece had many drawers. Her new dress was in there. She slid out of bed and ran to the five-drawered chest and pulled her dress from the middle drawer.

The fire had gone down. Sassy hopped about, first on one foot and then another, trying to keep her feet warm. She got down on her hands and knees and looked under the bed for her moccasins. She found them and slipped them on her feet.

Crazy white people, she thought. Building a fire in the wall where the heat of it would only reach a small portion of the room, leaving the rest freezing. If she was to sleep in this room again, she would be the keeper of the fire. And she would sleep on the floor beside it.

She saw something under the bed and pulled it out. It was a chamber pot. She sat looking at it, thinking about Mrs. Cutter. It was not as pretty as Mrs. Cutter's. She removed the lid. The pot was empty but the stench of it engulfed her. She almost threw it across the room. Elena did not trek to the woods to relieve herself like Mrs. Cutter.

The white people were so fussy and unclean. She replaced the lid on the pot and shoved it back under the bed. She had been too tired the night before to pay much attention to Mary's room. Mary had spent the night in Jake's room and Paul slept with his brothers.

She opened drawers and touched the different materials in them, rough and soft. Muslin and chintz and cottons and linens and a mixture of the two. Too many clothes, she thought. Why would anyone need so many?

She smelled the lamps and a silver-backed hairbrush. She lifted the lid from the tulip-embellished chest at the foot of the bed and found more bedclothes. She picked up a bit of lace from a chair back and forced her little finger through the tiny holes.

"Beautiful," she murmured.

The big room with its dying fire was even colder than the out-of-doors. There was ice on the inside of the windows.

She spied a box sitting on a small chest. It stood up on four little legs. She lifted the lid. Inside was a beautifully polished dark stone ring. There were other things, but the ring caught her attention. She had started to lift it out when she heard someone coming up the stairs. Quickly, she left the little box and put the lace back on the chair. She slipped out the door and gently closed it.

"Paul. I was wondering where you all were."

"We let you sleep as long as we could. Breakfast is waiting."

He escorted her downstairs to the kitchen.

All the family was gathered around a table eating a hearty breakfast. It was noisy and confusing to Sassy. The women ate almost as much as the men. Sassy held her own.

Prescott and Richard could not keep their eyes from her. Never had a prettier lady been at table with them. She seemed so strange—fascinating. Her manner was odd and she made no attempt to follow the normal ways. She did not seem to notice a difference. She took the food from her plate to her mouth any way she saw fit, preferred her spoon to her fork, and used her fingers often.

It was all Elena could do to keep from shaking her head and clucking her tongue. The girl certainly could not be brought out into local society until her manners were improved. But how to manage that? The servants would yammer if no one else did.

There was no way that Elena could hide the fact that the girl had been with the Indians. She was too wild. Her skin was brownish, turning yellowish now from the lack of sun. But that was not so bad.

A few of the farm women on the farthest reaches of land from Philadelphia were browned by the sun.

At least she had not been despoiled by the savages. The good citizens of Philadelphia did not always take kindly to women who had been ravaged by the red men.

Elena's heart was filled with sympathy for the girl. What a terrible life she must have had. Well, that was all over. She was safe now.

Elena made a decision. She would keep Sassy in this house until she had had a chance to correct the girl's manners. She would make a small wardrobe for her. And it would allow Sassy to see Paul. Something might develop.

After breakfast, Elena asked Sassy to help clear up. Just as they were finishing she said, "You will be needing a few new things. Paul is riding to the city today. Since he will not be underfoot, we may as well get started right now."

"What things do I need?"

Elena did not want to point out to Sassy that she only owned one dress, not counting that terrible deerskin. You could not consider that attire as anything wearable.

"Well, you will need some clothes. An everyday dress. And you will need a grander dress for the Sabbath and material for chemises. And probably something for get-togethers. And a shawl and a coat."

"Stop. My head is spinning just thinking about it." Sassy laughed.

"We will need to start on the Sabbath dress first. We can begin as soon as all the morning chores are done. I have some good material on hand. We can go into town for the day soon and look for the rest. Have you ever cut from a pattern?"

"No," said Sassy.

"I will teach you," said Elena.

The entire family, including servants, left bright and early Sunday morning. The women rode in the carriage and the men rode horse-back. They headed for the new church halfway between their farm and Philadelphia. There were fifty-two members, including children and the few servants who attended. Sassy had never seen so many white people at one time in her whole life.

She sat in her new cloak and gown and sang the old hymns her mother and father had taught her. She did the best she could, considering she had forgotten half the words. She made Jake and Elena proud. She felt oddly at ease in the church.

After the services, Elena briefly introduced Sassy to friends and neighbors, then whisked her away in the carriage. She did not want to linger and have too many questions asked too soon. She excused their early exit by saying that they needed to prepare for their trip the next day. Tomorrow she and Sassy were going to Philadelphia.

20

When they finished their shopping, Elena had the carriage driver take them all through town. They rode past the brickeries and book and print shops while Elena pointed out things she thought might interest Sassy. They wandered among the alleys and lanes. Elena showed Sassy the homes of Philadelphia's wealthier citizens and pointed down one road where William Penn had maintained his mansion just a few years earlier. He was back in England for the time being. But thanks to his genius and fairness dealing with the Indians, they had spared the colony the bloodshed and terror plaguing others.

On Water Street Elena and Sassy visited Jake and Paul at their small tannery shop. Elena's boys had started the business the previous year and it was doing well. She was very proud of them. Almost every venture they tackled was successful.

The four of them had lunch higher up on Third Street. Then the women walked the men back to the tannery. On the small bridge crossing Dock Creek Sassy looked down disgustedly and asked, "What is all that floating around in the water?"

It seemed to Elena that it was at least Sassy's hundredth question of the day.

"Oh," Elena said, "that is just the spillage from the tanneries. You must pay no mind to it. There are three or four tanneries right along here and they all empty into the creek."

Sassy thought of all the hides she and the people had tanned. The waters at home were still crystal clear. Of course, in all the years she had lived with the Tuscarora, she had never seen as many hides at one time as she had seen in Philadelphia in one day.

Furs and skins were piled high on the wharves waiting to be loaded into ships. Cargo sat all along the docks waiting to be carted into the warehouses that dotted Front Street.

There were enough hides to clothe her people for years. There was an abundance of food, too: in the penny pot taverns and teahouses, being loaded aboard and taken off ships, and displayed in the marketplace. She did not even know what some of it was.

Elena told her that the great ships carried pitch and tar and timber to places all over the world. They hauled sassafras and tobacco— anything that other people might use or want.

They started home around two-thirty. It was a three-hour trip. Jake and Paul would be staying in town the next few days, taking care of long-neglected business.

As they settled back against the cushioned seats, Sassy leaned toward Elena and said, "Thank you. Thank you for this day."

Elena smiled. The girl no longer wore the look of a scared rabbit although there was still wildness in her.

They were a little more than halfway home when Sassy thought she saw an Indian. He was standing on a rise in front of a small farmhouse. He held an ax poised high above his head. At his feet was a pile of firewood. A white man stood beside him holding a whip. Before Sassy could get a clear picture of the scene, the carriage passed on.

Sassy slumped back into her seat. She no longer wanted to look out the carriage window. The fun had gone out of the day. Old stories she had heard around her mother's fire entered her head. Stories about slaves. She remembered Long Feather and his missing first family. Stolen, the story went—stolen and taken to Pennsylvania. Although he never spoke of it, Long Feather had gone to Pennsylvania to look for them. He had returned alone. Maybe they had been put on one of the big ships and taken away. Many had been. Even whites, she had heard a trader say once.

Elena stirred and opened her eyes. She glanced at the girl. That hard, closed look was on Sassy's face again. The change that sometimes came over Sassy was frightening to Elena. As she stared, the feeling returned. The feeling that Sassy was trouble.

Drucy, the servant girl, was large with child. No one knew who the father was. As her usefulness was limited, it was decreed by Elena that the girl spend her final month of pregnancy at the Tyler place some eight miles from the Martin farm. In truth Elena did not want the bother and mess of the birth on her hands, and she did not want to encourage speculation as to the newborn's paternity to include her sons.

Priscilla Ann was easily maneuvered into the responsibility of accompanying Drucy and comforting her through the final stages. Thursday, bright and early, they would embark. To further distance the Martin men from Drucy's condition, the entire Martin clan went into town Thursday morning, leaving Drucy and Sassy with the house help and a few of the field hands. Sassy packed a lunch, loaded the old farm wagon with odds and ends, hitched up the horse team, and climbed aboard.

Drucy was screaming at her. "Miss Priscilla! Miss Elena told me not to let you out of my sight."

There was no getting away from the girl. Elena made her follow Sassy everywhere. She did not want anything to happen to her potential daughter-in-law. Now the situation was reversed and Sassy was to be the companion. Reluctantly, she allowed Drucy to get up into the wagon. She looked at the sun. "Not much after ten," she said, and drove the wagon out of the yard, heading west.

The ancient smell of the soil lay across the Pennsylvania hills. The horses pulling the wagon over the hard, rutted tracks felt the change in the weather. Sassy tugged back a little on the reins to keep the horses from going too fast for the burden they pulled.

"Miss Priscilla, Miss Elena is sure going to be mad at you. Driving these horses so hard."

Sassy glanced impatiently at the girl sitting beside her. Drucy's face was squinched up like she was ready to bawl. "Then, Drucy, drive this wagon for me."

"No, Miss. My babe is not long due. You are going to kill both of us, bouncing around like this. And you know I am afraid of horses."

Sassy pulled back a little tighter on the reins, slowing the horses to a walk. She really did not want to frighten Drucy. The girl seemed to be afraid of everything beyond the doors of the farmhouse.

"Drucy, who fathered that child in your belly?"

"Miss Priscilla, I will never say."

The fact that Drucy refused to tell anyone, even Elena, was a point of pride with the staff. No amount of threats or cajoling could get Drucy to reveal the name.

"Well," Sassy continued. "If I knew who the father was, he could be taking you to his farm instead of my taking you to the Tyler place."

They were on their way to the Tyler farm. Jake had bought it two weeks ago. It was due west of the Martin place, at the end of a rutted lane. There were no more houses beyond it. Mr. Tyler had died of lung fever during the previous winter. Not long afterwards, his wife had sold out and moved her three children close by Philadelphia.

Sassy made good time. She drove the wagon straight up to the porch and unhitched the horses and picketed them while Drucy began to unload lighter items from the wagon.

The house was two stories tall. It was small, with only four rooms in all, and sat on a narrow rise of land with a stream cutting along the side. There was a lean-to beside the house and a fenced-in barn around back. There was one window in each room with heavy wooden shutters that could be locked from the inside for protection. There had never been any trouble with Indians but there were slits in the shutters for shooting in case. The kitchen window had panes of a greenish colored glass. The rest of the windows were rectangular holes with nothing in them.

The kitchen was the largest room with a huge, river-rock fireplace across one wall. It was used for cooking all year and heating the house. In winter, the Tylers had slept in the kitchen. The only heat in the children's room on the second floor was from the huge chimney burrowing its way up toward the roof.

In the hot months, they had slept as far away from the fireplace as possible. The doors and windows were left open during most of the summer to keep the little house from becoming unbearably hot. Jake already had plans for additional windows and had ordered glass shipped from England. There were no reputable glass factories left in Pennsylvania; Tittery's—the last one—had closed twenty years earlier, Jake had said.

The land around the house and across the little creek was bare of all trees and shrubs and was kept clear so as to prevent Indians from sneaking up unseen. The fields were laid out across the creek.

Drucy had lunch laid out in the center of the floor. Sassy laughed. "If it was anybody else here with you, they would scold you. It is not time for lunch. But I am as hungry as you are."

"Miss Priscilla." Drucy spoke with her mouth full of chicken. "There is something I have been meaning to ask you. And since I am going to stay with you until my child is born, I will ask now."

"Well, what is it?" Sassy said. "If it is private, now is the time. We are all alone."

Drucy said, "It is . . . about your bow and arrows. I watched you shooting. Miss Elena was muttering about 'young ladies who behave like rowdy boys'."

"You are pursuing your question like a fox that lost his rabbit. Hurry up and say." Sassy had finished eating and her eyes were already searching the house, looking for something to do.

"I want you to teach me."

Sassy was startled. "Teach you? Do you mean to shoot arrows?"

"Teach me to shoot. Yes. From the first time I saw you, I wanted to learn."

"Why, Drucy, you are afraid to even step outside. Do you expect to practice indoors?"

Drucy shrugged. "I am not as afraid as you think I am, Miss Priscilla. Pretty soon I will not be alone anymore. Not ever again. I will have my baby to be with me and to take care of. I must learn to protect myself and my baby. And not just from Indians, either."

Sassy thought over what Drucy had said. The girl was an orphan and had been passed around from family to family since early childhood until Elena had taken her in. There was no telling what she had experienced in her young life.

"Clear up lunch, Drucy, then come on outside. I will set up the targets and get the bow and quiver out of the wagon."

Drucy's face broke into a smile. She was very pretty when she smiled. "I knew you would do it, Miss Priscilla. I knew you would help me. Then, after my baby comes, you can teach me to ride. On Sunday afternoons, maybe I can borrow a horse and take the baby for a ride. Maybe you will come with me."

On her way to the wagon, Sassy could hear Drucy chattering to herself. She must have a head full of dreams, Sassy thought. Dreams that nobody else knew about.

Sassy reached for the bow that lay in the bottom of the wagon. When she put her hand on it, the baby kicked and she felt as if she were suddenly somewhere back in time. Runs With The Wind's face came before her as clearly as though he were beside her. She swayed with emotion and nausea. The bow felt hot in her hand. She dropped the bow and sat on the ground beside the wagon.

She thought about how Runs With The Wind had made the bow for her. In its polished wood glowed his spirit. It was all that was left. Memory.

When she heard Drucy coming down the wooden steps, she rose

clumsily from the ground. "I had a little dizzy spell," she said in answer to Drucy's quizzical look. "Get the bow and arrows for me."

Sassy spent the better part of the day teaching Drucy how to shoot. Drucy was not the best pupil Sassy had ever seen, but what she lacked in skill she made up for in enthusiasm. She was determined to learn.

"I will make you your own bow," Sassy said.

Back at the house, Sassy began to feel faint. "Let me lie down a while," she said to Drucy. "Then I will help you with supper."

Well before nightfall, Sassy was burning with a raging fever. Each time Drucy looked in on Sassy, she seemed to be worse off than before. Sassy's hair was drenched with sweat, long silky strands stuck to her cheeks, and the color in her face was much too high. Drucy was afraid for her friend.

Drucy carried cool water in a bucket. She bathed Sassy's face and left a wet folded rag across her forehead.

In the morning Paul came by. Drucy met him at the door. "Oh, Mr. Paul, Miss Priscilla is sick with fever. Go get the doctor. Go get Miss Elena right away."

Paul rushed past her. Light from the little window fell across Sassy's sweating face. She did not look at all well. He called her name but she did not respond. All the pent-up love he felt for her came rushing forth. If he lost her, he would not want to live.

"Sassy," he called.

She moaned and turned her head.

The only thing he could do was ride for the doctor. He would stop on the way and alert Elena.

The sky was turning dark with clouds when Paul reached his mother's house. He burst into the parlor. Elena sat sewing by firelight. Startled, she looked up. "Paul. You look awful. What is wrong?"

"I need a change of horses. Sassy is sick with fever. I'm riding for the doctor."

"I should be with her," said Elena. "I will have Silas hitch up the wagon."

"I love her so, Mother."

She patted him on the shoulder, trying to keep her own worry from showing. "Stop. You look dreadful. I will go to Sassy."

While Elena waited for the wagon, she gathered up her medicines and put them in her leather drawstring bag. She was ready when Silas pulled up to the door.

She handed him extra lanterns and stepped onto the wagon seat. The air felt good despite her anxiety and she breathed it in deeply.

The jolting ride awakened her completely. She tried to calm herself but her thoughts went where they might. What a shame it would be if Paul lost Sassy. He would never get over it. Some men were like that.

In a remarkably short time she arrived at the Tyler farmhouse. Drucy met her at the door, looking pale and confused. Elena studied her face. "Poor child," she said. She called back over her shoulder to Silas, "Bring me the lantern from the wagon, will you?"

Elena picked up the one lamp in Sassy's shuttered room and carried it to the bed. Sassy was sound asleep. Elena could see she had a high fever. Examining Sassy, she could also see that the slight young woman was pregnant. Far too pregnant for it to be her son's child.

She turned to Drucy and said in a cold, hard voice, "Did you know about this?"

"No, Miss Elena. She's such a small thing, I had no idea she was in a family way." Drucy reached past Elena and covered the sleeping girl. "Miss Elena, remember why you came. Help Sassy."

Elena thought for a moment and said, "I will do the best I can for her. Now listen. Drucy, you love your Miss Sassy. I see it in your face. And you are very worried about her. If you will do something for me, I will do everything in my power to make her well."

"What is it? Miss Elena, I would do most anything if you would just get started."

"It is a hard thing for me to ask. It will be a hard thing for you to do, but you understand, it must be done. We must do it for Sassy's sake," Elena said.

"What is it, Miss Elena? What do you want me to do?"

"We cannot let people find out that she birthed a baby. What will they think? They will never accept her or the baby either. What will it do to Paul? People will laugh and gossip. And besides," Elena said, "I will see that your own child has everything. I will treat it as my own. What I want you to do is to say both infants are yours."

With a flash of insight, Drucy said, "It is Paul you want to protect, not Sassy."

"Can you not see?" Elena's patience was at an end. "I want to protect them both. And this is quite a disappointment for me, too. I have waited a long time for a grandchild. We must put our own feelings aside for now."

"Even if we do this thing, Miss Elena, what makes you think that Sassy will cooperate?"

"Sassy is not stupid. She will see the sense of it."

Drucy stiffened. "Hurry, Miss Elena." She pointed. "She needs you."

"Does that mean you will help *me*?" Elena said.

"Yes."

Elena reached out and pulled Drucy to her. She quickly hugged her and kissed her on the cheek. "Bless you, child. You will not be sorry."

With a sigh of relief, Elena ushered the girl out of the bedroom and closed the door.

The thought now occurred to her that maybe things would be better if Sassy died after all. Or else, if the baby turned out to be Indian, maybe they could get rid of it. Give it away. Or have someone take it into the wilderness to an Indian tribe. The Indians never turned down one of their own. Drucy could eventually be sent out on a ship—back to England or even the islands. Ships were always coming and going.

Elena shivered at her own chilling thoughts. She had known from

225

the start that Sassy was going to bring trouble. She had had the feeling. But she never dreamed it would be anything like this. The poor girl must have been raped. Maybe by all of the savages in an entire village. She had heard of such things. Whatever had happened no longer mattered. She was spoiled. She was unacceptable. They would all be better off if she expired. Especially Paul.

Elena sat beside the bed. She turned her lantern out but kept the little lamp burning.

She spent a fitful afternoon and night, sleeping and waking in the uncomfortable straight-backed chair. She did nothing for Sassy except to wipe her brow from time to time. "God's will," she said to herself. "God's will, either way it goes."

Small gusts blew through the slats of the window. The wind lifted the tiny strings on the drawstring bag that lay neglected in a dark corner of the room. Inside the bag the fever medicine lay alongside other herbs and medicines. Not once during the night did Elena touch the bag.

21

Breakfast was over with and Elena was back in Sassy's room. Sheer determination was all that kept her there. She had cleaned the room and washed Sassy and cleaned the room again. She wondered what she was going to do all day—sit in that awful chair? She did not want to stay out of the room too long at a time, in case Drucy went in alone.

Sassy's condition was unchanged. Drucy pestered Elena all morning about the doctor not coming until Elena screamed at her to be quiet. The doctor was no doubt occupied with another crisis. God willing, not another Indian attack somewhere.

Drucy, angry at Elena for shouting at her, grabbed a bucket and started for the creek. She was stopped by the bursting open of the kitchen door. She looked up to see a wild Indian standing in the doorway. He wore no clothing from the waist up and very little below. He carried a tomahawk raised menacingly in the air. A dirty, rolled-up blanket was under his arm. A knife and what looked to be a flute hung from his waist.

Drucy screamed. Elena rushed in and froze, her mouth hanging open.

The Indian glared at the women. He looked at the frightened one until the screaming caught in her throat and only a little gurgling noise was left in her. Then he turned his attention to the stupid one. The one he had watched through the window last night. The one who sat in the chair all night. The medicine bag was in the corner. He knew that the stupid one had not opened it once during the long night.

When Little Gabriel felt that his presence had terrorized the women into submission, he turned his head toward the closed bedroom door. "Sassy Sunshine," he said.

When it finally sank in that he was asking about Sassy, Elena said with relief, "Sassy. Do you know Sassy?" Was this the father? she wondered.

He ignored her. With a wave of the tomahawk, he entered the bedroom. As soon as he did, Drucy suddenly came alive. She ran out the kitchen door and was halfway across the yard when the Indian came headlong through the bedroom window. He rolled once on the ground and jumped back on his feet. He ran and caught Drucy by the hair and jerked her head back harshly.

"No!" he shouted, "Stay!" and pushed Drucy toward the house. The Indian walked her directly to Elena and struck the older woman with his open hand. It knocked Elena to the floor. Then the Indian returned to the bedroom with Sassy. Drucy sat at the table.

"Might as well wallow in hot ashes as try to get out of here," she said. Drucy looked across the table at Elena. "The great Miss Elena cannot fix this."

Elena said nothing. Her head was hurting and her elbow was bleeding from where she had fallen on it. She was every bit as scared as Drucy. Whatever the Indian meant to do, he did not intend to set them free.

The Indian came back. He grabbed Drucy's arm and pulled her up out of the chair. "Water," he said. He pointed toward the stove. He grabbed a cup from the open cupboard and went to the door and looked carefully in all directions, then returned to Sassy.

Drucy put water to heat on the stove. She stirred up the fire. In a little while, the Indian called from the bedroom, "Water!"

"You go," Drucy said to Elena.

Elena shook her head.

Drucy poured the water into a large open-mouthed crock and took it to him. He grabbed the crock from her, slopping some of the water onto the floor.

His blanket lay open on the bed. It was filled with leaves and small limbs and roots. They were scrubbed or rubbed clean, Drucy did not know which. She could not identify any of them except for the dried milkweed and small willow limbs. He had already shaved willow bark into tiny slivers and placed them in the cup. He poured some of the water over the shavings.

Her concern rose above her fear. "Mercy, what are you going to do to Sassy?"

Little Gabriel ignored her. He was taking medicines from the blanket and putting them in the crock. Drucy backed out.

"Stay!" He pointed.

Drucy hesitated. "I—"

"Stay!"

Self-consciously, Drucy sat on the far edge of the bed. She watched Little Gabriel prepare wraps. He took whatever materials he needed from the rooms—utensils and string from the kitchen, and cloths from both rooms. He looked inside the little cup and nodded. He lifted Sassy's head and had her drink.

He steeped the milkweed in another cup.

Little Gabriel paused in making his concoctions. He walked over and closed the bedroom door. He looked directly at Drucy and said, "She no fix." He nodded toward Elena in the kitchen. "She no fix Sassy Sunshine." He pointed at the window. "I watch. She sit. Do nothing."

It took only a moment for Drucy to understand his meaning. She searched the room until she saw Elena's undisturbed drawstring medicine bag. A cold chill walked up her back.

Little Gabriel put his hand on Drucy's shoulder. He touched her gently and said, "Stay. Help Sassy Sunshine. Little Gabriel come back. Take everybody." He pointed toward the forest.

Drucy wondered if she could believe him, trust him. Then she realized that there was no other choice.

Drucy went to Sassy. She would never leave her alone with Elena again.

Little Gabriel stood above Sassy. She was naked now except for the poultices wrapped around her neck and midsection. A stone lay on two sticks at the end of her feet. Little Gabriel asked the bad spirits to leave Sassy's body and enter the stone. Then he picked up his flute and played them an enticing tune.

Sassy moaned. Her head turned this way and that. Little Gabriel lay down his flute and spoke to the bad spirits again. He promised to take them to a cool and shady place where life was peaceful and long. He reminded them that if Sassy died, they would die also. He asked if it would not be better for them to enter the stone and be carried to a safe place far away from here. He picked up his flute and played again.

Sassy opened her eyes. She stared at Little Gabriel. There was no recognition in her eyes. Drucy watched closely. Sassy heard the music. Drucy knew she heard it because a calmness settled over her features when the Indian played his flute.

The savage was speaking in his own language. Drucy did not know what he was saying. He spoke in a flat, monotone voice. Periodically, he would stop and play his flute.

The droning voice went on. Drucy nodded off then awakened suddenly to a loud sound. Little Gabriel dashed through the kitchen and out the back door, holding his blanket in front of him. He crossed the road and ran down the hill to the creek and into the small stand of trees that surrounded it. He disappeared from sight.

Elena was sitting at the kitchen table, staring after him. Drucy came up behind her and said, "I think you should leave now."

"What? Leave?" Elena seemed confused. "Where should I go?"

"Go home," Drucy said.

"That Indian." Elena pointed to the window.

"He is not coming back."

A look of disbelief crossed Elena's face.

"He really is not," Drucy repeated. "You are free to leave."

Drucy turned and walked back into the bedroom, closing the door behind her.

Little Gabriel was only a mile from the house. He would have been farther but he was zigzagging, trying to fool the bad spirits in the stone so they could not find their way back to Sassy.

Near sundown he came upon a lovely place on a high bank above a small riverbed. It was just the kind that he had promised the spirits. There were plenty of shade trees, also clear ground in among them.

He found just the spot he wanted and carefully laid the blanket down. He undid his flute and played. Just as he had done in Sassy's bedroom, he played and then talked for a while. He spoke soothingly to the stone, reminding it that he had kept his promise. He called upon the spirits in the rock to keep their part of the bargain.

He was very careful not to disturb the stone too much as he unrolled its blanket. He did not wish to anger the spirits and have them jump from the stone onto him. When the stone was completely exposed, he lifted it with the two sticks and set it on the ground. Once the stone was placed where he wanted it, he did not play his flute or speak again. He gingerly stepped away and rolled up his blanket. He backed out of the little grove of trees, keeping his eyes on it. When he was far enough away that he could not see the stone anymore, he turned and ran.

Little Gabriel did not make camp until he was well away from the resting place of the spirits. He did not eat nor did he make a fire. He had not eaten since early morning, but he felt no hunger. Although he was far away from Sassy's house, he did not want to risk building a fire and being found by Jake or anyone else.

Under a heavy rock in the nearby streambed he placed the corner of his blanket, letting the water rinse it all through the night. There should be no trace of spirits in his blanket by morning.

Why had the elder white woman not helped Sassy Sunshine? The white people were a mystery to him. He had seen his first one when he was a very young man, thirteen or fourteen winters. He had watched them closely ever since, at trading posts and outlying farms. They were a great contradiction. They used many practical tools but would get lost and freeze to death if they strayed a mile or two from their homes in a snowstorm.

His new white wife at home was as big and strong as a man. He was very proud of her. She had not liked him much in the beginning but she eventually consented to their mating. When she came to be with child, her whole outlook had changed. Now she could not do enough for him. She was old to be having her first child, but many others were even older. She had such a warrior's strength. He named her Plough Woman, although he mostly still called her Mrs. Cutter.

Little Gabriel had first seen Sassy Sunshine when she was a small child up in the mountains. He had watched her family from a distance, never disturbing them. Years later, at a green corn festival held by The People of the Mountains that he went to with a cousin married into the Tuscarora tribe, he had seen that she was living with the Tuscarora as one of them.

Her family had chosen to live with the Tuscarora. They were not captives, not traders.

The father called the bright-haired girl "Sunshine." Others called her "Sassy." Sassy Sunshine.

It was strange how he had seen her at the Cutters and now at the little farm. His destiny was linked to hers.

The white people, they would be looking for him. He had hit the elderly woman hard, he had treated the younger one harshly. The white men's hearts would not be appeased because he had not killed anybody or because he had helped Sassy Sunshine. He knew enough about them to know that they would still come for him. Especially now with so many tribal uprisings to the south and the west.

He knew that he might be recognized easily. The flute would give him away. It always did. He could hide his flute but he would not get rid of it. It was sacred to him. Since he had learned to play, nothing really bad ever happened to him. It was the sacred flute that protected him.

It was almost dawn and still raining. The meadow was soaked from the downpour. Runs With The Wind and Takime pulled themselves forward on their elbows, dragging their feet in the mud. Yesterday's battle had lasted all day and they were both exhausted. They lay hidden in the woods during the night, without food or shelter. Daylight seemed a long time in coming.

They crawled past a severely injured Tuscarora. They could not stop to help him. They were traveling in as straight a line as possible, heading toward John Billips, who lay wounded near the center of the field.

When they reached him, he was facedown in the mud. Rolling him over on his back, they saw tiny sparkles of blood glistening on his lips. His eyes were closed and his breathing was shallow. One of his legs was shattered, and the bone protruded at a curious angle through his buckskins. Another jagged wound was in his chest.

In the dimness of the North Carolina morning, Runs With The Wind searched the field for the enemy while Takime quietly tried to make his father as comfortable as possible. The ground was littered with dead and fatally wounded Tuscarora braves and English colonists and their Indian allies. The decimation favored the colonists.

A few men were sitting up but no one was standing. Anyone who could walk or crawl had already evacuated to the adjoining woods.

"We will have to take the chance and carry him," Takime whispered.

Runs With The Wind nodded. He knew that somewhere downstream on the Trent River, under the command of Colonel Barnwell, the red soldiers and colonists were regrouping. If they were going to attack, it would most likely be at full light, although there was no need for another assault. For every one of the colonists killed or wounded, five or six Tuscarora had died. Most of the wounded were dying, too. The majority of the Tuscarora forts and towns had already been destroyed. There was nothing left but to fight in the woods and fields.

Runs With The Wind retrieved a rifle from a dead soldier and made a splint for Billips's leg. Takime lifted his father by the shoulders while Runs With The Wind lifted him at the thighs, trying not to disturb the broken leg. They bent over as far as they could without losing their balance, then swiftly made for the north woods.

They had almost reached the trees when a single shot erupted. It must have come from a wounded soldier. Takime heard the soft thud and felt Billips's body sag. Instinctively, he knew this final insult to muscle and bone had taken the life from his father. He did not slacken his stride.

They carried Billips deep into the woods. A gray dawn was rising when they stopped to rest. Takime carefully placed his father on the ground. He motioned for Runs With The Wind to help pile brush over the lifeless body. When he was finished, Takime announced quietly, "I am going back. It is over."

Runs With The Wind touched his friend's shoulder. "I know. You will not be alone."

On their journey back to the field of fallen blood, they stayed close to the path they'd taken while carrying Billips, but they did not walk on it. Ever cautious, they were even more so now. Since the Tuscarora massacre of one hundred, thirty colonists the Trent River, soldiers and Carolina militia had penetrated the forest for miles in all directions.

Bone weary, the pair reached the edge of the battleground. There was no indication that the main body of white soldiers was returning. Only one man was sitting up. He was most likely the one who had fired the fatal shot at Billips.

The two young men edged their way toward the English soldier. Sitting in the mud, the man was dead. Takime stared at the puffy white face with rage and hate. He picked up the spent rifle lying alongside the soldier and beat the dead man. His anger dissipated. He dropped the weapon and turned to Runs With The Wind, but he was not beside Takime.

Across the field Runs With The Wind was crouching over a prone body. As Takime watched, Runs With The Wind crashed his tomahawk down on the skull of the man beneath. He ran to another body and examined it quickly, pulled something from the man, and stuck it in his own shirt. Then he lifted his tomahawk and hit the man several times.

Takime began searching the dead and wounded for food packs and knives. The carbines were too heavy to carry more than one at a time and most of the powder was wet. How had the soldier gotten off that last shot? No matter. Takime had no more stomach for killing. Let Runs With The Wind do it. He would find supplies and look for wounded brothers and uncles. But most of the faces he stared into were dead. Very few belonged to The People of the Mountains. Many Arrows and Bear Paw had fallen weeks ago at the battle near the soldier fort. He had watched Long Feather and Skylook flee the field of blood yesterday. Skylook looked wounded, Long Feather did not. He had not seen Lame Crow for several days.

Takime stopped short. Snake, son of Great Hawk, lay at his feet. He was still breathing. He seemed to be sleeping. His face was calm and peaceful. Takime roughly jerked a buckskin shirt from some unknown Tuscarora's body and bundled his supplies in it. He brought the sleeves of the shirt up under his arms from the back and wrapped them around the back of his neck, tieing them as tightly as he could. Then he dragged Snake toward the woods.

As he entered the treeline he heard the call of a dove just barely

235

above the steady beating of rain. He knew it was Runs With The Wind and that he would follow soon.

Takime half dragged, half carried Snake for nearly an hour before stopping to rest. He was heading north, toward home. He knew he could not hide the drag tracks from the enemy, but he saw no sign of soldiers. Maybe they had gone back to their fort.

He searched the food packs stolen from the fallen enemy. Munching on jerky and soggy maize bread, he thought about the position he was in.

Snake was unconscious. His only visible wound was a huge lump on the side of his head with an open cut in the center of the lump. He was feverish but breathing easily. Every once in a while he would roll his head and move his arms and legs in a wild and uncontrollable manner. If there was any way at all, he would save Snake.

Leaving his own father's body under the pile of brush in this strange Carolina place was unforgivable. But what could he do? There was nothing to dig with. The ground was turning to mud from the continual rains. There were no rocks to pile over him and no caves to hide him in. But he could not leave John Billips for the animals or the colonists to desecrate. And he must get Snake to a safe place where he could heal.

Takime thought of the river. He could weight his father's body and put him in the river. No man or animal would find him there. He could carry his father to a place far above the field of fallen blood. It would be dangerous. He was more likely to run into the enemy along the river's edge than in the woods but he had decided: he would retrieve his father and take him to the river. But first Snake.

So as not to not leave a trail for others to follow, Takime lifted Snake and carried him bodily. In a secluded place among the pines, he lay him down and built a temporary shelter of pine boughs around Snake. It would help a little in keeping the rain from falling on him. He wanted to leave food beside Snake in case he awoke but food would attract animals. He climbed a tall pine tree and tied the food high up in the branches. By midafternoon he returned to his father. From several light, sturdy logs he built a travois and set off.

When he arrived at the river's edge it was black dark. The rain had not slackened and there was no moon or stars to see by. The river was high, running fast with the added burden of heavy rains.

Takime lifted his father from the makeshift travois, laying him on the ground as close to the river as possible. The downpour would dissolve his tracks before daylight.

He had found one heavy stone along the way and tied it on top of the travois with rawhide. It jarred and bounced against his father's body several times during the journey. He did not like that. Now he tied the stone to Billips's legs. He needed another for Billips's chest.

He searched for rocks along the riverbank as best he could in the darkness. It was not a rocky river, but he knew that most rivers carried some rocks and other debris in the spring floods, depositing them along the edges of the bank. Not far along, he stumbled over a half-buried rock.

Kneeling down, he ran his hands across the surface of the rock. It seemed about the right size but it was buried under the mud. He began to dig it out with his hands. It was hard work. When he was finished, his hands were raw and bleeding. He paid no mind to the pain or blood. He only wished he could do more for his father.

When everything was ready, Takime dragged Billips into the water. Fighting the current and the weight of the rocks, he walked against the strong river water until it reached high on his chest.

He stood for a moment, holding tightly to his father while the current tried to sweep them both away. He hugged Billips to him one last time. Reluctantly letting him go, he felt his father sink beneath the swirling surface.

Takime tried to stand in one position but the water buffeted him and pushed him downstream. There was little he could do but grope his way back to shore. Feeling empty and alone, he tried to find comfort in the prayers his mother had taught him. But there were no prayers in him. None for the white god and none for the Great Spirit.

His heart was filled with sadness as he made his way through the wet night. What would he say to Lydia? He could not even imagine her life without John Billips. And young White Cloud? And his own baby? His child would never know the strength of his grandfather.

Sassy—It would break her heart to know that her father lay at the bottom of a river. At least Runs With The Wind had been able to bury his father, Bear Paw.

Takime's thoughts were far from the path he traveled. He tripped over an unseen tree root and fell flat out in the mud. Lying there alone with the rain beating down on him, it came to him to stay there. Just stay there and sleep. Rest. He lay still and closed his eyes and fell into a hard sleep.

Something woke him. What? He listened carefully. The forest was too silent and he realized that it was the silence that had awakened him. The rain had stopped.

He sat up and brushed the mud from his clothing as best he could. He stripped a handful of young leaves from a low-hanging branch and wiped his face and hands.

It was still night but there was light across the land. He began to make his way back to Snake. The going was much easier with the coming of dawn.

Snake was wide awake when Takime arrived. He spoke Takime's name and motioned for something to drink when he saw him. Takime had no water to give him, but he offered food. Snake chewed slowly. Everything he did was done slowly: the movement of his head while looking around or the simple act of bringing food to his mouth. Snake was childlike and unsteady.

Takime watched, trying to decide what to do next. If Snake could walk, it would be best to keep moving. The farther north they went, the safer they would be. He decided to head northwest, back toward the mountains. There were too many farms and settlements along the rivers and coasts to stay where he was or go east.

Traveling would be much easier along the bottomlands but it would not be as safe. He did not think that Snake could survive another battle. He would keep close to the mountains.

"Stand up," Takime ordered. "We have a long way to go. We must begin. Now."

Snake tried to stand up. He used a pine sapling to support his weight until he was erect. He took a few shaky steps.

Takime encouraged him: "Good. We will rest often. If we rest often, you will go further in the long run."

They could not travel more than a mile without resting. Some of the time Takime supported Snake's body with his own. Snake was trying very hard. He wanted to reach the lodges of the People.

Runs With The Wind, Great Hawk, and Lame Crow caught up with them before dark. Each carried food, water, and weapons taken from the dead soldiers.

Great Hawk was wearing a soldier's hat. He handed it to his son. "You have fought well, my son," he said. "My heart swells with pride." He did not mention his other son, Bear Paw, father of Runs With The Wind, lying beneath the Carolina soil.

Snake smiled broadly and put the hat on his head. His belly filled and his thirst slaked, he lay down and quickly fell asleep. The four remaining looked at one another over the sleeping man's body.

"My son is greatly changed," Great Hawk said, "but he lives."

Runs With The Wind spoke to comfort his grandfather: "We do not know it all yet. It will be many moons before we know it all. Snake will become more like he was. It will take some time passing."

Great Hawk nodded. "Yes, I have seen this before. If the old shaman still lives, he will bring him forth."

Takime said, "Blackbird? Of course he lives. He has White Cloud and Bright Eyes looking after him. Who could be under better care? Now, when did you find one another?"

Runs With The Wind laughed. "While I was so busy in the field I saw another coming from the forest. It was Great Hawk. He saw me and decided to help. I think he only came for the hat."

"I tried to follow the soldiers," Lame Crow said. "But I tired of spying on them and I was alone. So I came back and found these two. They told me of the death of my friend, Billips. I am much saddened."

The four men talked of their plans for traveling home. Takime gave up his idea to skirt the mountains. They decided that they would traverse the bottomland. They would keep wide intervals between them so as to be less visible and also able to assist another if he was endangered or attacked. Or, if outnumbered and captured, at least the struggle would alert the others spread out along the trail. Someone would make it back to recount their bravery and pain.

They slept fitfully through the night. Great Hawk was much worried over his wounded son. Takime was anxious to see his family; he knew a baby had to have been born to him since he left. The face of Rainy Days was before him, and each time he awoke abruptly, he had only to think of her to fall asleep again.

Although they built no fire, Runs With The Wind saw golden sparks in the night. They flew from his Sassy's hair back into the firelight of his dreams, just the way they used to by the campfires at home. For days at a time, he tried not to think about her too much. But tonight, he let his mind roam where it would. He was going home.

22

Sassy sat on the edge of the bed folding up papers. She put them back in a narrow wooden box.

"Sit, Drucy. I want to tell you a secret. It is a very important secret. The reason I am telling you is that it may involve you."

Drucy had never seen Sassy so serious. She got a funny feeling in her stomach just looking at her.

Sassy said, "I am leaving here, Drucy. I am taking my horse and going. These maps will help me." She patted the box in her lap.

"Oh, no!" Drucy jumped up. "You cannot go away. Please do not leave me."

Sassy reached out and grabbed Drucy's arm, pulling her back down on the bed beside her. "That is why I am telling you this. You can come, too. If you want to."

Without even asking where they would go, Drucy said, "When are we going?"

Sassy laughed. "You better wait until I tell you all of it before you decide for sure."

Sassy patted the wooden box again. "There are maps inside this box that Jake and I drew. Some of the way here I have never forgotten. But some days were so rainy or I was so mournful that I didn't take notice of the route."

"You are going back where you came from," Drucy said.

"Yes. If I can find it."

"To the Indians?" Drucy could not believe her ears.

"Yes."

Drucy wrapped her arms around her knees and rocked back and forth, softly crying. "They will kill us. They will torture us and eat us," she moaned. "And you're barely well enough."

"I would like to ease your fears but I cannot. It will be dangerous," Sassy admitted. "But not all of the danger comes from the Indians."

The two girls sat silent for a while and then Sassy said, "My people will not harm you but I do not know the people around here. The tribes are at war. The doctor never came. I can't help but think a calamity delayed him or made it unsafe to travel."

Drucy interrupted: "Your people? You called them your people."

"Yes. They are my people. My mother and father and brothers are there. My husband is there. That is, if the men are back from the wars." She paused a moment, remembering.

"What? You have a husband?" Drucy stared at her in disbelief. "And he is fighting with the Indians?"

"He is one of them," Sassy said. "He is a chief."

Sassy told Drucy about her childhood and her growing-up years and about her marriage. She left many things out. She did not mention her father killing the King's soldier many years ago and the family's self-exile, nor the raid and the killing of the white settlers. She did not tell Drucy the name of her tribe. Some things were better left unsaid.

When she finished, she said, "Well, are you still coming with me?"

"Yes," Drucy said. "I cannot stay here without you. Elena would eventually dispose of me. Although that's hard to believe, deep in my heart I know it. I do not trust her anymore. She would probably sell me into servitude or give me away to the Indians. So I may as well go on my own."

"Well, then," Sassy said, "we have plenty to do. We must go in the morning. I have to memorize these maps. I can't take them or Jake will know where we went. Not that he or Paul would want me back after Elena is done with me, but the less anyone knows, the better for us."

Drucy said, "What do you want me to do?"

Sassy was not greatly concerned about how much food they should take. They could always hunt and she knew how to find berries and wild vegetables. They needed enough provisions to get through the first few days without having to stop to hunt or forage. They could use the time saved to cover their trail. Not that Jake or Paul or any of the white men were good trackers. They were not. But they could always get the services of one of the town Indians or a half-breed. She did not want to take any chances.

Sassy pulled a kitchen chair into the bedroom and sat in the pre-dawn light by the window, reading over the precious maps for the last time. Drucy took inventory of their supplies. Everything was ready.

Their destination was southwest. In order to fool anyone trying to track them, they set out traveling north. The northern woods were unknown to Sassy and it was difficult going for a while. She planned to head west about noon the second day and then south. She was not worried about getting lost but she was worried about the danger of meeting wandering Iroquois. Still, she was willing to risk running into the Iroquois rather than getting recaptured by the Martin family or other whites. Her bow at the ready, they rode north at a brisk pace.

The trees were throwing long shadows as Runs With The Wind chose his way carefully along the riverbank. Takime was not far behind. They were in a place unknown to them. Sometimes the woods were so thick that their horses could not penetrate, which was why they had chosen to follow the twisting, winding river. They had been traveling for many days, searching for the trail home.

They rounded a bend in the long chain of mountains and saw a group of strangers coming toward them. Although there were about twenty of them, six appeared to be women. There were several small children among them. Two women carried infants on their backs.

Runs With The Wind and Takime decided to approach. A war party would not include women and children. The men wore their hair in the style of the Mahican—shaved on both sides of the head with a roach of several inches running down the center. The clan was traveling with dogs but there was not a horse among them.

The two young men raised their arms in greeting. A Mahican signaled a sign of friendship. Runs With The Wind and Takime sat their horses and waited for the Mahicans to reach them. The closer they came, the more obvious it was that one of the women was white. She was a big woman. Her hair was fixed into one large plait at the side of her head. She had stuck a huge wildflower through the center of the plait, which flopped back and forth as she walked. She, too, carried an infant in a cradleboard on her back.

After the initial greetings, Runs With The Wind slapped the deer carcass strapped across the rump of his horse. He addressed the man who was obviously their leader, the one with a white man's flute tied to his breechclout.

"I would consider it an honor if you would share our meal with us," Runs With The Wind said.

Little Gabriel stared at Takime as he spoke to Runs With The Wind. "It is with pleasure that we accept your offer."

Neither man completely understood the other's words, but the intent was clear.

"Does the half-breed speak English?" Little Gabriel asked.

"Yes," Takime answered. "I do."

Little Gabriel turned his attention back to Runs With The Wind. "And you?"

Runs With The Wind nodded. "Yes."

Little Gabriel shook his head in amazement. "Much English talk in these woods," he said. He pointed to the big white woman. "My woman speaks English. Me, too," he said proudly, thumping himself on the chest with his fist.

Runs With The Wind and Takime smiled and nodded at the white woman. They both knew better than to openly acknowledge her before the right moment arrived. They would wait for an opportunity to speak with her.

Little Gabriel turned and said something to the men behind him. They immediately unloaded the deer carcass from the horse and threw it on the ground. Two of the women began skinning it where it lay. The rest dispersed to prepare a campsite.

Runs With The Wind and Takime climbed down from their horses. Runs With The Wind took the mounts away from the group. He figured he would have to keep a cautious eye on them, lest one of the Mahican braves decided to steal them.

Little Gabriel patted Takime on the arm. "You have rum?"

"No. No rum," Takime said.

Little Gabriel was not overly disappointed. If rum was around, he would drink it. But he was not like some of the braves who seemed to long for it. He was more interested in the half-breed. He still harbored a fascination with white men, even if he was now devoted to killing them.

"I have seen you before," he announced to Takime. "If I do not remember by nightfall, it will come to me in my dreams."

Takime studied the man's face. "I have no recollection," he said. "My friend with the horses will know."

"Is he the keeper of faces in his clan?"

Takime shook his head no.

After their meal was over, the men sat around the fire and smoked and talked. They conversed mostly in English and Runs With The Wind noticed that the white woman was never too far away. She was listening. Runs With The Wind spoke of the wars in the Carolinas and of the great Tuscarora losses and of the cleverness of the Iroquois in retaining the goodwill of the whites in the colonies closest to them while raiding Indian and white towns in farther territories. Little Gabriel told about the fast encroachment of the white men into the Mahican territories. He talked with pride about a man of his tribe who went to England to meet the great English mother, the Queen Anne.

They were in agreement: their way of life was changing because of the ever-advancing white men. Trees were being steadily felled to accommodate huge white villages that were always growing. The face of the earth was bare for miles and miles around them. Animals could not live without the forest, and Indians could not survive without the animals. The whites had hunted fur-bearing creatures to near extinction. And now that these were practically gone, the white men were turning to farming grains and tobacco. But they raised far more than they consumed. The surplus they bartered or stored. They were hoarders, these people. And their senseless grubbing had no end.

When the talking was over, Little Gabriel moved away from the camp to an isolated spot where he could play his flute to the music of the river and contemplate.

The white woman settled by the women's fire. Her eyes were still on Runs With The Wind and Takime. Runs With The Wind nodded for her to come to him. She immediately arose, dished up a portion of meat from the hanging pot, and took it to him.

Although his belly was full, he accepted the food and ate with pretended hunger. Between bites he said, "I am searching for a white woman. Stolen from us almost one year ago. She is my friend's sister. She is called Sassy. Have you seen her?"

Mrs. Cutter gasped. "Gar, yes." The words almost exploded from her broad mouth. "Stolen, you say. Are you sure?"

Runs With The Wind calmed himself and said quietly, "Yes, stolen. Tell me what you know."

"What makes you think she wants to be found?"

In a low, threatening voice Runs With The Wind said, "She wants to be found. She is my wife."

Mrs. Cutter left their fire without another word and returned to the women's fire. She was confused and frightened but she wanted to hear more. She quickly ladled more meat from the pot and returned to the men's fire. She handed it to Takime.

"Eat or they will become suspicious." Mrs. Cutter talked as Takime ate. "I love that girl," she said.

"If you tell me where she is, I will get you out of here," Runs With The Wind said very quietly.

Mrs. Cutter took a deep breath. She somehow trusted the young brave with the menacing frown. She would tell what she knew and then if they were lucky enough to reach Sassy, Sassy could make up her own mind about staying or leaving. As for his taking her out of there, she was not sure she wanted to go. Life was very good with the Mahicans.

"She is somewhere outside of Philadelphia," Mrs. Cutter whispered. "She is with a family called Martin. Jake and Paul Martin."

"White men? She is with white men?" Runs With The Wind was surprised. He had assumed Indians had abducted her.

Runs With The Wind grew cautious. The flute had stopped. He glanced toward the riverbank where Little Gabriel had gone for solitude. Little Gabriel was no longer sitting there. He was fast approaching the camp fire.

Little Gabriel stopped directly in front of Takime and said, "Sassy Sunshine's brother. You were adopted into the turtle clan of the Tuscaroras. But you are no half-breed." He was all smiles for having remembered. He turned to Runs With The Wind. "You are the son of Bear Paw, son of Great Hawk."

By this time Little Gabriel was laughing out loud. "Now my dreams will be peaceful for I have no memories to make.

"Sassy Sunshine is with child," he added. "I, too, expect a strong baby boy, like this one." He proudly lifted a month-old baby from a cradleboard and held him up for the visitors to see. Mrs. Cutter's big generous face broke into a grin at her husband's show of pride in yet another infant. She hoped he would feel as much for the child she carried in her.

Takime took the child from Little Gabriel's hands. "You have seen my sister?" He was careful to show admiration for the baby.

Takime glanced at Runs With The Wind to see how he was taking the news that Sassy was expecting a baby. His friend's face wore a mask of stone. Takime laid his hand on Runs With The Wind's arm in companionship and support.

Little Gabriel continued, "I spied from the edge of the woods near the house where she lives."

Runs With The Wind moved not a muscle. Takime decided to question Little Gabriel before Runs With The Wind could speak. Runs With The Wind had not been the same since they had quit the wars and learned from other Tuscarora on the trail that his wife was missing. He had taken to quarrelsome ways and you could not always count on him to hold his temper.

"Do you know where she is now?" Takime asked.

Little Gabriel nodded vigorously. "Yes."

"Can you tell us how to get there?" Takime paced his breathing, waiting for the answer.

"Tomorrow morning I will show you where she is. It will be a nice journey by walking horse." Little Gabriel pointed toward the hobbled horses.

Takime said nothing, waiting for Little Gabriel to finish. He was sure some sort of bargaining would ensue.

"My woman ride horse with me, you ride with him." Little Gabriel pointed to Runs With The Wind.

Takime smiled. So all he wanted was a horse. "You take me to my sister and I will give you the horse."

"Ah." Little Gabriel was pleased. He had never owned a horse. He had never even ridden one. He motioned to Mrs. Cutter to join the women. There would be much talking around his camp fire tonight and he did not want to be disturbed by women or children.

Mrs. Cutter walked to the women's circle, thinking over all that she had heard. Little Gabriel must trust her completely to allow her to accompany them. He must know that on such a journey she might tell Takime and Runs With The Wind who had killed her husband and all the others at Cutter's Place. She could also tell about the captives. And Takime was white. He would be certain to want to retaliate for such treatment of his people.

Usually, Little Gabriel went alone when he journeyed in white territory. Of course, she did not expect him to let her go near Sassy's house. He would keep her hidden out in the forest somewhere when he went there.

Since the conception of their child, Mrs. Cutter had gained a great respect for her new spouse. He was a gentle husband and a good provider. But even so, she could not see how she could live with her own conscience if she did not tell someone about the massacre. She sat down beside the other women but her attention was still on the guests.

Runs With The Wind was mostly silent for the rest of the evening. It would be a long night for him, waiting for the sun to rise and the journey to begin. He listened intently as Little Gabriel told the story of Sassy's sickness but he did not ask questions. It was enough to know that she was alive.

Little Gabriel offered to show them where he had placed the stone with the evil spirits in it although he hoped that they did not want to see it. It was best to leave such things alone. He questioned Takime closely about the southern wars, shaking his head sadly over the deaths of Bear Paw, Many Arrows, John Billips, and the others. He understood the consequences of the scattering of the Tuscaroras. His tribe, too, was being pushed further and further west and north by the whites' insatiable appetite for land and bounty.

There was a lull in the conversation while the men passed the pipe. Then Little Gabriel spoke: "I was going to get your sister one day soon. I promised the other female I would come. Tomorrow is a good day to begin." He sniffed the air. "Yes, tomorrow will be a fine day to start on such a journey."

Takime stiffened. "And where were you going to take her?" He wondered if Little Gabriel had intended to make her another wife or the wife of one of his braves. Or he might have been planning to trade her off to some other tribe, as was often done.

"Mrs. Cutter, my woman, likes the girl," Little Gabriel said. "I did not tell her I saw Sassy Sunshine. I was going to surprise her with the girl. A gift."

Takime chose his words carefully. He did not wish to offend his host since he had saved Sassy's life. He would always be grateful for that, but he wanted Little Gabriel to understand that he and Runs With The Wind were taking Sassy home.

Takime said, "I am honored that your woman thinks highly of my sister and sorry that you cannot give her as a gift to Mrs. Cutter. But Sassy is coming with us. She must live with her husband and her family. I am sure you and Mrs. Cutter will always be welcome in her lodge."

Little Gabriel nodded and stared into the low-burning fire. "Mrs. Cutter will like the other one just as well," he said.

Takime had not thought of that. Little Gabriel had not elaborated about the other woman. "Which other one?" Takime said.

"The one that helped Sassy Sunshine, not the one that let her sicken. She is a strong girl. The other one, the old one, I do not like her." Little Gabriel made a face.

Takime said, "Yes. Mrs. Cutter will probably like the other one." He could not be concerned with the fate of an unknown girl.

Takime felt Runs With The Wind leave the fire in the direction of the horses, probably to change their grazing area. Just to make sure, Takime decided to follow. He stood up and stretched. It had been a long day and he wanted an early start in the morning. He said to Little Gabriel, "First up wakens the rest."

Runs With The Wind hobbled the horses and lay down not too far from them. Takime made his bed on the opposite side of the small meadow. He knew the night would bring little sleep for either of them.

The next morning, breakfast was finished before daylight. As a rosy gray dawn rolled across the sky, Takime handed his horse to Little Gabriel and jumped up behind Runs With The Wind.

Little Gabriel's horse stood obediently while he mounted and helped Mrs. Cutter up behind him. Runs With The Wind motioned for Little Gabriel to take the lead. Little Gabriel gave his horse a mighty kick in the side and the animal bolted forward, almost dislodging Mrs. Cutter. The horse ran full speed along the riverbank.

Mrs. Cutter clung to her husband as he bounced around on the horse's back, trying to keep a good grip on its mane. He had dropped the reins. Arms and legs askew, they rounded a bend in the river and disappeared.

Runs With The Wind and Takime laughed so hard at this unexpected display that they could not follow right away.

When Runs With The Wind could catch his breath he remarked, "Good talker, bad rider."

"Yes," Takime agreed. "We better give him some time to control that horse before we catch up to them. He would not care to be seen like that twice in one day."

They walked their shared horse slowly toward the bend where Little Gabriel had vanished. It had felt good to laugh. They laughed all over again when they rounded it and no horse was in sight. By the time they caught up to Little Gabriel his horse was walking as sedately as their own. Mrs. Cutter was walking sedately beside it.

"Gar," she shouted as they rode up. "That horse will be the death of me and my baby." Several hours passed before Little Gabriel could convince her to climb back up.

23

Sassy chose to camp in the bottom of the second of three gullies. She figured no one could see the small flames unless they were right upon them. Since it was almost dark, the little smoke should go unnoticed in the night.

Drucy skinned the rabbit Sassy had brought her while Sassy gathered pine boughs for their beds. It was their fourth night in the woods and Drucy was just as scared to see the sun go down as she had been on the other three nights. Tonight was the first time Sassy had allowed a small cook fire.

She was a little anxious as she stripped small limbs from the pine trees. She had not told Drucy, but while hunting small game on foot, she had seen a huge bear in the distance. It was too far away to tell much about it. Luckily, she was downwind of the creature and she did not think that it was ever aware of her presence. It had disappeared over the ridge soon after she spotted it. She hoped it had not caught their scent or that of the horses.

Wolves had been near their camp last night, too. She had seen one slinking through the edge of the woods at daybreak. She had not seen any signs since, but they seldom traveled alone.

Drucy broke the silence: "Supper will be ready in less than an hour." She put her head over the steaming pot and sniffed. "This rabbit is going to taste good."

Drucy had taken very well to the outdoor life, loving the steady roll of the horses. She slept soundly out under the stars, wrapped tightly in blankets, blissfully unconscious of predators and problems.

Sassy finished making the beds and sat down. She and Drucy had actually become contented.

Runs With The Wind and her mother and father and brothers entered her mind. She sat and conjured up their faces in the fire. She was going home to the mountains.

The next morning they slept a little later than usual. After a cold breakfast, they quickly packed the horses and departed. Sassy was beginning to recognize the terrain. She turned in the saddle to see how Drucy was progressing. Sassy always took the lead but Drucy was never far behind.

"Whatever are you thinking about?" she asked Drucy. "With such a solemn face as yours, you will frighten away the sun."

Drucy said, "I am thinking how lucky we have been."

Sassy laughed. "You don't look like you are thinking about how lucky we have been. You look like you expect Lucifer to fall down on you from the trees."

"I am thinking that we are lucky he has not—or some strange savage."

Sassy turned back around and guided her horse over a fallen log that lay across the trail. Drucy was right. So far, they had been very lucky. But you could not spend all your time worrying about what might be around the next turn. They had such a long way to go. She would try harder to keep Drucy's spirits high.

They ate lunch in a tiny grassy meadow that suddenly opened up beside the trail. It was very pleasant there and they hobbled the horses to let them graze.

"We are not far from the Lake Above The River," Sassy said. "Our trail will take us above the lake. We might reach the big Susquehanna River tomorrow. This time of year it should be easy to cross. It was easy when we crossed it last year." Sassy glanced at Drucy to see how she was taking this bit of information. She knew that Drucy could not swim and did not like water.

Drucy spoke calmly: "What do you mean by easy to cross? Are we supposed to walk across it?"

"We could. I can go first and see if we can."

"Well, how did you cross it before?" Drucy asked.

"We walked. And led the horses. But if it happens to be deeper, we could ride across. We must be very careful either way and tie ourselves on securely. The water could rise as high as our shoulders in places or we might stumble on something and fall."

Drucy's calmness exploded. "Tie ourselves onto the horses' backs? Your mind must be addled. We are not tying ourselves to horses."

Sassy felt that she had said enough for now. They would just have to wait and see how the water was. She patted Drucy on the hand and said, "We will decide what is best when we get there. I can swim. I could bring you across."

That either satisfied Drucy for the time being or she decided not to think on it.

After lunch, they walked for a while to loosen their stiff, sore muscles. They had spent too much time in the saddle and their already overtaxed bodies were not used to it. There was not enough room on the old trail for them to lead the horses and walk comfortably side by side so they continued with Sassy in front and Drucy following.

By midafternoon of the next day, they were standing on the edge of the Susquehanna. It was a beautiful river. It was not so wide at this point. The sun sparkled across the water, and the heavy green of the trees on the shores reflected on both sides. The girls rested a while on its banks, quietly enjoying its lulling beauty.

The current was moderately swift but the water was down, exposing large rocks here and there.

After several minutes Sassy said, "Let me take Dear Friend across, and if everything goes well, I will come back across by myself and get you."

"All right," Drucy agreed.

Drucy cupped her hands to her eyes and watched Sassy's every move. She saw that Sassy and Dear Friend walked carefully but steadily all the way across without any problem. The water never came above Sassy's hips. Once, the horse seemed to falter and once Sassy stumbled and caught on to Dear Friend for support. But, all in all, they had little difficulty.

Sassy and the horse disappeared from sight on the other shore. They were gone for several minutes. Drucy began to worry. Just when she was sure that something was wrong, Sassy reappeared at the water's edge. She waved that all was well and stepped back into the water. Soon, she was across, wet and rotund and tired but pleased with her success.

"I hid Dear Friend in the brush," Sassy said, "in case anyone comes around. We cannot afford to be stranded without horses."

Sassy sprawled out on the ground to rest and let the sun warm her. "The water is cold and it was a struggle just to walk against the current. I need to rest a few minutes and then I will take you over," she said. "It is easy enough. You have to watch out for rocks on the bottom and the current is a swift, but when your turn comes, you won't have any trouble."

"I am going now," Drucy announced. "I will take the bay over."

Sassy was startled. "There is no reason for you to do that. I will take you."

Drucy stood her ground. "Why should you do all the work? I am just as strong and a little less pregnant, I suspect. The water is not high. I can walk it." As she spoke, she stepped into the water, pulling the horse along with her.

Sassy watched in fascination as Drucy carefully waded toward the middle. The middle was the deepest but it was less rocky.

Wherever Drucy had come from, she was made of good stuff, Sassy thought. There she goes, half-afraid of the horse and completely afraid of the water. I am lucky to have her as a companion.

The girl and the horse easily reached the far shore. Before heading into the forest to hide the horse, Drucy turned and waved. As Sassy stood up and waved back, three men stepped from the edge of the forest. One of them grabbed Drucy. The other two waded into the water, heading for Sassy's side.

Sassy scooped up her bow. Drucy screamed. All Sassy could do was run. She knew that she would be caught. One girl was no match for two or three men and there could be more. She looked back to see how far the men had advanced across the water. This time she recognized them.

"Sassy!"

Runs With The Wind was ahead of Takime. He was running through the water with abandon. He slipped and fell and rose again and fell again. By this time, Takime was beside him. Takime lifted him up.

"Go steady, my friend," Takime said. "She is not going anywhere."

Runs With The Wind grinned. He was drenched. There was a gash on his shin from hitting a rock. But his eyes were shining and his spirit could hardly be contained. He pulled away from Takime and continued his run through the river.

Takime followed more slowly. The girl behind him, the one with Little Gabriel, had stopped screaming. Takime looked back and saw that they were in deep conversation. Takime laughed. Little Gabriel, the talker.

Before Runs With The Wind reached shore, Sassy ran into the river and met him amid the swirling waters. They stood holding one another, rocking back and forth until their feet began sinking into the streambed.

Sassy and Runs With The Wind walked out of the water still

clinging to each other's waist. Takime raised a fist to the sun and howled. Sassy stood quietly. She walked to her brother and hugged him. "I knew I would see you again. But not this soon."

"We have been looking for you," Takime said. "Now that the search is over, we better get across the river and save your friend from Little Gabriel."

Sassy was surprised to learn that Little Gabriel was with them. "Little Gabriel," she said. "I have much to thank him for."

"I know. There will be plenty of time for that. We have a long trek ahead of us. Come."

Runs With The Wind put his hand on Sassy's arm to stop her. "First, I must tell you something."

Takime heard him and knew what he was going to say. He was going to tell her of the death of her father. Takime started to come back to the riverbank but Runs With The Wind waved him away. When Takime reached the river's midpoint, he turned again. He saw Sassy sobbing violently, clinging to Runs With The Wind for support. Her knees buckled and she slid to the ground. Runs With The Wind sat down beside her and held her in his arms, gently stroking her hair.

At the sight of it all, Takime's own eyes filled with tears. The death of his father was something he would never get over.

Runs With The Wind and Sassy crossed the Susquehanna side by side. Sassy could see that another woman had joined the group on shore. She recognized the huge bulk of Mrs. Cutter but her eyes and her mind were at odds with one another over the sight.

"Gar, girl." Mrs. Cutter pulled a wet and tired Sassy to her breast. "You are a blessed sight. Better than a piece of dry kindling on a blizzardy night. Never thought I would see you again." She thumped Sassy on the back. "Why, you are a lot plumper than the last time we met."

Sassy wept and laughed at the same time. The sight of her old friend was comforting.

"Well, we have been fruitful and multiplied."

A shadow crossed Sassy's face as she remembered that John Billips would never see his grandchild.

Mrs. Cutter realized what Sassy was thinking and said, "All things in their season. God rest your father . . . and Mr. Cutter."

Sassy nodded, guessing the details.

Little Gabriel interrupted their conversation. He spoke to Takime and Runs With The Wind. "That one"—he indicated Drucy—"does not want to come with me. She wants to stay with her." He pointed at Sassy. "It was agreed that I could have her if I took you to your wife."

Drucy stood wide eyed, dried tears streaking her face.

Sassy turned to her husband. "What! You gave away Drucy?"

Runs With The Wind would have given away his life to find her, much less Drucy. "Yes." What had he done wrong?

"Well, do something about it. Get her back. Drucy is coming home with us."

Runs With The Wind stared at Sassy. Amusement danced in his eyes. Sassy had lost none of her spunk. He would keep Drucy for her even if it meant destroying Little Gabriel. But, first, he would bargain. Runs With The Wind turned his attention to Little Gabriel.

"The girl for the horse," he said, pointing at the one remaining mount he owned.

Little Gabriel considered this. He had never owned a horse. Now he had one and was being offered another. One for him and one for Mrs. Cutter. It sounded like a fine bargain. But then, what about his unborn son. His forthcoming son would one day need a horse. Meanwhile, they could use the extra horse for a packhorse.

Little Gabriel said, "Yes, the horse for the girl. Now, what about her baby? The pregnant girl was mine and so the baby will also be mine. What will I get for the coming baby?"

Runs With The Wind stiffened. His hand crept to his tomahawk and tightened around the handle.

Little Gabriel saw and stepped back. He realized that he was greatly outnumbered.

Mrs. Cutter came to his rescue. "Please. No killing. One more horse is sufficient." She looked at Sassy. "Who would hunt for me and care for me? It is strange but he has been good to me despite what he done. I do not want anything bad to happen to him."

Sassy did not understand Mrs. Cutter's feelings for the man who had most likely murdered her husband, but she loved the older woman and respected her. She held up one finger to Runs With The Wind. He understood. He quickly unloaded his horse and handed the reins to Little Gabriel.

The tense situation was over and Little Gabriel was all smiles again. But he would remember. He would remember that he had been cheated. He settled his wife on her horse and then mounted his own. He did not know exactly where he was going but he knew it would be in the opposite direction from Runs With The Wind. He urged his horse into the water. Mrs. Cutter followed. She had expected to stay longer. With the sudden change in tempers, it was best to obediently follow Little Gabriel. She turned once and waved good-bye.

The little group on shore watched the two cross the river. When they disappeared around a bend in the trail, Drucy went to get her horse and Sassy retrieved Dear Friend. There was no thought given as to who would ride and who would walk or if they would all ride. They had too much to say to one another to be separated by the horses. Everyone walked, despite the advanced state of the women. They tied one horse behind the other and Takime, on foot, led them.

Once the trouble with Little Gabriel was over, Drucy lost all her fright and shyness. She acted as though she had always known Takime and Runs With The Wind. For the first time since the beginning of her journey, she felt no apprehension as the evening shadows lengthened. She hardly noticed the chill in the air when they stopped for the night. By dark, the change in the weather was noticeable to everyone. It was cold.

They sat around the fire talking, comforted by the warmth and the darkness surrounding them. When the moon had fully risen, Runs With The Wind and Sassy slipped off into the wilderness alone for she had felt the first stirrings. Her child was coming. Their infant was about to appear on earth under the night's canopy. She would squat down in the wilderness and her baby would dive headfirst into the world as befitted the warrior he would be.

Lydia was sitting beside the fire outside her lodge. She and White Cloud were having their morning meal when she heard a slight, rustling noise. She glanced up and saw Blackbird slowly approaching. The old shaman made his way to the fire and, without speaking, sat down between Lydia and White Cloud. Lydia dipped food from the pot hanging over the fire and put it into a bowl. She handed the bowl to Blackbird. The three ate in silence. Black crows called in the distant trees. Lydia knew that Blackbird was calling on her to tell her something important. He seldom left the comfort of his lodge anymore. The deep chill that had invaded his old bones years ago never left him now. He was much too ill to go visiting.

Blackbird finished his meal and handed the bowl back to Lydia. He poked White Cloud in the side to get his attention, but he spoke to Lydia.

"I had a dream," he said.

Lydia stared at the old man. When she heard his words, fear ran through her. What could the old man have seen in his dreams? Please, God, she thought, not any harm to another member of my family. She drew in her breath and waited for him.

Blackbird looked first at Lydia and then at White Cloud to make sure they were paying strict attention. "Sassy comes," he said.

"What?" Lydia could not believe her ears. "What did you say?"

Blackbird attempted to hush her by holding up one skinny hand. "Sassy comes," he repeated. Although he was certain that White Cloud understood him, he signed the words as he spoke.

Lydia could not contain her questions. "When? Where is she now?"

Blackbird said, "She comes."

He would not speak again until Lydia quieted down.

Ashamed of her outburst, Lydia hung her head and waited. She realized what a great effort it had taken on his part to come to her fire in the first place. He must have more to say.

"She will ask for a new name and you must help her and accept it. She will not see me," the old man said. "Her eyes will never rest on Blackbird again."

"Is she hurt?" Lydia could barely get the words out.

"She comes with Runs With The Wind and Takime." Blackbird looked into the flames of the fire while this news sank in. He took his walking stick and poked around in the fire, gathering his next words from the sparks and small blazes that arose.

Blackbird looked at Lydia and his eyes were sad. "Sassy lives," he said. "It is our life's way that dies. Our life's way should continue under the sun forever." With one hand he lifted his walking stick and pointed it at the sky and with the other he shaded his eyes. "It is the last of the long sun days for us," he said. "For the Tuscarora. For The People of the Mountains."

He rose slowly and leaned on his stick. "Tell them to leave these mountains." He moved his arm in a circle, enclosing the surrounding lodges. "Tell them all to go. The time has come."

Blackbird paused. His tired body swayed back and forth over his walking stick. He steadied himself before he spoke again. "They must leave after after the ice turns to water again, but before the spring. Tell each of them. Tell them Blackbird had a dream."

The sun was warming, but Blackbird pulled his leather cape tight around his shoulders. He folded his withered hands around the top of his walking stick and leaned forward. "White Sister, will you tell them?"

Lydia felt burdened by the enormity of his request but she nodded yes. What could she do? There was no one else to hear him. There was only White Cloud.

Satisfied with her answer, Blackbird began to slowly make his way to his lodge. After a few steps, he hesitated as though just re-membering something. He turned to White Cloud and pointed to-ward the distant crows. They were noisily chattering at each other.

Lydia called after him but he would not look back. White Cloud ran after him but he turned and scolded the boy, telling him to go away. Obediently, White Cloud went back to his mother.

He wrapped his arms around her and laid his head against her stomach. She ran her fingers through his long blond hair to comfort him.

As she held her son she thought about all the times Blackbird had been right in his predictions. She pulled White Cloud's head back so that he was looking directly into her face.

Although she had strong doubts, she firmly said, "I believe him, son. You must believe him, too." She smiled and held him out at arm's length. "We have no time for sorrow. There is too much to do. Your brother and sister and Runs With The Wind are coming home. And there is that other thing to consider. The leaving."

She stood by the fire with her hands on her hips and her head cocked to one side. "Why did he say those things to me?" Lydia asked her son. "Who would ever listen to me? Why has he chosen me to deliver such a message?"

Lydia looked sharply at her son to see what he thought of all this. She read many things in his alert young face. There was intelligence and understanding tinged by sadness, but there was no fear. This was the only home he could remember and now he must leave it. And go where? Where would they all go? Blackbird had failed to tell her where they should go.

"Come. We will clean ourselves and dress in our best. If we are to deliver this message, then we will call a council meeting."

It was noon by the time the council meeting was over. Lydia's nerves were as stripped as the willow branches lying in the corner. Her fear that no one would listen had proved untrue. Everyone listened but many did not want to leave their homes. They could see no reason to do so.

Blackbird was old and sick and frail. He was respected by everyone but he no longer held the influence over the people that he once had when he was younger and stronger.

As for Sassy returning, they were more confident that this would take place. If Sassy lived, most of them believed that the young warriors would return with her.

"Well," Lydia said to White Cloud when they were alone, "we did all that we could do. Now let us go to Blackbird's lodge and tell him of the grumblings of the people. He may have more words to give us to make them listen."

They entered Blackbird's lodge together. In the dimness of the room they could see the old man sleeping, covered with his many blankets.

"We will come back later," Lydia whispered to her son.

As she started to leave, White Cloud grabbed her arm and held it tightly. Lydia looked at him and, for the first time that day, saw fear. He was afraid of something in the room.

Her eyes adjusted to the dimness and she looked around, trying to find whatever had upset White Cloud. Nothing looked out of place. Nothing seemed to have been added or taken away.

White Cloud suddenly gave one of his strange cries and ran to Blackbird. He threw back the covers and stared down at the old, shrunken body. Even Lydia could tell from where she stood. The old man was dead.

White Cloud ran from the room and Lydia made no attempt to follow him. It was useless. When White Cloud wanted solitude no one could find him.

Lydia walked closer to the pile of crumpled blankets and stared at the body of the man who had meant so much to her and her family. Tears rolled down her face. She reached down and pulled the blankets back over him, covering his shoulders.

"You were cold for so long," she said. "I will see to it that you are buried with many blankets."

She recited the Twenty-Third Psalm and left the room. The villagers watched her walk back to her lodge.

Oak Leaf was the second one to enter Blackbird's lodge and the people heard her cry out in dismay and disbelief. Soon others of the village arrived. They gathered to dress him in the finest skins and moccasins. He would be taken to the grave place on the other side of the greenbrier path. In time he would have been moved later to the lodge of the chiefs where the bones of many reposed. But by then the Tuscarora would be gone and Blackbird would remain with the earth forever.

Lydia came back with her best blanket and handed it to Oak Leaf. She stayed, helping to prepare the body. The evening turned cool. The heat from the fire burning in the center of the ceremonial grounds felt good on Lydia's face. She sat with the women on the edge of the clearing.

The entire village had turned out to mourn. Even the young ones who did not know him well seemed to understand that a great shaman had died. They listened to the wailing of the women, then ran to the men to hear their songs and tales of Blackbird's deeds.

White Cloud sat at the feet of the warriors, trying to catch every word and gesture, accompanied by the soft beat of a drum.

Yellow Bird came to sit beside Lydia. She brought Speaks Softly and Rainy Days, who carried Lydia's grandchild in her arms.

Yellow Bird said, "We have come to say that we believe in the message you gave us. We will prepare all winter to move. We have told the men."

Lydia nodded.

"There are many who will come with us," said Yellow Bird.

"There are many who will not," Lydia replied sadly. "There are all of those left in the southern forests."

The women sat in silence for a while, thinking of the past and how good it was. Then Lydia spoke again: "Why was the message brought to me?"

Speaks Softly said, "There were three messages. Two of them were for you. He did not have strength enough left in him to visit other lodges."

"Yes. Of course. That is why he came to me," Lydia said.

Yellow Bird added, "We believe the messages."

Lydia stared across the sacred ground at White Cloud. He sat at the feet of the men, his head cocked attentively. Yellow Bird touched her shoulder gently.

"And Takime comes," Rainy Days said. "He is coming home. I feel it." She was holding her son in one arm and nervously fingering the carved wooden pendant around her neck with the other hand. She was not like the older women, content with their lives when their men were away. She had seen a great deal of death and destruction in her young life. She loved her son with every breath she took, but no one could take the place of Takime.

Speaks Softly reached for her grandson. Rainy Days placed him in her arms.

"Your feet will not walk in these hills," Speaks Softly said to the sleeping boy. "But then, your mother was born in another place, too." Sadly she added, "We are forever leaving our fathers' bones behind and going on."

Speaks Softly passed the baby to Lydia. Lydia rocked him in her arms and hummed an old tune from her childhood, thinking of all that needed to be done for the move in late winter.

They owned few possessions but many would have to be abandoned. They still managed a small herd of horses. Not as many as before the men went to war, but enough to use as packhorses. Mostly, they would need to carry food—enough corn and beans to get them through the summer. At least through a planting season. This year's harvest had been a good one. There would be plenty of food. Each person could take a change of clothing, food, weapons, and little else.

"We will need to repair all of the baskets," Lydia said aloud. "For carrying the food supply. Tomorrow, we can begin gathering cedar chips to dry over the winter for the babies' diapering."

Lydia shivered and moved closer to the fire. It was turning a little cold. "And we will go toward the northwest," she said. "Remember? Years ago Blackbird said we would go west. And the Iroquois are strong there. They must help us."

The women nodded in agreement. Yes. They would go northwest. Tonight, they would mourn Blackbird. Tomorrow, they would begin the preparations for their journey.

It was then that the sentries called and the riders emerged from the trees and The People heard an infant's wail.